On Lock

Dany Mack

Acknowledgments

I would like to first thank God for giving me the gift to write. A special thanks to my parents for birthing me and for not putting me up for adoption. Thanks to my grandparents on earth and in heaven. Thanks to my grandma Georgia Mae for listening to me rant when I had nobody else to talk to about my dreams. I would like to send a special thank you to my cousin Jeremy for believing in me so much that I asked for money and he gave it to me. I'm still in shock about that. I would like to thank my brothers Chris and Elliott for their support, growing up with me was not easy I'm sure. I know it must be hard to have such an awesome sister. To my cousin Josh, thank you for the late nights and early mornings helping me with so many things I could not began to name. You were heaven sent exactly when I needed you and our journey together has been awesome. I want to thank my little cousin Stephanie for agreeing to be my personal assistant when I had nobody else to turn to. I want to thank my editor Tara Steverson, my graphic designer, I'm Your Plug LLC, for designing an amazing book cover, and all my Facebook friends that motivated me to continue writing. Finally, my amazing daughter Addyson Alease, I did this for you baby! Always follow your dreams!!

Facebook: Story Time With Dany

Instagram: Authordany_mack

Twitter: IamDany_Mack

Email: Authordanymack@gmail.com

"Make the money, don't let it make you."

-Diamond from Players club

Chapter 1

All I could see was red in his eyes. I knew he was going to kill me and BJ from the look in his eyes. He pulled his pistol out and put it to my head. I screamed and started crying telling him not to do this! BJ jumped up with his hands in the air.

"Look Fred, you just got out of prison. It's not worth going back for the rest of your life because of what we did," BJ pleaded.

Fred pointed the gun at BJ. "Killing y'all would be worth my while and I wouldn't have no regrets." BJ stared at the gun and then POW!!

The Beginning

Let me take it back to the beginning. My name is Lisa Davenport and Fred is my husband. We live in Philadelphia, Pennsylvania. Fred has been locked up 8 years in for violating his parole from a previous drug charge. We have 3 kids together and I've been with him since we were 15. I was there for Fred when he had nothing and when he had millions from the drug game. BJ is Fred's best friend. For the past 3 years,

I've been having an affair with him. I know y'all thinking I'm a thot but it was nothing I ever wanted to happen. My kids call him uncle and he helps Fred move weight while he's away. This provides us the same lifestyle we had before Fred got locked up. Every morning BJ takes Fred Jr. and Freda to school and he picks them up. BJ even brings me lunch everyday and makes sure I always have what I need. He is a lifesaver for me and the kids, and Fred too.

About 3 years ago I had a company Christmas party for the part time job I had and I really didn't want to go. BJ surprised me and bought me the most beautiful red dress. He even had a makeup artist and a hairstylist come to the house and style me. About 2 hours later he came dressed in a tuxedo that had to be custom made by God himself. Now I never looked at BJ in a sexual way but damn tonight he made me super wet.

"Why are you all dressed up BJ? You must have a date?" I said jokingly.

"Yea with you silly." BJ flashed his million-dollar smile. BJ was super fine even though I considered him family. He was about 6'4 with smooth, caramel skin. His eyes were tight like he was Chinese. He looked a lot like Tyson Beckford the model, except he had tattoos all on his face. BJ was definitely the biggest dope boy in the city since my husband left and he had enough women to keep him occupied.

"You didn't have to come BJ. I really didn't want to go myself, but I guess we can turn up tonight. Wait! Who's watching the kids because Rosa has the weekend off?" Rosa was my nanny and housekeeper.

"I paid Rosa to stay the weekend so don't worry about anything I have everything covered and I'm going to take care of you tonight." BJ gave me a look that made my kitty jump. I mean it had been almost 5 years since a man has touched me down there besides my gynecologist. I kept that thought out my head because I would never betray my husband in that way.

I was finally dressed, and I was looking good as hell in this dress BJ picked out. I walked down the stairs and it felt like I was going to prom. Everybody was waiting and watching me come down the stairs.

"Mom you look beautiful!" Fred Jr. said hugging me.

"Thanks baby and y'all be good for Rosa she was supposed to be off this weekend," I told the kids.

"Don't worry about me I am glad to be here," Rosa said. I'm sure BJ probably paid her enough for her time.

"Ok well let's go BJ."

We headed to the venue and BJ pulled out his Porsche. We made it there and the looks on my coworkers' face let me know that I was looking like a million bucks myself. We talked, had a few drinks, and mingled with my coworkers until it got late, and everyone began to leave.

"I really enjoyed myself tonight BJ. Thank you so much. I'm definitely done drinking though because I am tipsy," I laughed to BJ.

"Well, let's get you home."

BJ helped me in the car. I dosed off and BJ was waking me up telling me we were home. He took my heels off and walked me in the house. BJ put my things on the table, picked me up, and took me upstairs. When I realized we were in my bedroom, I told him thanks and that I could handle it from here.

"Ok. I'm glad you had fun. I will see you guys tomorrow," BJ said staring at me with this weird look.

"Are you ok to drive? You can stay here tonight in the guest room," I told BJ.

"No, I better go. I will see y'all tomorrow."

BJ left and I took my dress off and got in the shower. I heard BJ calling my name like 5 mins after I was in the shower, so I just jumped back out and grabbed my robe.

"Hey, you left your clutch in my car and I was letting you know I was putting it on your bed." BJ's eyes never stopped looking at me head to toe like he was ripping the robe off me with his eyes.

"Ok, thanks again BJ."

I felt really uncomfortable, so I waited for him to leave but instead he walked closer to me and grabbed my ass and started kissing me. I couldn't resist and I started kissing him back. He laid me down and started kissing between my thighs and I lost control. I imagined it was my husband until I opened my eyes and saw BJ. I pushed him off me.

"BJ stop! You know we can't do this!"

I couldn't believe what just happened. This is my husband's best friend and I know this is wrong, but my body was so weak. To have somebody kiss me with so much passion and love I felt like it was Fred.

BJ walked over to me apologizing "I'm sorry I don't know why I did that Lisa, please forgive me I promise I won't ever do it again."

I heard what BJ was saying but the only thing I could say was "Fuck Me."

BJ didn't say a word. He laid me down and licked between my legs until I couldn't stop shaking. Then he pulled out a monster that made me buck my eyes. BJ finally eased inside of me. All I could do was grab him and he pulled back and looked me in my eyes. I couldn't look at him so I turned my face but he fucked me like I was the last woman on earth and his nut was the only thing to save his life!! He seemed as if he had been waiting to do this his whole life. BJ felt so good and I was trying not to moan loudly, but he was definitely bigger than my husband. I couldn't help but moan and scream as I nutted all over the bed.

As soon as I was about to cum all over his dick, I heard a voice say "Mom are you ok?" It was Fred Jr.

Chapter 2

"Fred I'm ok go back in your room." I said panicking.

"Uncle BJ, what are you doing in here? Were y'all just having sex?" Fred Jr. screamed.

He ran out the room and I jumped up putting my robe back on while BJ put his clothes on. "Shit BJ, he's going to tell Fred about this! That's a grave for me and you!"

BJ looked like he saw a ghost. Then he turned to me and said, "It would be worth it for you Lisa, I would die for you."

I looked at him disgustedly. I didn't say a word to him. All I could think about is getting to Fred Jr. and making sure he doesn't tell his dad what he thinks he saw.

"Fred!" I yelled out. Nothing. "Fred Jr. where are you baby?"

He walked out the bathroom holding his cellphone. "Dad wants to talk to you." He looked at me and shook his head.

My heart was beating so fast at this point I felt like I was about to faint. I saw BJ walk out the bedroom and I pointed at the phone letting him know it was Fred. I could barely breathe and my hands were sweating. Fred still had that much control over me and he was locked up. All these years, I never cheated on him until now. The worst mistake of my life was to do it with his best friend.

I put the phone to my ear. "Hey baby," I said very weakly.

"What's wrong baby?" Fred asked. He seemed actually concerned so I guess that means Fred Jr. didn't say anything to him.

I had to think of something quick to say so I told him I wasn't feeling good and I think the kids were worried about me.

"Fred Jr. called and he sounded upset but then he said you were calling his name." Fred sounded so concerned. Meanwhile I'm still thinking about fucking his best friend and that I want more of him.

"Yeah I think he heard me vomiting and got scared but it's late baby and I just want to lay back down." BJ just seemed to be in a daze.

"Ok baby I love you I'm going to call you and the kids later, get some rest I'll have BJ pick you up some medicine and bring it to you."

I almost dropped the phone when he said BJ's name. "Ok I

love you more baby. Goodnight."

I hung the phone up and BJ looked up at me like a lost puppy. I was disgusted with myself and with BJ. "I need you to leave please."

He didn't say a word. I couldn't even stand to look at him anymore. I walked in my bathroom and turned the shower on. I stayed in the shower for about an hour. I cried most of the time I was in there and it was more for Fred Jr. more than anything. I felt like I failed my kids by betraying their father. A few minutes of temptation may have just destroyed years of everything I built.

I woke up the next day and I really thought everything was a dream until I looked at the text from BJ. He had called about 5 times and sent about ten texts. It was Sunday so he didn't have to take the kids to school today so there was really no reason for him to be calling me. Most of the texts were just him apologizing and saying he's going to talk to Fred Jr. "Shit." I couldn't even think what was probably running through my son's mind. I thought about it and letting BJ talk to him might not be a bad idea. Fred Jr. just became a teenager, so I know he had a million questions about sex but to walk in on me and

BJ was not how he needed to learn.

I got out of bed and got dressed and went downstairs. We had an amazing home and it was huge. I loved our spiral staircase it just made the home look so grand. It's definitely a nice upgrade from the two-bedroom apartment we started in.

"Where is everybody?" I screamed when I made it downstairs.

"Mommy come in the theater room."

I walked in the movie room where we had the projector screen set up. The kids, BJ, and Chanel, the bitch of all bitches, were all there. Chanel was BJ's sister and she came around from time to time.

"Hi you guys." I said very dry.

"How are you feeling Lisa?" BJ jumped up quickly and offered me his seat.

"I've been better." I said sarcastically. I walked over and sat between my kids.

"Hi Lisa." Chanel said with a smirk.

The bitch knew I didn't like her but dealt with her only because of BJ. She tried to fuck Fred before we got married and when I found out I tried to break her jaw. So ever since then we are cordial, but she knows I don't fuck with her.

"Chanel." I said and looked back at the movie.

She stood up and touched BJ on the shoulder, I guess to tell him she was leaving. He got up to walk her out and then I saw Fred Jr. at the refrigerator. I got up and when he saw me, he hurried back up the stairs. BJ came back in the house and he pulled me in the dining room.

"I'm sorry Lisa. What happened was nothing planned. I want to move on from this and pretend like it never happened."

"It did happen and that's what is fucked up about it." I whispered to BJ. "We fucked last night and we can't change that. I'm more concerned with Fred Jr. and him seeing us."

BJ had this look of confusion on his face. "I'm going to talk to him now and let him know it's not what it looked like. I already came up with something to say."

There was nothing he could say to clean this up. "Ok what could you possibly say BJ?" I guess he going to say his dick slipped in my pussy.

"Let me figure that out. Fred Jr. looks up to me, so I hope I can convince him that we are all family and that you are like a sister to me."

I bucked my eyes. "The way you fucked me last night BJ, would you fuck Chanel like that?" I asked.

"Whoa!" Chanel walked in the dining room holding a wallet in her hand. "BJ you left your wallet in my car."

She had her mouth wide open. Fuck! I knew Chanel had heard enough to know my life was officially over.

Chapter 3

The one time I cheat on my husband and everybody is finding out in less than 24 hours. I was not cut out for this shit and I felt like I was going to have an anxiety attack. I walked out the dining room and went upstairs. I sat on the end of my bed and just thought about when me and Fred got married. That was the best day of my life and he seemed so happy.

Things were never perfect between us because Fred, being one of the biggest dope boys, he had his fair of getting caught with women when we were younger. I always forgave him and he always made it up to me. I'll never forget when he was cheating with this girl Ashley and she was trying to make sure I found out about it. Well I did because in those days I was like an FBI detective. I always found out everything. She tried to say her daughter was Fred's baby and it ended up not being his.

I left Fred after that and he literally, for almost 7 months straight, sent me a gift every day. He sent roses, jewelry, and money. Fred even sent me and my friends on a trip. I wasn't impressed because I knew he had the money now, so I still could care less about the gifts. One night he came by my apartment and knocked on my door. He said he had a surprise for me and to just give him a chance to talk. I told him he had 5 minutes. I walked outside and saw a man playing the violin. I turned my head and saw an all white Porsche with a bow on it and Fred dropping to one knee. I could not believe he was proposing to me! I cried and obviously I said yes. He was the only man I loved, and this 5-carat ring made it a lot easier.

Somebody knocked on my bedroom door, it was BJ.

"Lisa look, I talked to Chanel and told her it's not what she thinks and she's not going to say anything."

I rolled my eyes. "Chanel is a fucking bitch that wants my life. I don't care if that's your sister or not, I know she hates me." I don't trust a soul and I damn sure don't trust a bitch with no soul like Chanel.

"Where are the kids? I need to get them lunch." I got up and started to walk out the door.

"I paid Rosa to take them to the arcade and get pizza so don't worry about that. You just take some time to yourself." BJ turned to walk out the door.

I couldn't help but to think about him licking and sucking my clit. I had a flashback of him turning me over and fucking me from the back and kissing my butt cheeks. The way he gently grabbed my breasts and sucked them one by one and licked on my navel had me soaking wet. I needed it again and I couldn't help myself.

"BJ!" I called his name.

I went to the door and he was halfway down the stairs.

"What's up?" He asked.

"I need you."

That's the only thing that I could think to say.

He turned around and walked back in my bedroom. I locked the door. He sat on the bed not saying a word. I took my clothes off while he watched. Then, I walked to him and kissed him. BJ stood up, sat me on the bed, and started eating me out like it was his last meal. I came twice before I knew it. He took his clothes off and I just stared at his dick, admiring it. BJ started kissing on my breasts; I grabbed him and put him in my mouth. I licked and sucked him until he let out a moan. Under his breath, all he was saying was, "Shit Lisa." He stopped me, stared in my eyes, and laid me back. His long dick slid inside of me and I could feel him in my chest. We fucked for at least 30 minutes and I know I nutted 10 times. Afterwards, we both just laid there trying to catch our breath.

"What are we doing BJ?" I asked him after a few minutes.

He turned and looked at me and grabbed my face and kissed me so passionately. His kiss made me wet all over again. Then he went back down and ate me out until I nutted again. I knew this was going to be an addiction hard to break.

After BJ left I took a nap and my phone woke me up. It was Fred calling.

"Hey baby!" I answered. I'm always happy to talk to my husband but this time was a little weird.

"Hey my favorite girl." Fred had the deepest sexiest voice ever.

We talked like normal until it was time for him to go. I told him the kids were still at the arcade and that I would have them call later. Before I could get off the phone BJ was calling. I hung up with Fred and answered BJ's call.

"What's up BJ?"

"I need you to meet me at the Green Room in an hour, it's about business."

I knew what that meant so I told him ok. I got out of bed and hopped in the shower and got dressed. I knew it was money to be made.

I made it to the Green Room. I had on my skinny jeans, black red bottoms, and an all white Gucci tee. I try not to over dress when we're doing business so that I won't draw attention. I must admit, I'm not a bad looking woman. Everyone says I favor Gabrielle Union, but I have hazel eyes.

I saw BJ in a VIP booth in the back so I made my way to him. I started feeling horny just looking at him. He had on all black and some diamond earrings that you could see from across the bar. I made my way to him and 3 Italian guys. I introduced myself to them and we got right down to business. The Italians own a lot of restaurants in New York and New Jersey and we were about to buy two of them. Don't get me wrong, the Italians were big drug pins too. They were known to move 50 million dollars worth of Columbian cocaine in two days. That's a huge feat.

I drank about 2 glasses of champagne just to unwind. Finally, we came to an agreement to get both restaurants for $100,000 apiece. I signed the paperwork. Our lawyers had already approved of the contract so it was a deal. They bought us another bottle of champagne to celebrate. We drank and talked for another hour or so before I got up to leave.

"It was a pleasure doing business with you and I can't wait to do more." I shook all the guys hands as I left.

"Lisa the pleasure was all mine." He kissed my hand.

I started walking away when I heard BJ calling my name. I turned around and to my surprise the first person I saw was none other than Ashley. What are the chances of me running into her of all nights. She still looked busted as ever and obviously she wasn't making any coins from how her heels were leaning. I walked back toward BJ because I wanted her to see me looking fly as usual.

"BJ!" I screamed a little louder so she could see me.

She looked dead at me and of course I pretended like she was invisible. I saw her stare me up and down and turn back to her drink. BJ finally caught up with me and hugged me.

"We just became a little bit richer." He seemed so excited about buying the restaurants. I know BJ always wanted to be a chef but he got caught in the drug game. When you're in it it's hard to get out.

"Yes I think I may go buy me a mink as a gift to myself." I said laughing.

"Well, if it isn't BJ and Lisa."

The bitch had a lot of nerve to even part my name from her

lips. Ashley stood up to hug BJ. He gave her a church hug and stepped back because he knew I wasn't going for that. I stared at her and didn't say a word.

"I understand Lisa, but we have no beef. That's been so many years ago and he married you, so you won." This bitch tried it!

"Bitch I was winning before I married him and I will forever win if you're the competition." I was tipsy enough to hit the bitch but I kept it classy.

"Ok Lisa, I get it. I'll make sure to tell Fred I saw you guys next time he calls," she said with an evil smirk on her face.

Before I knew it I choked her. "Bitch!"

The only word in my vocabulary for the next 5 minutes was stupid and bitch. BJ and security came to pull me off her. She was not going to disrespect me in my face about my husband. BJ pulled me off and pushed her out the way. He pushed her so hard that she fell on the floor and she touched the back of her head and it was bleeding. We ran out the club and to my car. BJ hopped in the driver side, so I jumped in the passenger seat. He started the car up and then started laughing hysterically. I mean he was laughing so hard that I started laughing.

"That bitch really tried it. She knows I don't play about Fred, and what she mean when he calls her again? I will murder that bitch!"

I was turnt up now and I had been drinking so I was feeling good. BJ just kept laughing. We stopped at the light and before I could say a word, a black SUV pulled up and started shooting at my car. I screamed and ducked down in my seat. Then I heard them pull off burning rubber.

"Omg BJ did you see who it was?" I looked over at BJ. He had been shot and wasn't moving.

"Shit!!"

I had to think quick before the police made it because, believe it or not, the police didn't like us. I jumped out the car and tried pushing BJ over. Two guys ran over to see if we were ok.

"I will give y'all $100 apiece to lift him up and put him in the passenger seat."

They looked at me strange. "Ma'am we can call the ambu- "I cut the little short dude off mid-sentence.

"Either move him for $100 or move out my way because we

22

are not waiting on the police or ambulance."

They saw how serious I was and they lifted him up. I gave them $100 apiece. As soon as I got ready to drive off, I saw a silver Mercedes ride up slowly and who else but Ashley is sitting in the passenger side. She pointed her fingers at me like a gun and started laughing. That didn't bother me at all, but the person driving the Mercedes was a guy named William. Everybody called him Big Will. Big Will had money but he was known for robbing, stealing, and killing. Why was Ashley with him and did she set it up for me to be shot because they shot up my car! The craziest part about it all is that Big Will was BJ's sister Chanel's boyfriend.

Chapter 4

So, we got to the hospital before the police came because I didn't need any issues. Fred might have been in jail, but he was definitely well known and being his wife, I was plugged in too. I pulled up to the emergency room. By this time BJ is awake and looking around, but not saying anything. I run in the door to get help

"I need a doctor! My brother has been shot!" I yelled to the nurse.

The nurse ran out and called the EMT's over to help. They got BJ on a stretcher and rolled him into the emergency room. The nurses were asking me questions about him as we rushed to the back. They asked about what he was allergic to and I had no damn clue. I've been knowing him for years but never knew a lot about his personal life. BJ was very private and I respected that. I gave them the information I knew. They told me that he had to go back into emergency surgery and it would be about 5 or 6 hours. BJ had been shot 5 times and they needed to remove the bullets immediately. I had to consent to the surgery, but I was honestly scared to do it. I called Chanel to let her know what was going on. She answered on the first ring.

"Hello." She sounded like she was sleep even though she answered right away. "Chanel BJ was just shot." I said as calm as possible.

"What?!" Chanel screamed. "OMG is he dead?" She asked.

"No he needs emergency surgery because he was shot five times and they're asking me to consent because I brought him here. I just wanted to call you and let you know what was going on." I was literally shaking at this point.

"Well sign it Lisa if it's going to save his life! Where are y'all? I'm on the way right now! Send me your location now!"

Before I could say ok she hung up. I sent her my location and about 15 minutes later she was walking through the door. Chanel lives across town so she had to run every light getting here.

"Chanel I'm over here." I raised my hand so she could see me.

She walked over and I could tell she had been crying. "Lisa what happened?"

I thought about Big Will. I didn't really know how to say it, but I just told her. "Big Will shot him five times, well he didnt pull the trigger, but he had him shot five times." I said staring at her.

Her eyes bucked. "My Big Will?" she asked.

I nodded my head. I told her the entire story from the Green Room until now. Chanel was beyond pissed.

"I'm about to call him now and tell him he almost killed my brother! That dumb fat bitch!" Chanel yelled and everybody in the hospital looked at us.

"Sit down Chanel and let's be smart about this." I whispered to her and sat her down.

I would be pissed too but dealing with Fred I learned a lot about the streets and the best way to get someone is when they least expect it. The bullets were really for me so Ashley and Big Will had to pay.

The surgery took 8 hours. The doctor came out and told us that BJ was doing fine and that he was even trying to talk. They were moving him to ICU to monitor him, so we couldn't stay. We could only see him for a few minutes. By the time we walked back, he had already fallen asleep. Chanel kissed him on the cheek and we left out. I had already got my car towed and was calling a car service to pick me up. Chanel offered to take me home. On the way there we talked about how to retaliate against Ashley and Big Will.

"I know you are upset about BJ being shot and the fact that

26

you know Big Will is cheating on you. You have to be smart Chanel and stay 2 steps ahead though," I explained to her.

I put a plan in motion that I knew would at least get Ashley to talking because that bitch tried it saying she's been talking to Fred. I was going to make sure she didn't have to talk to anyone else's husband at all. Before I could say another word Fred was calling me.

"Hey baby," I answered the phone.

"Hey baby, where are you because the kids said you didn't come home last night?" He was in prison and could still keep up with me.

"Baby, BJ was shot last night after we made the restaurant deal." I told him.

"What the fuck!?" I could hear the concern in his voice.

"He's ok baby. He had surgery and the doctor said he should make a full recovery." I tried to ease his mind because I knew that was nothing he wanted to hear.

"Who the fuck did it Lisa because..." He paused. I'm sure he remembered where he was and didn't want to say the wrong thing.

"Baby it's ok we don't know who did it, but I'm just glad BJ is ok." I looked at Chanel to let her know that this is something that the women were going to handle this time. I have always let Fred take care of things since we were young. Now that BJ was in the hospital, I had to step up to the plate.

"Fred, as your wife you know that I'm always in your corner. Just know that you have a wife that will forever hold it down by any means necessary." I meant what I said because I knew Fred was thinking about the money we could lose also.

"I love you Lisa. Keep me updated but I have to go." Fred sounded like he had lost his best friend.

I know being in prison wasn't easy for him and some days he just wasn't in the best mood. With something like this happening I know he wished he was home. Fred could whistle and have somebody murdered that's how much power he has. I might not be Fred, but I was damn sure about to whistle.

When we got home, I let everyone know what happened to BJ and that he would be ok. I needed a hot shower and a change of clothes because I felt disgusting. I told Chanel to come back

28

later because the plan was effective immediately. I ended up taking a bath so that I could soak, relax and just gather my thoughts. I had Rosa bring me a glass of wine and I got my plan together for Ashley and Big Will. Once I felt refreshed, I got out the tub. I threw on a black tee, black jeans and put on my Air Max. It was time for business.

When Chanel made it back over here, we jumped in my Range Rover and headed to the west side where Paco lives. Paco has been around the family almost as long as BJ, but Paco is not affiliated with the drugs. He's a straight killer. He doesn't talk much but rumor has it that he's killed about 30 people in his lifetime, if not more. It's always good to have a shooter on your team. We made it over to Paco's and I called him to tell him to come outside.

"Paco we are outside are you home? I don't see your car." I asked.

"Yea I'm here. My girl just in my car. I'm coming outside now." Paco hung up the phone. A few minutes later he jumped in the truck.

"Hey ladies. Let's ride out."

I told Paco about everything that's going on and how the

29

bullets that hit BJ were really for me. Paco was beyond pissed. He said that him and Big Will had words before so he was ready to get him back. The plan was on and it was showtime. Chanel called Big Will like everything was normal and told him she was horny and asked why he hadn't called her.

"Baby, I called you and it went to voicemail. You know Big Daddy gon feed you this dick whenever you want it." Big Will said.

I rolled my eyes as I let them finish talking and he was heading to Chanel's house just like I thought. I took Chanel back to my house to get her car then we went to her house. About an hour later, Big Will made it to Chanel's house.

"Hey Big Daddy!" Chanel said as she kissed him. We were watching everything from the loft upstairs.

"Did you miss me baby because I missed you?"

He picked her up and sat her on the kitchen table. As he parted her legs, he kissed her aggressively. His tongue slowly moved his way down to her pussy and began working its magic. Chanel was moaning and grabbing his head. She got louder and louder. I could tell she nutted.

"Sit down in the chair baby and let me please you." Chanel turned her speaker on and R. Kelly began playing. Big Will turned and smacked Chanel on the ass. He pulled his pants down as Chanel grabbed his dick and spit on it. Chanel devoured his dick and Big Will began moaning loudly.

He couldn't see us coming down the stairs. Paco pulled out a machete that was so big it scared me just seeing it. Chanel was going to work and Big Will never saw what was coming next.

"You never sucked me like this before baby! Damn, I'm about to nut!"

Before he could get his nut, Chanel scream loud as fuck. Suddenly, Big Will's head rolled across the kitchen floor. I looked at Paco and Paco looked at me. I dropped the machete on the ground. I had just cut Big Will's head off myself.

Chapter 5

I couldn't believe what I just did. "Omg!" Chanel screamed. I stared at Big Will's head on the ground. Paco got the machete and started cleaning up everything. I thought it would be blood everywhere, but it really wasn't much besides some coming from the head.

"What the fuck did I just do?" I asked. Nobody said a word.

"You ladies go to the hardware store and get some drop cloths used to paint with and some heavy duty trash bags. I will stay here and clean up." Paco seemed to know what he was doing and I'm pretty sure this isn't his first time cleaning a crime scene. My phone rang and I screamed. It was Fred Jr.

"What's up Jr.? I can't really talk." I answered the phone.

"Mom where are you?" He asked.

"Why? What's up?" I did not have the right mindset to talk to my babies when I was staring at a dead body.

Fred Jr. sounded like he was crying. "Immigration just came and took Rosa!"

I knew this was a joke. The kids were playing but it wasn't a good time. "Look I'm really busy and I can't play right now ok Fred."

I was about to hang up when Fred Jr. got louder. "Mom I'm not playing! They really just took Rosa and she was screaming and crying!"

Fuck! Could this get any crazier? "Fred did they say anything else about why they were taking her? Are they still there?" I asked.

"No. One of the guys asked me how old I was and I told him. He said I was old enough to be home but to call my parents because we wouldn't see Rosa for a long time."

Fred Jr was clearly upset about what was going on. I thought about Megan, the girl that watches the kids when Rosa is off, and figured I better call her to watch the kids.

"I'm about to call Megan to come over until I get there. I'm on my way baby."

I know he was terrified. I hung up and called Megan. She told me she was out with her boyfriend but when I offered her a thousand dollars, she said she would be there in 20 minutes. I explained the story to Chanel and Paco. They couldn't believe Rosa had gotten deported. Chanel and Paco decided they would go and get everything so that I could get back home.

"Are you going to be ok Lisa?" Paco asked me.

I wanted to say no but I was better than I thought. Cutting Big Will's head off was like the birth of me. I was feeling untouchable. With Fred in prison and BJ in the hospital, I knew I was next in line to make the business run and I would do that by any means.

Megan had made it to the kids. I felt good knowing they were safe, but I had to clear my head before I went home. I drove for about an hour outside the city so I could get away from all the noise. Finally, I pulled up to a back road. Remembering that I had gym clothes in the back of the truck, I pulled them out and put them on. I changed clothes because I realized I had blood splattered all over the ones I was wearing and I didn't want any evidence on me.

I called Paco to see what they were doing. His phone went to voicemail. I called again and got the voicemail again. Chanel's phone went straight to voicemail when I called her too. That was weird. I didn't need anymore surprises. I called both phones again and the same thing happened. As I was still standing on the side of the road making my phone calls, I realized a black truck was flying down the road towards me. It came speeding by me so fast that they almost hit me. I jumped back, shut the trunk, and got in my truck before I got ran over.

The black truck went down a few miles and made a U Turn. It came back flying towards me again, so I put my truck in drive and sped off before they caught up to me. When I got on the road, I realized they were either trying to catch up to me or they were trying to pass me. I sped up and started calling Paco and Chanel again. I called about twenty times and still nobody answered. The black truck had caught up to me and it was riding my tail. If I had stopped they would ram into the back of me. I think that's what they wanted. My phone rang. I had never seen the number before but I answered it.

"Hello?" I heard laughing.

"Slow that thang down Ms. Lisa." I heard the laughing get louder.

"Who is this?" I asked.

"This is Phil, Big Will's brother. Remember me?" He said in this raspy voice.

"How did you get my number?" My heart was beating so fast I thought it was going to jump through my chest. He knew I killed Big Will and now he was going to kill me.

35

"Your number is all on Facebook on your boutique page. Slow down, we were just having fun with you beautiful." Whoever was riding with him was laughing even harder when he said that.

I started to curse him out but I didn't. I just let them pass by me. As the black truck passed by me, I looked Phil dead in his eyes and he just smiled. I thought I would pass out while I was driving so I stopped at the first store I saw. Finally, I got a call from Chanel. She said that both of their phones had died but everything had been taking care of. I told them to meet me at the Ritz Carlton in an hour so we could move on to the next plan. Ashley wasn't going to get off that easy.

I stopped by my boutique to get some clothes then I reserved a suite at the Ritz Carlton. My boutique, Looks by Lisa, was shut down but I was going to have a relaunch in the next few months hopefully. I wasn't going to do business at home around my kids but I wanted to be somewhere as comfortable as my house, so that's why I got a suite. I ordered room service then got in the shower. I tried to wash away all the shit that just happened in the last few days.

I thought about BJ. I needed to check on him. My mind was filled with scenes of him fucking me. It was amazing how

36

gentle and rough he was at the same time. I didn't have to tell him what I liked, it's like he already knew my body. Just thinking of his kisses and his tongue licking my pearl tongue made me touch myself in the shower. Before I could even get started good I heard somebody knocking at the door. I jumped out and put on a robe. It was room service. I had ordered steak and lobster with the works, hors d'oeuvres, fruit tray, and a bottle of champagne. It was a celebration bitches! I was ready to take over the kingdom and show what the king had taught the queen.

Chanel and Paco finally made it to the hotel by the time I had gotten dressed.

"You had to get The Ritz Carlton huh?" Paco asked laughing. He grabbed some grapes and started walking around the room.

The room was huge and we were the only ones on the top floor so we would not be disturbed. I pulled out a cellphone and sat it on the table. Chanel and Paco looked at me.

"It's BJ's phone, I got it before he went into surgery." I knew BJ had the connects' numbers and I needed to get to work. I was pretty sure by now there were a lot of people mad. Paco had done small runs for us before, so I was putting him in charge over one side of the territory, the pick ups, and drop offs. This was a pay increase for him so he was anxious to do it. BJ had about 10 voicemails from Victor and I knew that meant to call him ASAP.

The phone rang once. When I answered it, al I heard was "What the fuck is going on!" He sounded furious.

"BJ was shot 5 times this weekend. This is Fred's wife. You'll be doing business with me for a while." I said very calmly.

"Is this a fuckin joke?" He started speaking something in Spanish. Then my phone rang, it was Fred.

"Speaking of Fred this is him calling." I said to Victor.

"Oh yea? Well if that's Fred, ask him what's the password."

I answered the phone. "Hey baby." I felt more powerful than ever talking to my husband today for some reason.

"What are you doing my lovely wife?" Fred asked.

"I'm on the phone with Victor and he told me to ask you what's the password."

I was on the phone with Victor Sanchez, one of the biggest drug lords of the Mexican cartel. Fred was big, but Victor was like The Godfather of it all.

"Burritos." Fred said.

"Huh?" Was Fred hungry or something. "Fred what's the password that Victor is talking about?" I asked him again.

"It's burritos. Them Mexican sons of a bitches love burritos I guess." Fred started laughing.

That was the dumbest password ever. "It's burritos Mr. Sanchez." He didn't say anything. I didn't say anything either.

"2662 Mac Arthur Blvd. Meet me there in an hour," Victor said and hung up.

"Fred, I'm going to hold it down until BJ is ok so don't worry." I just knew he was about to go crazy, but he didn't.

"Baby I know you can handle it, but I just don't want you involved in it." Fred seemed calm about the entire situation and I wasn't expecting that.

"Fred I've promoted Paco and he's going to be making drops

for me. I wanted to get some suggestions from you on who else we should promote too."

Fred didn't say anything right away, but he gave me two names, Smoke and Rico. I knew exactly who they were. They were stone cold killers. I heard so many stories about them but every time they were around me, they were always respectful. I talked a little while longer to Fred and we got some plans together before I met with Victor. I was just glad that I had the blessing of Fred so now it was time to lock the streets down.

Chapter 6

I changed into one of the dresses I got from my boutique. The formfitting red dress fit my body perfectly as I slid it on. I felt powerful and this dress was definitely going to demand some respect when I walked in the room. The address led me to a Chinese restaurant, like the old ones you see on tv or in the movies. It was only about 3 people there; I walked in with full confidence. I didn't know how Victor looked so I told the lady at the front who I was there for. She told me to follow her and she took me through double doors that led to the back. The back of the restaurant was very nice compared to the front. We walked in a room that had a long red velvet couch.

She told me to have a seat, so I did. "Mr. Sanchez will be right in," the Chinese lady said.

"Ok, thank you."

About a minute later he walked in. I was not expecting him to be fine as fuck! Victor Sanchez was about 6'3', muscular, and had the body of a football player. The tailored suit he was wearing had him looking like a million bucks. He had the straightest and whitest teeth I've ever seen. His body was almost identical to The Rock.

I stood up to shake his hand. He stopped walking and just stared at me. "Wow! Nobody said Fred's wife was this beautiful. I will try to behave." He said flashing his smile.

"Thank you Mr. Sanchez. I will let Fred know of your compliments." I said smiling back.

He walked over and pressed the intercom button on the wall. "I need someone to bring me a bottle of Rosé please and two glasses. Please sit down." He pointed at the seat at the table.

I sat down as he found some music to play on the speaker. He played classical music which I wasn't expecting. "Let's get to business shall we." He said. "Wait before we start, how is BJ?" He seemed concerned.

"He's going to be fine. He just has to recover." I explained to him how everything happened, and he couldn't believe it. He offered his frontline men for retaliation. I declined but thanked him. By that time another lady brought in the champagne and glasses. I needed a drink bad, so I wasn't going to refuse a glass.

"Have a drink with me?" Victor asked.

"Sure, I need one." I stood up to get my glass.

"Let me play some music we can vibe to then we can set a

date for our next meeting."

Victor was so charming. He was so sexy that I couldn't help but imagine if he was packing or not. I tried not to look down but I had to see if I could at least find a dick print or not. Victor caught me staring; I tried to play it off. I pretended like I didn't see him notice me staring.

"Lisa can I ask you something in the most respectful way possible?"

I could only imagine what he wanted to ask me. I did not want to curse this man out. "Sure. Just be careful what you say to me Mr. Sanchez." I told him.

He started laughing. "I better not say anything then. I must say though, you are a beautiful woman. I admire you for handling such business like you are."

I sipped my champagne and just nodded my head. I couldn't help but to think how he would feel inside of me. I finished my glass and decided to pour up another one. The Isley Brothers song *Between the Sheets* started playing and I guess that was Victor's song because he started dancing. He grabbed my hand and then we started dancing. Victor grabbed my ass and I didn't stop him.

He started kissing my neck and I began unbuttoning his pants. I wanted to feel his dick grow in my hands so I pulled it out. It was everything I was hoping it would be! Victor picked me up and put me on the couch. He kissed me passionately and slid my dress off. My whole body felt the pleasure of his tongue and my entire body tingled when he started licking my clit. Victor moved his tongue fast like he was speaking Spanish on my pussy. I damn near said "Aye Papi!"

Victor made me cum on his tongue and then he fucked me like he hated me. He turned me from the back, smacked my ass, and pulled my hair. I loved every minute of it. He was rough compared to BJ, but I really liked how he took control and fucked me with no remorse. When he started choking me and we both nutted at the same time, I swear it was magical. We both lied there naked for about 5 minutes without saying a word. Victor finally leaned over and kissed me, then he started putting his clothes back on.

"Wow that was amazing! You are amazing Lisa!" I loved his Spanish accent.

I stood up and put my dress back on and poured another glass of champagne. "Well I guess we can shake on the deal then huh?" I chugged the glass and poured another one.

"Lisa just know that no one will be able to beat your prices from today forward."

He held up his glass for me to toast. I definitely needed the best prices in town, but I didn't think it would be because I fucked my husband's plug. This new sexual freedom was going to get a lot of people hurt.

I made it back home and I was tired as hell. I have had one hell of a week but I have never felt so in control of my life. I had always done what Fred wanted me to do, however I was fine with that because I loved him. But now I was in control and I was calling the shots. The kids were all upstairs asleep and I'm sure they were tired from Dave and Busters so I didn't wake them. Megan was still up watching tv when I came in the family room.

"Megan you are a lifesaver. Here's $500 just to thank you again." I handed her the money.

"No thank you. I'm always here if you need me so please just call and I'll be here for you guys. I love those kids," she said smiling.

If I could make $2500 in 3 days I would be smiling too. I thought to myself. "Thank you, Megan. I will definitely let you know when I need you again."

As I was saying that my phone rang. It was Victor. Megan

waved bye so I could answer the phone.

"It's not important, I will walk you out sweetie." I walked her to her car and I walked back in the house. My phone started ringing again and it was Victor.

"Hello." I answered.

"I can still taste you on my lips and it's driving me crazy. I wanted to make sure you were home safely." He had the sexiest voice I had ever heard.

"Yes, I'm here and I'm about to shower and call it a night." I started walking upstairs to my room. I checked on the kids first and they were sleeping so peacefully.

"I did not want anything more than to tell you that you are beautiful and I can't stop thinking about you. I hope you sleep well and it was great doing business with you." Victor told me.

"Thank you and we will schedule our next meeting very soon." I said with a giggle. We hung up the phone and I got in the shower so I could get some sleep.

Knock! Knock! Somebody woke me up banging on my door

the next morning. I jumped up because it scared the hell out of me.

Knock! Knock! "Who is it?" I asked.

"Mom it's me why is your door locked?" It was Fred Jr.

I got out the bed and put my robe on to open the door. "I must've locked it last night baby, are you ok?" I thought something was wrong.

"You have a delivery downstairs." I wasn't expecting anything. I started walking downstairs and my living room was filled with roses.

"Omg! Are you sure these belong here?" I asked one of the delivery guys.

I grabbed the card out his hand. It had my name and address and the note said, "Pleasure doing business with you." Victor sent these flowers. Where was I supposed to tell my kids they were from?

"Who are they from mom, daddy?" Frank asked.

"No, they are for Uncle BJ. I forgot that they were coming."

I counted and there were 24 dozen roses sent to me. My pussy immediately started jumping with just the thought of him. I feared for my life soon as those dirty thoughts crossed my mind. I had really gotten ahead of myself. Victor was a very powerful man and he had so many connections. I didn't want him falling for me and creating problems for my husband in jail. I got nervous because I never told him where I lived so I wondered how he knew to send flowers here. My phone started ringing and it was Paco.

"What's up Paco?" I answered.

"The drops went perfect and we just doubled our profits. We are literally about to take over the streets with the lick you were able to get." Paco sounded like a kid in the candy store.

"Ok, meet me at the Ritz at 3. I'm about to take my kids out for lunch." The kids started jumping up and down and dancing.

"See you then." Paco hung up and then Fred was calling.

"Hey baby!" I answered. "I miss you so much!"

Fred started laughing. "Baby I miss y'all more, what are y'all doing?"

I told him we were about to go to lunch and deliver some

flowers to BJ in the hospital. I walked away from the kids to tell him about the drops.

"Paco has been handling things really well and I was able to negotiate on the prices to get them a little lower. We will be able to double our profits." I explained how it was beneficial so that we can add more into the fund for our restaurants and open them up sooner.

"Sounds like you got things handled out there baby. I'm proud of you."

It meant the world to me to hear Fred say that because I really only wanted to make him happy. "That means so much baby, do you need anything?" I asked.

"No my beautiful wife, but I will be sending you something for all your hard work." Fred said. I had been working harder than he thought but I always liked surprises.

"Ok thanks baby. You are the best husband ever!" We hung up and I went upstairs to get dressed.

I took the kids to lunch and to the park, then we stopped by the hospital. I had the kids grab a vase and we took the flowers to

BJ's room. When I made it there, I noticed that there were two officers by his room door and it freaked me out. I kept calm and we walked up to the door. The police officers actually moved out the way and went to sit in the corner.

"Hi BJ! You must have security at your door?" I asked him still looking out the window at the officers. He tried to say something but I stopped him.

"No don't talk. I was only trying to see what was going on. The kids are here and we have flowers for you."

We put the flowers all over the room for him and sat down. The kids were talking and pulling out their phones showing him videos. I decided to take a walk to the nurses station for information. I asked the nurses how BJ was doing and they said he was healing extremely fast. His recovery time wouldn't be long as they thought. I was happy to hear good news; that was one less thing to worry about. I walked back in BJ's room, but I noticed how the cops had been staring at me while I talked to the nurses.

"Time to go kiddos." We said our goodbyes and as I walked out the door one of the officers stopped me.

"Excuse me miss, is it ok if we talk to you?" he asked.

"I don't have time right now, what is it about?" I put my

50

sunglasses on so he knew I was not with the bullshit.

"We wanted to ask a few questions about how your friend got shot." He pulled out a small notebook.

"I don't know anything sir. Come on kids." I tried walking by him and he stepped in front of me.

"Ma'am, do you know if he has any enemies?"

I giggled. "We all have enemies, but I don't know who would want to harm him. He's always been a great person and he loves my kids sir. I wish I could help but really I have to go." I proceeded to walk off and they didn't stop me.

I had Rosa meet us at the movies so the kids could have something to do while I met Paco. I made it to the Ritz and we really did double our profit in a few drops.

"This is definitely game changing Lisa. You should have been moving weight with Fred." Paco said laughing.

I gave him his cut and then my phone rang. It was Chanel Face Timing me. I picked up the phone and Chanel asked me would I come by. It looked like she had been crying so I let her know I was on the way. Me and Paco left the hotel and I headed to Chanel's house. I stopped and got a bottle of wine and some Hennessy just in case she needed to talk and drink. I never thought me and Chanel would be close but after the last few days I think we were basically bonded for life.

"Hey Lisa, I'm glad to see you." Chanel opened the door and hugged me.

"Are you ok? I have alcohol," I said holding up the bottles.

"Yessss!" Chanel laughed and got us both some glasses.

Chanel started telling me how sad she was about BJ. She was having nightmares about Big Will, and her bills were behind. Normally BJ takes care of everything or either Big Will would.

"Everything is going to be ok. I can help you with bills until BJ comes home and these shots of Hennessy will start helping you with the nightmares."

I poured us 5 shots a piece and after we drank that we drank 5 more. We turned on some music then started laughing and talking about everything. Some old R. Kelly song came on and Chanel started dancing with me.

"Come on Lisa, loosen up some! Let's take another shot!" She was screaming by this point and obviously she wasn't a drinker.

"Ok I'll take another one." I took the shot and started dancing with her.

Then Chanel grabbed my face and started kissing me. I jumped back at first but then I started kissing her back. She slid my dress down and started kissing my breasts and licking my stomach. Chanel pulled my panties off and told me to sit on the table. She started giving me the best head of my life. I almost instantly nutted! Then she started eating my ass and then back to licking my pussy until I squirted.

"Omg!" I jumped up. I had never squirted before and I was terrified. "Wait Chanel, I'm not gay and we definitely can't be doing this." I started putting my panties back on.

"Lisa lay your ass back down on the table and I'm not playing."

I stared at her, turned around and laid back on the table. Chanel ate me out until my pearl tongue was throbbing and numb. She stood up and walked in the bathroom. I just sat there for a minute and then I took another shot of Hennessy. The part that scared me the most was that I liked it and I knew I was going to let her do it again.

Chapter 7

Chanel had just turned me out and I liked it. When she got in the shower I put my clothes on and left. I was starting to not even recognize myself anymore. I was a murderer and I was committing adultery after only being with Fred most of my life. It was addicting to the point that I knew I was going to do it again.

When I made it back home and saw that the kids were in the game room, I went upstairs and ran some bath water. I got a wine bottle and glass to take with me in the tub. I turned on some old school music and just relaxed. Everything that happened ran through my head. I thought killing Big Will would have been traumatic for me but it wasn't. It awakened a monster in a good way. I was no longer just Fred's wife, I was making a name for myself.

My phone rang and it scared me. I knocked over my wine glass. It was Victor. Just seeing his name on my phone made my pussy skip a beat. "Hello?" I answered.

"What are you doing beautiful?" He asked me in his sexy voice.

"I'm taking a bath right now. I'm actually about to get out." I picked up the glass and grabbed a towel to get the wine up as I put on my robe.

He asked me what I had planned for the night because he really wanted to see me. "I've been out all day and I really wanted to just stay home and relax.

"I understand. I wanted to take you to my favorite restaurant. It's a Jamaican place and you can wear something comfortable." He said to me almost begging.

"Ok, well I don't want to be out late. I am wearing my adidas track suit so no fancy places, ok." I couldn't resist him. I had to go with him. In just a couple of days we made 15 million dollars because of him. It's nothing like rich sex.

"Would you like a car service to pick you up or I can text the address to you?" he asked.

I had him to text the address to me so I could leave whenever I wanted to. I got dressed and by the time I was downstairs the kids had fallen asleep. I didn't feel as bad knowing they were sleeping. I kissed them on the cheeks and I left out the garage door.

The address led me to what looked like a small airport. I called Victor. "I'm at the address but it didn't bring me to a restaurant." I said confused. /

"No, I see you beautiful drive down, I have the jet waiting for us." Victor said laughing.

"Jet? What do we need the jet for Victor?" I asked.

I pulled up by him. He opened my door and kissed my hand. Then he had one of his guys park the car as he escorted me on this huge plane. When I walked in my mouth dropped. It was all gold and white everything in there. The seats were white, outlined in gold, and there was white carpet. The carpet was so white and plush it looked like snow.

"Wow this is beautiful." I walked down the aisle and the flight attendant seated me and poured us champagne.

"I thought you said we were going to a Jamaican restaurant and you have me on a jet. Where are we going?" I was excited but nervous at the same time. I mean this dude was almost a billionaire he could take me anywhere in the world I'm sure of it.

"Well the best Jamaican food is in Jamaica, right?" He said laughing.

"You are very slick I see." I started laughing.

The flight wasn't long and we landed in Jamaica quickly. It was beautiful. He had an SUV waiting for us as we got off the plane to drive us to the restaurant. Once we made it I realized that it wasn't anyone else there, just us.

"For the place to be good there sure aren't any people here." I said jokingly.

"I rented it out so we could enjoy each other's company. I hope you don't mind," he said seductively.

"Of course I don't mind." I walked in and the atmosphere blew me away. It was a gorgeous restaurant and the servers were all lined up waiting for us. There was a table set up outside with champagne on ice. We sat down and Victor asked if he could order for me.

"Sure I don't mind." I told him.

He ordered for us and then we talked until the food came. It seemed like I've known him for years. We were talking about so many things; the conversation never was dull. The food was delicious! I literally wanted to lick my fingers, but I resisted the urge.

"That food was amazing! I see why this is your favorite restaurant." I told him.

"Yes! I'm so glad you like it because I fly here once a week to eat. Hopefully you can come again." As he was talking he pulled out the biggest bankroll I had ever seen. He put so many hundreds on the table I lost count. I have been accustomed to my lifestyle but with Victor this was a whole new level. He was definitely the head honcho.

We made it back to the plane to leave but I actually wanted to stay a little longer. However, Victor said that he had something important to get back to. He walked me to the very back of the jet. To my surprise, there was a bedroom with a king bed and white and gold Versace covers. It had a walk-in shower connected to it with white and gold tile from top to bottom. Everything was so beautiful and elegantly placed. He closed the door and we immediately started kissing.

The sexual tension had been there all night. I wanted to fuck him on the table at dinner but I kept it classy. He started taking off all my clothes and then he began licking me from head to toe. Victor feasted on my pussy like it was oxtails and gravy, not missing a drop. He turned me over and ate me from the back until I screamed.

Somebody knocked on the door. "Are you guys ok? It was a

little turbulence." It was the flight attendant making sure we were ok but I didn't feel any turbulence besides Victor's mouth.

"Yes, we are fine. Thank you," Victor said as he started kissing me again. I stopped him and asked how long has she been working for him. He said about a year and that she was one of his best.

"Do you think she would fuck us?" Victor bucked his eyes. I think I shocked him with that question.

"Well Lisa that is something I would not know. You can find out, but I will not ask her." He started talking so fast it sounded like Spanish.

"Ok I'll ask. What's her name?" I put my clothes back on and walked back out to the front. Her name was Jennifer and she was beautiful. It took me about 5 minutes, but I convinced her. When I walked back in with her Victor's eyes got even bigger.

"Hello ladies," he said.

"We brought shot glasses." I held them up for him to see.

We started taking shots of patron and then me and Jennifer decided to take a shower together. We stripped and got in the shower. I had only let Chanel eat me out so I didn't really have a clue what to do, but I just went for it. I started kissing her and touching her breast. Jennifer grabbed mine while we kissed and then she started kissing my neck and playing with my clit. Victor was watching the whole thing sitting on the bed. We kissed some more and then we just started washing each other.

Once we came out the shower, Victor was in his boxers and his dick was so hard that I couldn't help but grab it. "Looks like you are ready for us to have some fun with you." I pulled his boxers down and massaged it.

"Jennifer come suck his dick." I told her.

Jennifer walked right over and started sucking it like a baby sucking a pacifier. While she did that I laid him back on the bed and I sat on his face so I could get my nut. We were all moaning by at this point. Victor moved us both out the way. Then he grabbed me, turned me over, and started fucking me so good from the back to the point that I was trying to push him away. He flipped me back over and put his face so close to mine it scared me. It was like he was looking me deep in my eyes, almost to my soul. I turned my head and pushed him back.

I grabbed Jennifer to come sit on my face, but I didn't know what I was doing. She stopped me and then went down and started eating me better than Chanel had. Victor came and sucked on my breasts and kissed me while Jennifer devoured my pussy! I started shaking until I moaned so loud and came right in her mouth.

"We have reached our destination." The pilot came across the speakers.

Jennifer jumped up and started putting her clothes back on. "I have to go get everything ready for the landing. I have to have the pilots paperwork ready," she said.

"Ok Jennifer. Give me your number." We exchanged numbers quickly and she left out.

Me and Victor kissed. He stared at me and grabbed my face. "You are full of surprises, I never met a woman like you before. You're different." Then he kissed me again with so much passion. I just hope he wasn't falling for me because even though I enjoyed every moment together with him, it was just sex. I just had my first threesome with him and I loved it! But, at the end of the day, my heart will always be with Fred. I just hope everyone can keep a secret.

Chapter 8

Everything was going so smooth with business and we were bringing in profit like never before. It's been a few weeks and we have made almost as much as we did in a few months last year. Paco was handling every situation thrown at him without hesitation and BJ was finally back to himself for the most part. He was just released from the hospital a couple days ago, but he was in great shape. He got out and he jumped right back to work. BJ couldn't believe how great the numbers looked. I was a favorite on the streets because I had the best prices and of course walking into meetings with a skin tight dress on always made things go smoother. I was about business before anything and they loved that about me too.

Since BJ was out the hospital, we were about to fly out and meet up with the Italian guys we bought the restaurants from. It was time to start getting all the renovations done. Since BJ's been home, we have been back to strictly business. I knew being out of town together might get things heated again. So instead of it just being the two of us, I invited Paco to come. I really didn't want to be alone with BJ. What happened between us was a mistake and it wouldn't happen again.

I was running some last minute errands when Chanel called. I hadn't talked to her since we had our encounter a couple weeks ago.

"Hello?" I answered.

"Hey Lisa, what are you doing?" She asked. I guess we were going to act like nothing happened which was perfectly fine with me.

"I'm just out and about running errands, what's up?" I don't know why but I was nervous as hell on the phone with her.

"I been wanting to talk to you but didn't know what to say. Do you think you could stop by so we could talk?" She sounded like she was in tears.

"Is everything ok Chanel? I know what happened last time I stopped by. I'm going out of town tomorrow so I don't really have much time." I explained to her.

"I understand if you can't make it, but I really need to talk to you about something as soon as possible." I told her I would come by later when I was finished handling some things, but I didn't have time for Chanel's games.

Once I finished handling my business. I promised my friend Monica I would meet her for drinks around 5 at this little bar called Divas. It was an all female bar that was completely ran by women. There were only women bartenders and even women security guards. It was a place for us to go without worrying about being hit on by men. Monica and I had been friends since college. While we didn't talk often, we always met up and had a good time when we could. Even though I thought I was running late, I actually made it before her.

I ordered a Strawberry Hennessy and waited on her to make it. I was sipping my drink when I noticed this lady in the corner that looked so familiar. She was short with curly hair, and she resembled Tracee Ellis Ross a lot. I tried not to stare but I couldn't quite put my finger on where I knew her from.

"Bitccchhhhhh what's up?!" It was Monica.

Monica was full of life. She's the friend that you always want on your team because she keeps it real as fuck. Monica can do hair, file your taxes, or change a tire. She can fight and pretty much anything she can't do, she knows someone who can. Monica will surprise you though because she looks like a librarian. You never expect when she turns up.

"Bittccchhhh!" I said hugging her.

"Girl why did it take your ass a month to meet up with me when I been trying to hold this tea that I have to tell you?" Monica said laughing.

"Wait I didn't know you had tea bih, spill it! You could've called me and told me." I said sipping some more of my drink.

"Well I needed to tell you this in person girl." Monica said.

"This must be good if we needed drinks." I said laughing. "Go ahead, order a drink and I'll start a tab." I held my hand up so the bartender could see me.

"Well Lisa, I can't drink for a few more months."

I looked at her with my hand still in the air. "Say what bih?" My mouth dropped.

"I'm pregnant and I want you to be the God Mother!" She said excitingly.

"OMG!!! Yasssssssss!! Congrats!!" I couldn't believe it because Monica has had a few miscarriages, so I knew how important this was for her.

We hugged and she told me she was almost 4 months, but wanted to make it through the first trimester before she told me. I've heard a few stories about the guy she had been dating but I never met him before.

"Wow I'm so happy and I can't wait to spoil my God baby." I

hugged her again and I ordered me a couple shots to celebrate.

We started talking about everything and she showed me the sonograms. "The last month has been kinda rough for us because Tim's brother was murdered." Monica said.

"Wow are you serious?" I asked.

"Yes, somebody cut his head off and then they found his body on the other side of town." I almost spit my drink out and I knew my heart was about to jump out my chest.

"Are you ok Lisa?" Monica asked.

I couldn't even talk because it felt like my heart was in my throat. "Yes, I'm fine. That's just so sad. Wow what happened?" I tried to look calm.

"The police aren't sure because there were no fingerprints or any evidence, but it has really gotten the best of Tim."

I took my other shot and ordered another one. "What was his name?" I was just hoping that this was a coincidence and she didn't say who I thought.

"You may have heard of him, they call him Big Will."

I thought I pissed my pants when I heard her say Big Will. I was about to have a panic attack if I didn't get out of that bar. "No, I don't know him, but I really have to use the restroom give me one second."

I went to the bathroom before I passed out. I paced back and forth and sprinkled some water on my face. I texted Chanel and told her to call me in 5 minutes so I could use that as an excuse to leave the bar. I walked back out once I pulled myself together. I had to get away from Monica for now though.

"Girl those shots had me spinning." I lied.

"Well, I won't have any for a while so enjoy enough for me." We both laughed and then my phone rang. I thought it was Chanel but it was BJ.

"Let me take this."

He was calling to check on the departure time for the flight and to make sure I had everything I needed. When we got off the phone, I made up an excuse to leave Monica anyway so I could get out of there. We hugged and said our goodbyes. I told her I would throw her baby shower for her and when I got back in town, we could link back up. That's the least I could do since I'm the one who actually killed the baby's uncle.

Chapter 9

I pulled up to Chanel's house but I was not in the mood to play games with this bitch tonight. I had a flight in the morning and I needed to finish packing my things. I went to the door and before I could knock she opened it. As we spoke to each other, I could barely look at her or the kitchen table. I sat down on the couch and pulled my jacket off.

"What's up Chanel?" I asked nonchalantly.

"Lisa I think I'm going crazy. I've been having nightmares about Big Will," she said kind of quietly.

I really didn't know what to say because I hadn't had any, and I'm the one who cut his head off! I looked at her so she could finish saying whatever she had to say. She went on about how Big Will keeps coming to her in her dreams and he's basically trying to kill her.

In one dream, she explained how he tried to suffocate her. She said she woke up not being able to breathe it felt so real. Then she told me that in the past couple of weeks, she's been doing cocaine and she couldn't keep living like this.

"So what do you want me to do Chanel?" I was confused.

"I'm going to the police Lisa. I need to get this off my

conscience."

I know she didn't say what I thought. "Chanel please don't bring the word police up around me." I looked her dead in her eyes.

She stood up and pulled her cellphone out. "I'm sorry but being in my right mind is better than money."

I don't know who the fuck she was calling, but I knocked the phone out of her hand and kicked it.

"Bitch I will fucking kill you before my kids lose their mother to the fucking prison system! They already don't have a father!" I was so close to her face I know she could smell the alcohol on my breath.

"Look you don't understand. I was the one who set him up so I will take the blame. I can't fucking live in fear anymore." Chanel started walking backwards but before she could move I grabbed her by the fucking neck.

"Bitch you won't be having anymore nightmares because you will be in hell with Big Wil!."

I started choking her hard as I could. I slammed her head in the wall and she passed out from that. I grabbed a vase and started hitting her as hard as I could with it. Then I made her face unrecognizable with my 4 inch stilettos . Chanel's phone started ringing and it scared me so bad that I jumped. I walked over to grab it and saw that it was 911 calling back. I panicked but I know if I didn't answer they were going to be here before I could clean the place up.

"Hello?" I tried to sound as much like Chanel as possible.

"We have a call from this number and were calling to see if you need medical or police assistance." The operator said.

"I'm sorry my nephews had my phone playing and called 911." I just pray that they didn't hear anything on that call.

"Ok well you could be fined if this happens again ma'am." The lady said.

"It won't happen again." I apologized and hung up the phone. I wiped my prints off Chanel's phone then pulled out mine. I called Paco.

"Hey, can you come over to Chanel's and help me take the trash out?" I asked. "Make sure you bring the heavy duty bags because I made a big mess."

I hung up the phone. I hated to kill Chanel but before I go to jail, I will kill whoever gets in my way. I just hope I had enough time to find a dress to wear to her funeral because I know BJ is going to need me there to help console him.

Paco made it and cleaned up everything. He was going to dispose of the body but he had a weird look on his face.

"Are you ok?" I asked him.

"Yes, but Lisa why kill Chanel? That's BJ's sister and this could get ugly." He sounded concerned.

"Paco, the only thing I needed you for was to clean up. Don't ask many questions on why." I really didn't have time for the bullshit anymore. I was the head bitch in charge and what I wanted to happen was going to happen.

"Be ready at 5am. I will pick you up for the flight in the morning," I told Paco as I grabbed my keys to leave. As soon as we were heading back out the door Chanel's phone rang. We both looked at each other. Paco grabbed the phone and we walked out the door.

We made it to New Jersey the next morning and checked into our hotels. I was beyond tired and had a few hours before we met at the restaurant. I decided to shower and take a nap. Right before I dosed, off someone knocked on my door. I didn't get up immediately because I wasn't expecting anyone. They started knocking harder and I sat up. I grabbed my phone and saw that I didn't have any missed calls from Paco or BJ.

"Who is it?" I asked. Nobody said anything. I called Paco.

"What's up Lisa?" He sounded like he was sleeping too.

"Are you at my door?" I asked.

"No I was taking a nap is everything ok?" Paco said. I had no clue who was at my door but I got up and asked again who was it.

"Lisa it's me, Charles, and Katherine." I rolled my eyes.

It was my aunt and uncle. I forgot I told them I was coming into town and I wanted to see them. They didn't even give me a chance to take a nap but I opened the door.

"Hey you guys!" I said excitedly and hugged them.

"Wow this is a huge suite you got here." They came in looking all around. I rarely get to see family so anytime I'm in town I always make sure I give them a call.

"You guys didn't waste any time coming to see me huh?" I said laughing.

I hugged them some more then we sat and talked for about two hours. I ordered us all room service. Soon, Paco and BJ came by to meet them. We talked about all the old days and I bragged on my kids and how smart they were of course. We finally said our goodbyes because I had to get ready to meet at the restaurant in about an hour. I told them I would try to see them again before we left.

I hopped in the shower and got dressed. A navy blue dress that fit every curve I had was my weapon of choice. I paired it with my nude Christian Louboutins; I was definitely looking like a snack. My hair was styled bone straight and my ass was sitting up just right. I was here to let the big boys know that the queen was in town.

We all made it to the restaurant and it looked even bigger with it empty. Fred and BJ wanted the restaurant to be urban because they thought it would attract more younger adults. I wanted a full out chic and upscale restaurant for New Jersey and a more artistic urban restaurant in New York.

"Wow Lisa! You definitely look better every time I see you." Marco said as he kissed my cheek.

Marco was the oldest one of the men. He was also the sexiest one. He really didn't look Italian. He looked more like Ricky Martin and sounded like Robert De Niro.

"I see you are in your Louboutins, very classy." He said laughing.

"Well, I ruined a pair yesterday, so I need to get another pair while I'm here. These are definitely bloody shoes." They all started laughing. I thought back to Chanel and how I had stomped her face in with my pump.

"So good to see you guys again, especially since I got shot after I saw y'all last time," BJ said shaking their hands.

He introduced them to Paco then we walked around and looked at everything. Paco wrote down estimates for some of the things I had in store. Once we got done looking at that restaurant, we drove about two hours to New York to look at the other restaurant.

We finally made it to the location of the second restaurant and it was beautiful. It had gorgeous chandeliers and gold accents everywhere. It was perfect.

"Wow, I know exactly what I want for this one. I'm going to actually make this one my upscale place."

I walked around admiring everything. I wanted new flooring throughout. The current flooring looked really old and run down. Other than that, there were only minor changes needed.

"I am in loooovveee! BJ, you didn't tell me how nice it was! The pictures definitely didn't do it justice."

Thinking about the price we paid for both restaurants, I felt like it was a catch to it. "Nobody is going to come shoot us up in here right fellas?" They laughed hysterically.

"No of course not. The friendship that we have with Fred is worth more than money," Marco said. "Fred saved my life and I will forever thank him."

I heard about the time Fred shot and killed a guy that was about to shoot some guy but I didn't know it was him. "I didn't know that but that's my husband. Fred is definitely loyal to you if you're his friend." I thought about me and BJ and how wrong we were. I almost felt like crying in that moment. I'm listening to them talking about my husband being a hero, and here I was becoming a disgrace.

Chapter 10

We made it back to our hotel in New Jersey. I was super tired so I quickly showered and got ready for bed. I had a missed call from Victor, but I decided not to call him back. Instead, I FaceTimed my kids and said goodnight to them. When I finished talking to them, I found something on tv to fall asleep to.

As I was dozing, off my phone rang and it was Victor again. I answered the phone because it could have been about business and the money had to keep flowing.

"Hello?" I answered.

"Hello beautiful, how are you?" He asked.

"I'm fine, but I was going to sleep. I've had a long day and I'm exhausted." I told him. I got up to get a bottle of water and I looked out the window. There was a couple in the apartment building fucking.

"Omg I can see some people having sex." I kind of ducked down. If I could see them I'm pretty sure they could see me.

"This is weird as hell, I could never live in New Jersey or New York, everything is too close."

I of course couldn't help but be intrigued so I kept watching. The guy had started eating her out and he looked like he was starving. He turned her over and began eating her ass. She looked like she trying to escape! My freaky ass was getting so turned on that I forgot Victor was on the phone until he said hello.

"Victor I'm sleepy can I call you in the morning?" I fake yawned.

"Yes, get your beauty sleep. Goodnight."

I hung up the phone and resumed my live porn show. By this time, she was sucking his dick like it would save his life. She was sucking his balls like there was no tomorrow. I continued to watch as he nutted and she swallowed. They started fucking hard and he nutted in like five minutes. I was probably more disappointed than she was.

The guy grabbed his phone to answer it, said a few words, then hung up. He moved and walked to the bathroom, I'm guessing, and then she sat up and started yelling at him. She had to be upset about him nutting fast or whoever was on that phone. When he came back in the room, he started putting his clothes on. They were obviously having some type of argument because she grabbed his arm and pushed his head. All of a sudden, the guy started beating the fuck out of that girl!

I ducked down to make sure they didn't see me then I started back watching. The girl picked up a lamp and hit him with it. The guy pounced at her and grabbed her neck. He was choking the shit out of her. Her eyes looked like they were about to pop out. "Oh shit!" I said to myself.

Her eyes started closing and she finally just collapsed in the bed. I was panicking because I couldn't believe what I just witnessed. I was wide awake by this point. The thing that shocked me most was the fact that he just put on his hat and walked out the door like nothing happened.

I didn't know what to do. I couldn't call the police because I might end up behind bars myself. That wasn't an option. I couldn't sleep knowing that girl's body was right across from me and I didn't do anything. If that was my daughter, I would want somebody to at least do that much for me. I slid some jeans and a t shirt on and went to the lobby. There was nobody there. When I walked out front I saw a guy on his phone.

"Hey, I don't have my phone but can you call the police? I just heard some loud screaming coming from that building." I asked the guy.

"Oh wow sure." He pulled out his phone and called. He said exactly what I said and he gave them his name.

"Thank you so much, I hope it wasn't anything serious. My name is Lisa." I stuck my hand out to shake his.

"Hi Lisa, I'm Blake. He shook my hand and he rubbed it a little and smiled at me. Blake was not my typical type but he was definitely cute, for a white guy.

"Nice meeting you Blake." I turned to walk back in the hotel.

"Wait can I ask you something?" He walked behind me.

"Sure, I guess." I had a confused look on my face.

"What do you moisturize with? You're the softest thing I've ever felt."

I couldn't help but smile at how corny that was but Blake was actually cute. He looked a lot like Channing Tatum but he had that New Jersey swag that was turning me on a little.

"Cocoa Butter and magic." We both laughed.

He asked if I had a boyfriend and I told him I didn't. It wasn't a lie because I actually have a husband. Blake was looking good enough to have some fun with so I invited him to my room.

When we got in the room, we took some took some shots of Hennessey and Patron that I had earlier. He asked me did I smoke. Normally I don't, but I needed to get high. We smoked two blunts and then I suggested a game of Truth or Dare. We started playing and I asked him truth or dare.

"Truth, I better start off easy," He said.

"What's the freakiest thing you've ever done?" I asked. He told me about the time he and his friends had an orgy in Mexico.

"Ok your turn." I told him.

"Ok Lisa, truth or dare?" He asked smiling.

"Of course I'm going with dare, duh!"

Blake dared me to kiss him anywhere on his body. Since I started he game I had to go hard.

"Take your pants off." I stood up.

"Take my pants off?" He repeated after me.

"Yea take them off so I can kiss you and your boxers."

He hesitated until he realized I was serious. Blake stood up and pulled down his pants and boxers. I was actually pleasantly surprised because I always heard white men were small down there. Blake was packing! I got down on the floor and kissed the tip of his dick. You would have thought I was a snake charmer the way his dick jumped.

"He is excited to meet me already huh?" I laughed. I stood up.

"Ok truth or dare?" I asked.

"Wait, you can't just kiss my dick and not expect me to be ready to pounce all over you right now," Blake said with his dick getting harder and harder.

"Blake, truth or dare?" I asked again.

"Dare." He grabbed his dick and started stroking it.

"I dare you to eat my pussy until I say stop," I commanded.

"How did you know that I was starving?" Blake asked with a devilish smile.

He laid me down and lifted my legs up like I was a baby and began licking the skin off my pussy. He knew exactly where to lick. Blake's mouth was so wet that I couldn't help but to bust nuts back to back. Every time I wanted to say stop he got even better. He turned me over and ate my ass until I nutted again.

"Stop." I moaned.

"Oh, you want me to stop?" Blake said smacking my ass.

"Stop and fuck me," I moaned. My pussy was getting wetter just thinking about his dick sliding inside me.

When he slid his dick in, my pussy tightened around it. Blake had a thick one and it felt so damn good. He actually knew how to fuck and I enjoyed every minute of it. He wanted to fuck in the ass but I wasn't quite ready for that yet. Blake was definitely a freak. We both came back to back until we couldn't move. It wasn't bad for my first white guy. Before Blake left he asked for my number to keep in touch. I gave it to him and we said our goodbyes.

After he left, I looked out the window to see if the police had made it to the girls apartment. It looked like nobody had found her yet. By this point I knew she was dead. I really hoped somebody would find her. Before I turned around, I saw the dude walk back in the apartment. I ducked down quick as hell hoping he didn't see me. He stood over the girl's body like he was trying to wake her up, then he looked straight at me. I stooped down for what felt like 5 minutes and then looked back at the apartment. He had closed the blinds. "Fuck!" I said out loud. I guess I would just have to hear about it on the news when they found her body.

My phone rang and scared the shit out of me. It was Blake.

"What's up Blake?" I answered.

"I just want to feel you one more time." Then I heard a knock on the door. It was Blake and he came back for more. As tired as I was, that dick was standing up and I was ready to take a seat.

We didn't say anything to each other, we just started fucking. I grabbed his dick and told him to lay back on the bed, but he stopped me.

"I want you to do something for me."

He told me to lay upside down on the bed with my head hanging. As soon as I got in position, he fucked my mouth. I didn't gag. I took all his dick like a pro until I felt him bust down my throat. He moaned so loud; I knew I had created a monster. He turned me over and started hitting it from the back. Blake liked it rough. He grabbed my hair, smacked my ass then called me a slut.

"Look don't call me no slut, I'm not into that shit," I warned him.

I had to let him know not to call me out my name. He only saw a woman that was beautiful and freaky, but he didn't know I was a cold blooded killer. We fucked so long and hard that I don't even remember falling asleep. A knock at the door woke me up and I jumped up. I put my robe on and opened the door.

"What's wrong?" I asked, still half asleep.

Once I realized that I wasn't at home, it was too late. It was BJ.

I was looking at him and BJ was looking at Blake in my bed.

"Wait BJ." I said frantically. He shook his head and just walked off.

Chapter 11

"Blake come on and get your stuff it's time to go." I woke him up and I grabbed his pants and shirt off the floor.

"Wow I can't even get a good morning after you were just moaning my name?" He tried to kiss me. I moved my head.

"I have somewhere to be in 30 minutes. I hate to rush you off." I lied. I needed him out of here so I could get myself together before I saw BJ again.

"I can take you, get dressed." Blake stood up and grabbed his boxers.

"No I'm fine, you can leave." I wanted him to hear the attitude in my voice.

"Ok well somebody woke up on the wrong side of the bed." He walked in the bathroom and started pissing.

"I have some important things to do before I fly back out" I had all his stuff and I handed it to him as he walked out the bathroom.

"Ok. Let me at least take you out before you leave."

He grabbed his stuff and started putting on his clothes. This dude really didn't pick up on hints that it was just a one night stand. I should have realized that when he came back to the room last night.

"Sorry, I really have a lot to do. I'll call you if I have any free time." I reached for my phone like I was going to save his number but then he grabbed my phone.

"You have lost your damn mind! Give me my phone!" I got loud and tried to grab my phone out his hand. This little white boy just didn't know who the fuck I was.

"I was only going to call my phone with yours to see where it was." He said handing me my phone back. "I see it under the bed. Damn, I'm sorry Lisa." He picked his phone up off the floor.

"You know what Blake, just leave please." I walked to the door and opened it for him. He walked out the door looking at me the entire time but didn't say another word.

I took a shower and got dressed. The only thing on my mind was BJ and how his face looked at that door. It seemed like I broke his heart and that broke my heart. I know I could never have sex with BJ again because when feelings get involved things can get ugly. I called Paco to see what they were doing.

"Are you guys dressed?" I asked him.

"Yes. I was just about to head to your room to see if you were you dressed." Paco said.

"Ok, well when you guys come down we can go to brunch." I hung up the phone with him.

I hoped there were no bad vibes between me and BJ. I heard a knock on the door so I opened it. It was only Paco. I was hoping BJ didn't pull a stunt and make things awkward, but I played it cool.

"Oh, where's BJ?" I asked.

"He's coming. He was on the phone." I closed the door behind Paco.

"Ok, gotcha." I asked him what they did last night and then I told him about the guy killing the woman. He couldn't believe it.

"Damn Lisa, your life is like a fucking movie. Why didn't you call us or something?" Paco asked.

"I wasn't scared but I was fucking shocked. Plus, I didn't know what happened after that."

I told Paco how I got this white guy to call 911 and how the killer dude ended up closing the blinds. That was all I knew. Somebody knocked on my door and I got up to open it. I guess

BJ finally got off the phone. I was so nervous opening the door. The scene from earlier this morning kept playing in my head. I tried to have a calm look. Hopefully BJ wouldn't even bring it up. I opened the door and it was fucking Blake.

"What are you doing back at my room?" I yelled at him.

"Lisa who is this?" Paco asked standing up.

"Oh, you kicked me out your room so that you could bring another dude right up? You are a nasty hoe ass bitch!" Blake screamed at me.

"What the fuck did you just say to me?"

Before I could move Paco had him by the throat. Blake wasn't a skinny guy but Paco had him off his feet. He turned bright red in the face until he looked like a damn tomato.

"Paco let him down, let him down!" I screamed.

I closed the door before someone called security if they hadn't already.

"Blake if you don't want to die, you will get the fuck out my hotel room and pretend you never met me. Now this is no threat, this is a promise. Act cautiously." I said very calmly. I don't know why I was even giving him a chance to live.

"Fuck you bitch, you're only good for sucking this dick." Blake screamed.

Before I could blink my eye, Paco hit Blake so hard I heard his jaw bone break. Blake went sliding on the floor like they were in a boxing ring. Paco stood over him hitting him again and again until I grabbed Paco's hand and stopped him.

"Paco don't do it! This is not the time nor the place." I yelled. Paco stopped and I looked at Blake's face. Paco had his face twisted already. He definitely broke some bones in Blake's face.

"Blake I need you to get up and get out of my room and pretend you never met me." I repeated myself.

He had so much blood coming out his mouth that I knew he was going to go to the police. If a white boy tells the local police that a Mexican man and black woman had him jumped, Paco and I were over with. I couldn't take any chances so I helped Blake up.

"I'm going to clean your face up." I took him in the bathroom and had him sit on the toilet. I cleaned his face, but his jaw and his nose were broken. I told him to get an uber to come pick him up, then I asked him his price.

"My price?" He could barely move his mouth.

89

"How much is it going to take for you to act like none of this ever happened? No police involved; we go our separate ways." I washed my hands and I looked at him and waited for him to answer.

"You're fucking serious right now?" He shook his head. "Ok, well give me twenty-five thousand dollars and we have a deal." He shrugged his shoulders.

"Ok one second." I walked to one of my Gucci duffel bags where I keep cash and grabbed the money. I try not to carry much cash, but I had seventy-five thousand on me to shop with for the trip. I walked back in the bathroom and I made him stand up.

"Before I give you this money, I need you to say something on video for me." I didn't care that he could barely talk, but I wanted him to know that this was his life on the line.

Paco had walked in the bathroom to watch. In front of the camera, I made Blake say his entire name, address, and parents' names. He showed his ID and he said his social security number.

"That's just a little security in case you think this is a joke." I gave him the money and he looked at us like he was being punked'.

"Ok goodbye." I said.

He walked out the bathroom and walked out the door. As he was walking out, BJ was just about to knock. I think BJ was surprised to see Blake again coming out the door especially with his face fucked up. Blake walked right by him and went down the hallway and got on the elevator.

"What's going on?" BJ asked. I was beyond embarrassed.

"It's a long story." I looked at Paco and you could tell he was still on edge.

"We could have saved that money and killed his ass." Paco said.

"Saved what money?" BJ looked confused.

I didn't say anything because it was my fault for inviting someone, literally off the street, in my bed. What had gotten into me? I was slowly turning into a nympho and I had to pull it together.

"I can explain everything BJ." As soon as I was about to tell BJ what happened, my phone rang. It was my aunt. I forgot that I told her I would see them again before we left.

"Hi Aunt Katherine. I haven't forgot about you guys." I answered the phone.

"Lisa, where are you?" My aunt sounded like she was crying.

"I'm at the hotel. what's wrong?" I asked.

"Charles had a heart attack and he didn't make it." It felt like somebody kicked me in the stomach. Uncle Charles was like a daddy to me. This really hit home. My aunt started sobbing louder. Just saying those words probably killed her inside. Tears started running down my face and I couldn't say anything. Me and Aunt Katherine just sat on the phone and cried.

I hated going to funerals but, after the news I got in New Jersey I knew I had to get ready for a tough one. I offered to pay for the arrangements so that my aunt could pull herself together and not worry about finances. Uncle Charles had an insurance policy, but my aunt didn't work anymore. That was money she could keep and save.

My kids didn't remember him, but they were a big help in keeping me smiling. I had been working on getting Rosa back, but I was doing it behind the scenes because I knew the kids missed her. My kids didn't want to go to the funeral, so I got in touch with Megan to watch them for the weekend.

"Are you guys sure you don't want to go with me and just stay in the hotel during the funeral?" I asked them.

I knew they would rather be home instead of going to New Jersey but I still asked. They did have everything a kid could dream of. A game room, a basketball court, an indoor pool and I was building a room for a rock climbing wall. The kids had it made.

I had been really worried about BJ. He had been going crazy since Chanel was still missing. I had to play along with him. It was easy for me to cry thinking of my uncle, so I would act like I was crying about her being missing a few times so he didn't expect me. Deep down I felt bad because I killed BJ's sister, but Chanel had it coming either way. BJ had his own team going around and asking questions, even posting flyers with her picture on it. He also offered a half-a million-dollar reward to anybody who had information. It had been a week since I killed her. No one had come forward about anything, not even her body. I knew one thing for sure, I wasn't going to tell on myself.

I made it back to New Jersey and my aunt wanted me to stay at her house. I knew it was a bad idea because when I get around family we always argue, especially me and my cousin Katrina. We call her Trina. She always starts some shit with me, it never fails. She's the cousin that felt like somebody owed her something, but she never tried to be anything more than a show off. When you see Trina, she looks like a million

93

bucks, but she don't have a pot to piss in. She's always dressed up and her hair is always laid, but she doesn't even have a car. Her priorities in life are messed up and because I'm doing good, she hates me. I was staying for my aunt's sake. I just hope nobody pushes any buttons because I'm already on edge.

There were so many people at my aunt and uncle's house that I had to go upstairs to hide. I was starting to feel like my anxiety was about to kick in. I took some Xanax pills to relax. I sat on the bed and I must have dozed off because I heard somebody close the door. It woke me up. It was dark in the room, but I saw a shadowy figure. I grabbed my phone to shine the light on them. It was Shawn, Trina's trifling boyfriend.

"Oh hey Shawn. What are you doing in here?" I asked.

"Is that you Lisa? I'm sorry I came in the wrong door." He looked shocked.

"I'm glad you woke me up because I wasn't trying to fall asleep." I stood up and stretched.

"Keep doing that Lisa and imma try to come through your door tonight too." Shawn said looking at me like he was picturing me naked.

"What the fuck did you just say?" I asked him with a scowl on my face.

He started laughing. "I'm joking, don't take me serious." He started walking back out the door.

"Shawn, the first time you try me I promise you won't try anybody else." I closed the door behind him and locked it this time.

After I freshened up, I called and checked on my kids before heading back downstairs. I could hear Trina and her sister Pam's loud mouth before I made it down. I was going to try to say hi to everybody and just float around the room.

I guess Pam spotted me because I heard her call my name. "Lisa! Hey cousin."

I turned and looked then started waving and walking towards them. "Hey you guys." I hugged everybody except Shawn. I caught him looking at my titties and rolled my eyes.

"How's everybody been?" I asked.

"Clearly not as good as you," Trina said looking me up and down.

I knew it was about to start but I just ignored her. Trina was my cousin and she was drop dead gorgeous, but she had no real hustle about herself. She always attracted bum ass men, and I

95

guess because I didn't, she hated me for it. Trina was about 5'8", had the prettiest legs, and perfect hips. She had a smooth, caramel complexion and beautiful hazel brown eyes that were mesmerizing. Trina kept her hair in almost any hairstyle you could think of and they all looked good on her.

Pam was just as beautiful. She wore her hair natural and you never saw her in anything flashy. They could almost go for twins, but Pam was so much nicer that Trina.

"How are the kids?" I asked just trying to change the subject.

Me and Pam started talking and catching up about the kids. We were having small talk about everything until Trina obviously got jealous.

"Pam can you come help me grab something out the kitchen?" Trina interrupted us.

"Ask Shawn to help you, I'm talking." Pam started back talking to me.

"Pam seriously, I need you." Trina looked like something was wrong, but you never could tell with her.

"Go ahead Pam. I'm going to walk around and try to talk to everybody. It's no problem." I didn't want to be around Trina much longer anyway.

I started walking around and talking to my cousins who I hadn't seen in years. I got a chance to see some of my aunts and uncles. I really was enjoying myself. That was until Trina walked out the kitchen.

"Lisa, you low down bitch!" She came out the kitchen screaming.

Everybody got dead silent. I didn't even say anything myself because I know she wasn't talking to me.

"You tried to fuck Shawn upstairs? Are you kidding me?" She was dead serious because I could see Pam telling her to stop. I just knew this was not happening to me right now.

"Please don't insult me like that Trina. Nobody wants Shawn but you, clearly." I said rolling my eyes.

"Where the hell is Shawn because I know he didn't tell you anything like that." I walked to where Trina and Pam were but at this point I was steaming mad.

"Lisa, let's just go in the kitchen," Pam said before I could even get near them.

As soon as we walked in the kitchen, I choked the fuck out of Trina. "Look bitch, cousin or not, you are not about to keep

97

playing with me."

By this point Pam was screaming at me to let her go and tried to get my hands off her neck.

"I'm sick of her always starting shit with me! Where the fuck is Shawn?"

I walked back in the living room looking for him. He was walking back in the house, I guess he went outside to smoke a cigarette. I walked up to him and slapped that nigga so hard his hat fell off his head.

"Look you dusty son of a bitch, don't lie on me or my pussy! I wouldn't fuck you with Trina's pussy so just know you have been warned."

By the time I turned around to walk off from him, Trina punched me so hard in my face that I almost fell backwards. Everybody at this point in the house was trying to break everything up and figure out what was going on. My aunt was crying hysterically and that pissed me off even more. Instead of me beating Trina's ass like I should have, I just walked away.

"If we can't come together in a time like this, then we will never come together. Trina, don't you ever think I would risk my marriage for somebody who can't even afford to buy the brand of tissue I use for my house." I went and apologized to my aunt and told her I was going to stay at a hotel. I was ready for this funeral to be over so I could get back home.

I got a hotel on a different side of town from my last stay here. I had showered and was finally in bed, looking for something to watch on tv. After flipping through the channels, I ended up watching the news to see what the weather would be like for the funeral tomorrow. They were showing a breaking story. It was about a woman's body being found and her name was Kimberly Murphy. I had a gut feeling she was the girl I saw get killed. They showed a picture of her and sure enough it was her.

I felt like I knew her. I was glad they found her body. The bastard had obviously taken her to the pier and dumped her body. Someone saw it floating. The police were still looking for a suspect and asked the public if they had any information to let them know. My life felt like a Lifetime movie. It was going so crazy lately. I just wanted to go to sleep and not think about anything.

I woke up at 2am and my stomach was growling. I couldn't order room service this late, but I remembered there was a diner right across the street. I got up, put on some clothes, and went downstairs. It had gotten pretty cool outside and I didn't even have a coat on. I ran over to the diner as fast as I could. I sat down and looked over the menu and decided to go with a t-bone steak and scrambled eggs.

The diner was really nice. It was actually kind of cozy and looked really clean. They didn't take long cooking my food either. After enjoying my meal, I paid and got up to head back to the hotel. There were a few cars coming down the street, so I had to wait to cross over.

As soon as I stopped, somebody grabbed me from the back. I dropped my to go box and tried to look back, but they put a towel over my face. Whatever was soaked in the towel when I breathed it in made my whole throat burn. I started coughing and tried to fight back. Suddenly a truck rushed up. Whoever was behind me pushed me in a black SUV and put a pillowcase over my head. They were speaking Spanish and it sounded like there were 3 of them. The last thing I remember is somebody unbuttoning my pants. I was paralyzed. I could not move my body at all. Then, I just passed out.

Chapter 12

When I woke up, I could still hear them talking but the truck wasn't moving. We were just sitting in the truck like we were waiting on somebody. I heard one guy say that the boss needed to hurry up. I didn't know if this was a random act or if someone had been watching me and waiting to kidnap me. I sat as still as possible because I didn't want them to know I was awake. One guy's name was Jose and the other's was Octavio. They were saying some more things in Spanish when the 3rd guy must've noticed somebody pulling up.

"That looks like the boss." The guy in the back with me lifted me up and took the pillowcase off my head. As soon as he took it off, I spit in his face.

"You stupid bitch!" He yelled out and slapped me. "The nasty bitch spit on me." He had a really heavy Spanish accent.

My throat was still burning a little. I should've kept my spit instead of using it on that asshole. We all got out the car and there was another black SUV that pulled up. They walked me to the door and sat me inside.

"Hello Lisa. Can I offer you a bottle of water?"

To my surprise, I saw two Jamaican guys. I thought that was strange because the other guys were Mexican. However, I was more confused on how they knew my name.

"Who the fuck are y'all and what do you want with me?" I asked.

"We will get to that soon but take the water. I know your throat is burning." I grabbed the water bottle and sat back.

"Lisa, we don't want to harm you, but we will if you don't cooperate.

"You better kill me before I kill you because y'all have fucked with the wrong one." I didn't have any connections in Jersey besides the Italians, so I didn't know what they wanted with me.

"My name is Barkley and this is Marley. We're twin brothers and we run New Jersey and New York." He said.

"We were informed that you purchased two restaurants from the Italians. Is that correct?"

This had to be some beef they had with the damn Italians and I was just caught in the crossfire. "Who wants to know?" I said sarcastically.

"Look bitch, don't play with me. We are about to pull up to that restaurant because there is something that belongs to me in there."

I realized that we were in New York, so I guess Jose and Octavio's job was to get me here to go to the restaurant. "Well when I bought the place everything in it became my property." I said to Barkley.

"I will allow you to live or I can kill you and still get in the restaurant to get what belongs to me. Your choice." He shrugged his shoulders. I decided to play it cool because I wanted to make it back home to my kids. They didn't realize that they had kidnapped the wrong woman.

I opened up the doors to let them in the restaurant.

"What are you looking for and do you know where it is?" I asked.

"Yes. Marley go get it." Marley went to the back.

"How do you know who I am? Who told you that I bought the restaurant?" I asked Barkley.

"It's public record and I also have my way of finding out things." He said.

I continued to observe him. He kept a very mean look on his face. I got a chance to get a good look at him. Even though him and Marley weren't identical twins, they did look alike.

"It was still there." Marley held up a diamond the size of a grapefruit.

"Wow that's a huge diamond." I said amazed.

"Beautiful Marley! Let's get out of here."

They gave me all of my things and told me if I went to the police, they would come back and kill me. They just didn't know that I would find them and make them regret this night forever.

I took an uber back to the hotel. By this time, it was almost 8 in the morning. I didn't have time to sleep so I got in the shower and got dressed for the funeral.

I called Paco. "Do you know anything about some Jamaicans in New Jersey or New York?" I had to get some information on them.

"Nah, I don't really have my connections there but BJ does." Paco told me.

I was really trying to avoid BJ so I decided to call Victor instead. Victor was well known all around especially if there was something to do with the drug game.

"Beautiful, where have you been? I haven't heard from you. I miss you Lisa." Victor answered the phone. I knew this might be a bad idea to get him involved but they asked for it.

"I've been going through so much. My uncle passed recently and last night somebody kidnapped me!" I said. "It was some Jamaicans and I've been scared ever since they dropped me off at my restaurant and left me there."

I explained to him how everything happened and he was furious. "I will get to the bottom of this and they will never forget your name. Be with your family and try not to worry about anything. If the names they gave you are their real names, I will have this taken care of before you get out the funeral."

I knew Victor was dead serious. We hung up the phone. I finished getting dressed and headed to be with my family.

The funeral service was nice. My uncle went out in style. After the funeral, we all went back to my aunt's house to sit around and eat. Victor had called me twice while I was in the funeral, but I was scared to call him back. As soon as I was about to call him he sent a text saying he just landed in New Jersey. Why did I even get Victor involved is the question?

He called me again, so I got up and answered the phone. "Hi Victor, I just read your text. You didn't have to come here." I said.

"If someone does something to my woman, it is a must I protect her and be by her side." He started saying something in Spanish and I just shook my head.

Did he say his woman? I knew then, Victor had lost his mind. "I'm with my family but I can meet you wherever."

Victor started laughing. "Lisa, I don't think you know how powerful I am. I know where your family lives and where Fred's family lives. When you are connected with me in this dirty drug game, you have to have collateral." Victor explained to me.

"Well I don't want you coming here, I will meet you back at my hotel. I'll send the address." I hung up the phone and texted him the hotel address.

Once I made it back to the hotel, I pulled up just as Victor was. His driver opened the door for him and he got out, apparently so excited to see me.

"Wow! You keep getting more beautiful every time I see you." He kissed me and my pussy automatically got soaking wet.

I knew he was getting infatuated with me, but I couldn't help wanting to feel his dick inside of me right then and there. "Where are your bags?" I asked him.

"I just hopped on the plane after you called me because I wanted to make sure you were ok. I can buy a few things while I'm here." He grabbed my hand and we went to my room.

We couldn't make it in the room good before we were taking our clothes off. Victor unzipped my dress and then took it off me. He unfastened my bra and sucked on my breast until I started moaning. He licked all the way down to my navel and then pulled my panties off. I was standing butt naked. He stepped back and looked at my body, ready to devour it. He laid me on the bed and started sucking my toes, then licked all up my thighs. Slowly, he started licking on my clit and then gently began sucking on it. I started moving like crazy because it felt so fucking good. Victor turned me over and smacked my ass.

His dick slid in so gently as he began stroking me from the back. He wasn't rough with me, he took his time. He bust his first nut pretty quick, but his dick was still standing hard. Victor guided me on top of him so that I could ride his dick. When he laid back, I started riding him slow. He moaned my name and that made me start riding him faster. That shit turned me on and made my pussy juices flow down his dick. I bounced on his dick until I came twice. He pushed me back off him and started eating my ass. One thing I loved about Victor was that he was not selfish in the bedroom. He always made sure I got mine. We fucked a little longer until we both passed out.

"That was amazing Lisa. You are something else." Victor said playing in my hair.

Victor's phone started ringing and he answered it. Whoever he was talking to must have told him some good news.

"Excellent! Yes, bring it right up." He hung his phone up.

"Let's shower baby. I have dinner coming up." He kissed my forehead.

We took a shower together and took turns drying each other off. Soon, we heard a knock at the door. Victor left out of the bathroom to answer it and I finished drying off. When I walked out there were three little carts with big silver platters and champagne on ice.

"Wow you got fancy huh bae?" I was starving and couldn't wait to eat.

"Yes. I got some steak and baked potatoes for us and I have a special dessert."

He lifted the top off one of the platters. The steaks looked so juicy! I couldn't wait to eat. We sat down to eat and drank a glass of champagne.

"Ok I'm ready for the dessert now Victor." I told him as I finished my potato.

"Come." He grabbed my hand and we walked back to the other platters.

"Lisa, I know this is something that just happened but no matter what, I want you to know that I am here to serve you, hand and foot, no matter what you need from me ok." Victor was looking me in my eyes like he was trying to reach my soul. I really didn't know what to say so I just didn't say anything.

"No matter what ok Lisa?" As he finished saying that, he lifted the top off the platters. I literally almost passed out. It wasn't a fucking strawberry cheesecake. He had just served me Barkley and Marley heads on a platter.

Chapter 13

As crazy as it may sound, I was super turned on by Victor's charm. I was honestly starting to like him. I've never had a man treat me the way Victor has, not even Fred. I know if he was home he would give me the world, but Victor was right here in the flesh. He was the man. I can't explain it any other way than that.

"Well you ruined my appetite for cheesecake." I said laughing and I kissed Victor.

"You must be impressed if I got those sweet kisses." He grabbed my ass and kissed me again.

He put the tops back on the platters and started kissing my neck. We kissed a little while longer and then we just cuddled. I didn't know much about Victor personally besides him being heavy in the drug game. I learned that he has two sisters and that he was the only boy growing up. He's from Mexico but grew up in California for most of his life. His entire family was involved with drugs in some way and they kept a tight knit operation. We both got to know each other more and it felt good to just be relaxed and held.

We were dozing off when my phone started ringing. It was BJ. I didn't answer it and just let it go to voicemail. He called right back so I decided to answer and just play it cool.

"Hello?" I answered sitting up in the bed.

"Are you ok? I haven't heard from you since you been in Jersey." BJ said.

"I'm fine, besides the fact I was kidnapped." I stood up and put on my robe.

"Lisa don't play like that." He said, sounding really concerned.

"BJ I don't play the radio so why would I play about being kidnapped." I let him know that I was serious.

"Ok so what do we need to do? Do you know who they were? What did they want from you?" BJ asked a hundred questions at a time.

I explained to him how everything went down and how it had been taken care of. There was no need to worry. He said he was still going to call the Italians to see who those Jamaicans were and to make sure there were no more surprises. Victor had sat up and started listening to our conversation. I didn't want him getting the wrong impression, so I cut BJ off.

"I'm perfectly fine. Trust me, I'm always protected." I looked at Victor and smiled.

"I will call you and Paco when I have time to discuss some new business ventures." BJ tried to say something, but I just hung up.

"That BJ likes you." Victor said. My heart starting beating fast as hell for some reason.

"BJ is like my brother. That is Fred's best friend." I said to Victor not trying to sound nervous.

"I see how he looks at you. It's the same way I look at you. He is in love with you Lisa." Victor said so seriously. I knew BJ liked me, but it made me nervous that Victor could see that.

"Wait, are you trying to tell me that you're in love with me Victor?" I asked.

He started laughing. "Do not make this about me right now, this is about BJ." I knew only a man that was infatuated or in love would do what Victor just did. When you are as powerful as Victor, there are different ways you show affection.

"I was only asking because I might be in love with you too." I walked over to him and slid my robe off.

We started kissing and Victor licked my entire body so slowly I felt like I would explode. This time, we made love and I could feel our bodies climax at the same time. Victor looked me in my eyes and kissed me again so softly.

"I love you Lisa and I vow to make you love me too." He whispered in my ear. I was speechless but a part of me wanted to tell Victor that I loved him back.

Victor left out early the next day and I went to my aunt's house before I flew back out. Trina was there and so was Shawn. If it wasn't for my aunt, I would kill them both. I just ignored them and sat by Aunt Katherine.

"I was coming by before my flight to let you know I love you. If there is anything you need, let me know." I told her.

"What I need nobody can help me with but Father God." Aunt Katherine said. She seemed to be out of it and was in tears.

"It's going to be ok. Uncle Charles is in a better place." I tried to comfort her.

I've never seen her like this before. Her and Uncle Charles had been married 42 years so I couldn't imagine what she was going through. I hugged and kissed her before I left. Thankfully Pam was coming through the door as I was leaving.

"Hey Pam, I'm glad to see you. Will you keep me updated on Aunt Katherine because she's still taking this pretty hard." I asked.

"Yes of course I will. She's going to be fine, it just takes time." Pam said. I made sure she had my number. We hugged then I got in my uber to head to the airport.

I made it to the airport and got checked in to board my flight. The shit that happened to me while I was here was crazy. I couldn't wait to talk to those fucking Italians. They were next on my hit list if they didn't have an explanation for this kidnapping ordeal. The flight attendant walked around and told us to make sure our phones were off. I reached for my phone to put it on airplane mode when I saw 3 missed calls from Pam. Before I could try to call back, she sent a text saying my Aunt Katherine just had a heart attack and didn't make it.

"Omg!" I screamed out. Everybody on the plane gasped. I'm sure I scared the fuck out of them.

"Ma'am is everything ok?" The flight attendant asked.

"No, I have to get off this plane right now!" I was crying out of control by this point.

This had to be a dream. Aunt Katherine was the mother I always wanted. I knew I shouldn't have left her because something just didn't feel right. They let me off the plane and I called Pam back.

"Please tell me that this a dream Pam?" I asked as soon as she answered the phone.

Pam told me that Aunt Katherine asked for a glass of water and when she came back she was slouched over on the couch. "Everybody is still here. We're waiting on the coroner, but Lisa she's gone."

Pam started crying and it made me cry too. "She died of heartbreak. She couldn't live without him." I had no other explanation than that. They both were just so full of life and now they both are gone.

I made it back over to Aunt Katherines house and everyone was still just in shock. I saw Pam and went over and hugged her.

"Can you believe this?" I asked.

"This really hurts. Two funerals in a week!" She shook her head.

I grabbed my phone and called Megan to check on the kids. I made sure it was ok for her to stay a little while longer. I missed my flight and had to book another one. I talked to the kids and they were so busy with their friends that were over they rushed me off the phone. I didn't tell them about Aunt Katherine because I didn't want to ruin their mood. As I was hanging up the phone, Victor was calling.

"Hey." I said sounding down.

"What's the matter Beautiful?" He asked.

"My Aunt just passed before I could even leave Jersey." I explained to him what happened and couldn't help but start back crying.

"Lisa I'm so sorry. I wish I was there with you right now." He sounded concerned.

"I'm about to find a flight back for tonight. There isn't much I can do here anyway." I just needed to get back home to my kids.

"I will send my plane for you. You don't have to book a flight." Victor said.

"You don't have to do that." I told him.

"I insist Lisa. I have a prior engagement, so I can't make it. I will have it fueled up and on its way to you. Talk to you soon." He hung up the phone.

Victor was full of surprises. He was charming as hell and it actually made me smile to know he had my back. I went back in the house and started talking to some of my other cousins that I didn't get to see at the funeral. We all had the same expression of disbelief on our faces. Trina walked in and instead of her acting normal for once, she comes right back in with the bullshit.

"Lisa you missed your flight to make sure your name on the will?" Trina started laughing. "You don't give a fuck about nobody but yourself and your criminal ass husband."

Before I knew it, I grabbed Trina's head and pushed it in the wall. I stopped myself once I realized where I was because if I kept going I knew that I would kill her.

"Look bitch, Aunt Katherine isn't here to save you anymore! Do not fucking test my gangsta today!" I yelled out.

Everybody was dead silent. Trina looked at me holding her mouth, but for the first time she didn't say a word.

"What's going on in here?" My cousin Grace walked through the door and everybody looked at her. She looked at Trina's face and then at me.

"Forget I asked. Come on in babe, but watch your step." She walked in and she opened the door for I guess her husband or boyfriend which, was backwards. I didn't care though, I was just ready to get out of this house.

"Hey everybody this is my fiancé Blake and our new baby girl Faith." Grace said. When I saw Blake walk in my aunt's house, I knew there was going to be a third funeral that week...mine.

Chapter 14

I played it cool because I had everything I needed on Blake. When he saw me, he almost dropped the baby carrier. He nearly tripped over his own feet. Grace walked in hugging everyone. When she got to me I couldn't help but notice how she smelled like Blake.

"Hey cousin." I tried to act normal.

"Lisa! I have not seen you in about 10 years since I was a little girl in pigtails. I hate I missed Uncle Charles funeral, but my baby is only a few weeks old so I didn't make it." Grace explained to me.

Grace was looking great to have just had a baby. "You look amazing and congrats on everything!" Blake was still standing by the door and he wouldn't look our direction.

"Trina, I see you must have rubbed somebody the wrong way for the last time." Grace shook her head and started hugging some more of our cousins.

I went upstairs to go to the bathroom and to think of an excuse to leave. I started having flashbacks from me and Blake fucking, and I was embarrassed. I was used to fucking millionaires and I let this little boy have his way with me. To make things worse, I find out he's engaged to my cousin. I called Fred because he usually called me at a certain time no matter what, but he hasn't been on schedule lately. The phone just rang. I hung up and called again but it did the same thing.

"That's weird." I said to myself. One thing about the prison system you never knew what was going on but i just hoped he was ok.

I went back downstairs. I didn't see Blake or Trina in the living room. I quickly hugged Pam and let everyone know I would be back in a few days. I got my stuff to go outside and wait on my Uber. When I walked outside, the first person I saw was Blake. He was on the phone talking to somebody about moving cars. I heard some of the conversation before he realized I had walked out, then he walked back in the house not even looking my way. Whoever he was talking to was trying to get a lot of cars shipped somewhere tonight. I'm sure whatever he was doing was illegal by the way he was talking on the phone.

I heard the door open back up and saw that it was Grace and Blake. I hope like hell she was not about to introduce this son of a bitch to me.

"Lisa before you leave I wanted you to meet my fiancé Blake." I wanted to fake a smile, but I couldn't. I gave him probably the nastiest look I could. I was surprised how well he heals considering how Paco beat his ass.

"Blake this is my cousin Lisa. This is the rich cousin I was telling you about." Grace laughed.

"Nice meeting you Blake." I said.

You would have thought he shitted on himself the way he was rocking back and forth. "Same to you." Blake didn't even look at me when he said it.

"I can't wait until you meet Fred, he's so fun to be around until you make him mad. Right Lisa?" Grace started laughing again.

"Yes, that's true." I kept a straight look on my face.

"Who's Fred?" Blake asked. He probably thought Paco was Fred and was terrified.

"That's Lisa's husband. When does he get out?" I looked at Grace and before I could curse her ass out my Uber pulled up.

"Well I have to get to my plane, but we will catch up when I get back." I hugged Grace. I saw a beautiful ring on her finger so I asked how long they been engaged.

"He just proposed last week. It's 2 carats." Grace held her hand out to show me. It was definitely a beautiful ring.

"Blake you must have a good job to afford a ring like that." He bucked his eyes and just shook his head up and down. I

121

started laughing and walked to the Uber. I guess my cousin can't say I never did anything for her because I am sure my money is what bought that ring.

I headed towards the airport even though Victor told me it would be a few hours before the plane would make it. I was going to find a restaurant or a bar to wait at until then. My phone rang and it was BJ.

"What's up BJ?" I answered.

"I just talked to Marco and he said he wanted to meet you and explain about the Jamaicans. He keeps apologizing for everything."

I really didn't want to talk to them because they really put us in a fucked up situation. "BJ, I feel like they knew something wasn't right and that's probably why they sold both restaurants so cheap." I said to BJ.

"Well if you don't want to meet with them I understand, but I would like for you to have a better understanding since you had to go through that." BJ explained.

I thought about it and I did want to know why that diamond was even there in the first place. I told BJ to have them meet me at a bar by the airport so that we could talk.

Once I made it to the bar I found a booth and ordered a Strawberry Hennessy. Not long after I made it, I saw Marco come in. I held my hand up. He was by himself and that was even better because I didn't need anybody adding in the story and distracting me from the truth.

"Lisa, I am horribly sorry about what happened. I can't imagine what you were going through." He apologized.

"Marco, please tell me what the hell is going on?"

He sat down and shook his head. "Barkley and Marley are big in the game, especially in New York." He started telling the story. "We linked up with them when we first bought the restaurant in New York. We had mutual friends." He kept explaining. "We did a lot of business from Morris Park to East Bronx. They were pretty cool, so we had a meeting with them on the money tip."

Marco continued to explain how they were heavy hitters. They were millionaires, but they stayed pretty low key. He also told me about a third brother named Jaheim that was younger than the twins. He was pretty crazy too.

"Well, they only used me to get the diamond out of the restaurant. How did that come in play?" I asked.

"BJ mentioned the diamond. Lisa, I had no idea there was a

diamond in there. I would have gotten it myself honestly."
Marco said sincerely. I believed everything he was saying but I
was still pretty pissed.

"So why did you guys stop talking if you were business
partners and friends?" I stopped the waitress to get me
another drink.

"It's very hard doing business with friends, I'm sure you know."
He went on to tell me how the money was never right
whenever they worked together.

"If the supply was for five hundred thousand, they would bring
four hundred and seventy thousand. Those mistakes added up
quickly." Marco explained. "A lot of the wrong people got killed
until I found out it was the twins." Marco said he was
devastated when he found out that it was them stealing from
them.

"My brothers and I confronted them right away and they
blamed some of their workers. They even offered to make it
right by replacing the money we lost." Marco said they
completely cut ties with them and that's only been a few
months ago.

"We wanted to leave the restaurant business alone and jump
into other avenues of money. That's why we sold the places so
cheap, it was never about the money for us."

He went on to explain how relationships are important to him and his family and that they would handle Barkley and Marley for me.

"No need Marco, it's already been handled." I told him.

The waitress sat my drink down and I guzzled half of it before he said a word.

"What do you mean it's been handled?" He asked.

"Do you think somebody is going to kidnap me and it not be handled Marco?" I drank the rest of my drink and asked for a glass of water.

"How was it handled Lisa? I feel so bad this happened to you?" He seemed to be in disbelief.

"If I say it's handled, just know it's handled." I pulled out my phone and sent the kissing emoji to Victor. He handled that and didn't even know the full story of what happened. I knew he was down for me.

"They won't bother another soul ever again or steal from anybody else." I sipped my water the waitress had brought out.

"Lisa, if you guys did something to them please let me know because believe me Jaheim is coming for revenge." Marco said.

"We didn't do anything wrong. They fucking kidnapped me! I don't give a fuck about revenge!" I had gotten upset. He thought I was fucking scared of two dead men and little brother.

"I'm just warning you about Jaheim. He doesn't play fair so it can get really ugly Lisa. I'm on your side, but this can easily turn into a war with the Jamaicans."

Marco ordered four shots of D'usse when the waitress came back.

"My hands are clean so there will be no war." I said.

"You said it was handled so your hands are not clean. If you had anything to do with it, they will find out." Marco sounded very serious.

The waitress brought out the shots and we got two apiece. "Drink up Lisa because shit just got real."

We took our shots and as we were finishing our last one, both of our phones rang at the same time. It was Victor calling me to let me know that the plane should be arriving in about an hour.

"You will have your favorite candy and fruit on the flight as well." He said. "I was hoping you flew to me so I put some

Hennessy on board, but if you don't there is also wine so that you can relax either way." Victor said laughing.

It was truly something about him that made my pussy jump and my heart skip a beat. "You are something else you know that." I laughed. "I will surprise you and I won't tell you what I decide." I started laughing again.

I could feel Marco looking at me. I tried to play it off by switching the subject to let Victor know that I couldn't say what I wanted.

"Ok, well let me finish this meeting and I will let you know what I decide shortly."

Victor laughed even harder. "Touch that pussy for me before I hang up, they don't have to know." He moaned on the phone. "I just want you to sit on my face and don't move until you cum in my mouth." I started twisting in my seat when I realized that Marco was still watching me.

"Ok I will do that. Thank you so much and I'll email those files to you." Victor was about to have me wet over the phone, so I knew I had to fly to him tonight. I needed him.

"You are so funny Lisa. I will talk to you later. Let me know when you board the plane." We hung up the phone and I got the check.

"Please let me cover yours, that's the least I can do." Marco said. He told me he would keep his ears to the street about anything the Jamaicans had going on and would keep me informed. We said our goodbyes and we left.

I was in the airport walking down to the terminal where the private jets landed. I couldn't hold my pee for nothing. I used the bathroom and went to wash my hands. I instantly got dizzy. I got a paper towel and put some water on it to put on my face. I started feeling better but then the next thing I remember is passing out on the hard bathroom floor.

Chapter 15

I woke up and had no clue where I was until I heard all the beeping noises. I realized I was in a hospital.

"Hi there, I'm nurse Hicks. I know you are probably confused, but you passed out in the bathroom and somebody called 911 in the airport." The nurse said.

"I don't know what happened, I guess I had too many drinks." I told the nurse. "Well that answered my question." The nurse grabbed her clipboard.

"What question?" I asked.

"Well I got my answer so I don't have to ask that question anymore, but I would like to say congratulations instead. You're pregnant."

"Is this a joke?" I tried to sit up but couldn't because of the IVs.

"I'm guessing you didn't plan this." Nurse Hicks asked.

How could I plan a pregnancy when my husband is in jail? I couldn't tell her that because I wasn't wearing a ring and this lady didn't know me.

"No, I have three kids already and I wasn't expecting anymore anytime soon." I tried to sit up again.

"You were dehydrated so we have to fill you with fluids for a while." She put another pillow under my head to sit me up some, but I couldn't move.

"Where is my purse and my phone? I was waiting on a jet to fly in." I tried to relax but my heart was racing a mile a minute.

"Your things are right here. Whoever the lady was that helped you made sure you had everything. She was very concerned about you," the nurse said.

I'm glad someone got help for me but I was ready to get out of here. "Can you pass me my phone please?" I asked.

She handed me my phone and of course Victor had called me about ten times. I called him back and he picked up on the first ring.

"Lisa, what is going on? I've been calling you, are you ok?" Victor asked.

"Apparently, I passed out at the airport because I woke up in the hospital." I told him.

"Lisa are you serious? What hospital are you at?" He sounded concerned.

"I don't even know myself, let me ask." I asked nurse Hicks for the name of the hospital and she said it was the Robert Wood

Johnson hospital, then I told Victor. Nurse Hicks walked out of the room so I could talk in private.

"What room number?" He asked.

"ER room 7." I told him.

"I'm on my way." He said.

"What do you mean you're on your way?" He had hung up.

I laughed to myself and shook my head. Victor was crazy enough to probably show up by the time I'm getting discharged out. I still was having a hard time believing this. Finding out I was pregnant was the last possible thing I wanted to hear. I was falling for Victor, but I honestly didn't know if he or BJ was the father. I knew it wasn't Blake because we used protection and I took a plan B to be on the safe side after he started acting crazy. I couldn't have a baby while Fred was locked up, he would kill me and the baby.

I called Megan to check on the kids and they were fine. I got a chance to talk to them and couldn't wait to hug and kiss them. I called BJ and told him about the meeting with Marco and what he told me about the Jamaicans. I didn't mention anything about the hospital to him at all. I told him I was waiting at the airport and that my flight got delayed.

"Well I wish we could get some time together to just talk." BJ said. "I don't want anything to be different between us for the kids' sake, especially Fred Jr." He said.

"I agree BJ. We do need to talk about everything and put it behind us."

I couldn't sneak around with him. I felt horrible for doing that to Fred. BJ was like his brother and we violated him like that.

"What do you mean put everything behind us?" BJ asked.

"What happened wasn't something that we can keep doing BJ, you know that." I told him.

"So you don't miss me or the way I put that pussy in my mouth?" He asked.

I was in a hospital bed but instantly got turned on. "I do miss you..." Before I could finish talking Victor walked in the room.

"Who do you miss besides me?" I couldn't hide the expression of shock on my face. I hung up the phone and put it on silent by the time Victor made it to me and hugged me.

"I was coming back to Jersey on the jet to surprise you but when I couldn't get you on the phone, I thought something happened to you." He said.

"You are full of surprises I see." I laughed.

"You surprised me this time though." We both laughed.

"What's wrong with you baby?" Victor asked. "I know you have been so stressed out and that's why I want to provide you with security." He walked to the door and there were two guys standing outside. They stuck their heads in the door and waved.

"Victor are you serious?" I hope he was joking.

"Yes, I want you to know that you are protected even when I'm not around." He said.

"No, and you need to get them from in front of my door." I didn't want or need that type of attention.

"Lisa please do this for me. I want my lady to know that she is safe." He walked over and grabbed my hand and kissed it. While he was doing that Nurse Hicks walked back in.

"I'm sorry to disturb you guys. Ms. Davenport can you take these prenatal vitamins and drink this water for me. It will help get some of those nutrients back for you and the baby." I gave her a look that could kill. I know this bitch didn't just say that in front of Victor.

"Why does she need prenatal vitamins?" Victor asked looking confused.

Nurse Hicks looked at me and smiled. That really pissed me off, but I guess she thought this was my boyfriend or husband. If only she knew.

"When I passed out, I found out it was because I'm pregnant." I told Victor.

"Wow, are you serious?" Victor asked.

He had a look of disbelief on his face. He stood up and asked Nurse Hicks for some privacy. Once she walked out I could tell by the look on his face that he was bothered by finding out that I was pregnant.

"Lisa are you really pregnant?" Victor asked. He sat at the edge of the bed and put his face in his hands.

"I'm not sure how this happened, but I don't think I want anymore kids right now." I really wanted to see how he would react to me saying that.

"Lisa I'm not telling you what to do but I know you have Fred and I don't want you to leave him for me." Victor said.

134

Honestly in that moment I was ready to take a chance especially if I was pregnant with Victor's child. I think all things happen for a reason and maybe it was meant for me to be with him. I didn't know if it was my pregnancy hormones or if I had fallen for him, but I started crying.

"I think I love you Victor and maybe this is just a way for us to be together." I expressed my feelings to him and for the first time he was quiet.

"Did you hear me Victor?" He shook his head up and down. I know this was probably just as much as a surprise to him as it was to me. We both just sat in silence for a few minutes.

"What's going through your mind?" I asked him. He seemed like he was literally praying. He had his head down and wasn't saying a word. I never saw him look stressed about anything until now.

"Lisa I can't have any kids with you, because I'm married too."

"Excuse me!" I know he didn't just say he's married. "I didn't hear you?" I know I heard that wrong.

"Lisa, I was going to tell you but I was waiting for the right time." Victor said.

He couldn't even look me in my eyes and tell me the truth. He kept his head down like a fucking coward. This is the same man that has probably had thousands of people killed and here he was acting like he was scared of me. I know I'm married to Fred and this was really only a fantasy anyway. Honestly, I would never leave Fred for anyone.

"The perfect time would have been before you started sucking on my pearl tongue or maybe before you ate my ass."

I hit the button for the nurse to pull me off this machine or I was going to do it myself. Nurse Hicks said she would be right down and I started trying to take the IVs out.

"Lisa don't hurt yourself because I'm stupid." He tried stopping me and then the nurse walked in.

"What are you doing?" She pulled my hands off the machine. "Your blood pressure is higher than it should be, have you been stressing about something lately?" She asked.

"I just buried my uncle and then my aunt passed after the funeral." I said it with no emotion because at this point I really had none.

"I'm so sorry to hear that. You know how important it is to take care of yourself," The nurse said.

"I really have to get back to my kids and book a flight home." I started pulling at the plugs again, so she knew I was checking myself out.

"Baby be careful, you don't want to harm the baby." Victor said. I gave him the look of death and rolled my eyes.

Once the nurse got everything off of me, she left to get the discharge papers for me to sign. I got up and I checked to see if my things were still in my bag. I had about thirty thousand in cash in my duffel bag and I was surprised it was still there.

"You carry that much cash with you when you travel?" Victor asked.

"I carry more." I got my stuff together so once Nurse Hicks came back I could just leave.

"Why are you going to book a flight and I have the jet waiting for us?" I didn't say anything.

"Can I explain myself at least?" He grabbed my hand and I snatched it back. "Lisa I am legally married, but my wife and kids live in Mexico." He said.

"Wife AND kids? You are full of surprises." I shook my head.

"We've been separated for three years but we have not gotten a divorce because she doesn't want to leave Mexico." Victor explained how he is no longer with her or loves her.

"I know you are married to Fred and I'm married to Isabella, so how could we bring a child into a situation like that?"

He had a point and I knew that I didn't have an option in the matter anyway. Fred would have someone to kill me or kill me himself if I had a child outside our marriage.

"I don't understand Victor because if you guys are separated why not just tell me?" Something didn't seem right about what he was saying. "I didn't know I would fall for you so fast Lisa and I didn't want anything to ruin what we have right now." He grabbed my hand and kissed my forehead.

"Well looks like you guys are good to go, I just need you to sign these two forms." Nurse Hicks walked back in. "You guys make such a beautiful couple." The nurse said smiling.

Victor grabbed me by the waist and kissed me on the cheek. "Thank you I'm the lucky one." He said. Him and the nurse laughed and I started grabbing my stuff and walking out the door.

"Lisa put those bags down." He had one of the security guards that was still outside the door get my things.

"I have a car service ready to take us to the jet." Victor said.

"You guys own a jet?" The nurse asked. We both looked at

her, but nobody said anything.

As I was walking to the elevator, I remembered that I forgot to get the name of the person that called 911 for me. I wanted to give them something for saving my life and not stealing my stuff.

"Nurse Hicks, can you give me the name again of the lady who found me?"

"I should be able to get a name from when they checked you in, one second." She looked on the computer and sure enough she found it. "Kenise Allen, there's a phone number also." She wrote it down and handed me the sticky note.

"Thanks so much." Victor was still waiting by the door for me to come out and the security guards had already put my things in the SUV. I walked right by him and got in the truck and didn't say a word to him.

On the way to the airport, I called the number for Kenise hoping she would answer. I called twice but nobody picked up.

"That is so nice of you to give that lady something," Victor said. He tried to rub my leg but I stopped him. My phone rang. It was Kenise calling back.

139

"Hello is this Kenise?" I answered.

"Who is this?" She asked.

"I'm the lady that passed out at the airport. They told me you saved my life." I explained to her what Nurse Hicks told me and that I wanted to meet her and thank her.

"You don't have to do that, it was just the right thing to do." She said.

"Well I wanted to give you a token of gratitude for making sure I was taken care of," I told her.

"It's just honestly not a good time. Right after I left the hospital I got a call saying they found the body of my boyfriend and his twin brother with their heads cut off."

Chapter 16

I was definitely in hell. This could not be my life. I couldn't even think of words to say because I was so shocked. I was literally speechless.

"Hello?" Kenise said.

"OMG, I'm so sorry to hear that. I just can't believe that happened. I'm completely shocked." I tried not to sound nervous.

"This is really tough for me. I can't believe this." She started crying.

I put my phone on mute. "This is fucking unbelievable." I told Victor. "You remember the guys that kidnapped me, you know the ones whose head you served for dessert? Well, I'm talking to one of their fucking girlfriends." I couldn't believe this.

Victor looked at me confused. "What are you talking about Lisa?"

I just shook my head. "I don't want to bother you while you are going through this. I know how you feel. I just lost my aunt and uncle back to back." I told her.

"I'm sorry to hear that. I just need to take all this in right now." Kenise said fighting back tears.

"Well, I have to come back to Jersey for my aunt's funeral. Is it ok to call then and try to link up?" I asked.

"Yes, just give me a call." We hung up the phone. I could not believe how small the fucking world was.

"I don't know if God is playing some kind of sick joke, but I have to get out of Jersey quick." I told Victor.

"What are you talking about? Who was that?" He asked.

"The lady that made sure I got to the hospital told me she just found out her boyfriend and his twin were found with their heads cut off." I grabbed my head because I instantly got a headache.

"The guys that kidnapped you deserved to die. I feel bad for her, but I did this for you." Victor said something in Spanish but I just ignored him.

I didn't know if it was because I was pregnant or what, but I was feeling very emotional. I didn't know Kenise and she didn't know me, but she saved my life. The fact that I had something to do with the murder of her boyfriend made me nervous, but I knew I had to meet her.

We finally made it on the jet and I was beyond tired. I just wanted to sleep.

"Where's Jennifer?" I asked Victor.

"She's been on vacation the last few days. We have Samantha tonight," he said smiling.

"It's not going to happen." I rolled my eyes.

I hope he didn't think he was in the clear based off what he told me. Niggas lie everyday and I wasn't born yesterday.

"Wake me up when we land." I walked straight to the bed.

"Can I lay with you? I will behave." Victor said.

I just shrugged my shoulders. I took my shoes off and fell on the bed.

"Lisa be careful!" Victor sounded concerned. "You can't just do that while you are pregnant," he said.

"Victor, I have three kids. I will be fine, trust me." I snatched the blanket to let him know I was still mad and didn't want to talk to him. He took his shoes and pants off and laid down trying to cuddle with me.

"Victor I don't want to be touched or talked to please." I slid over as far as I could and closed my eyes.

"Ok Lisa, can we talk about this?" He sat up.

"I'm tired of talking. I just want to take a nap so when I get home I can have some energy for my kids." I didn't move.

"I know you are upset with me, but you are married too." He knew exactly how to push my buttons.

"You knew I was married from the jump so don't try to turn this on me." I sat up. Victor had a lot of nerve. I know I'm married and he knew I was married too.

"I'm not trying to do anything but understand how you can be mad at me for being in the same situation that you are in."

I wanted to curse him out but I didn't. "You know what Victor, you are absolutely right. I should have never gotten involved with you." I laid back down.

"Lisa I didn't mean it like that. I'm just confused right now."

I pretended like I didn't hear him. I didn't move.

"I love you and I just don't want to lose you," he said. "I won't lose you either and I mean that, no matter what."

Victor tried to kiss my cheek and I pushed him back. He grabbed my arm and bent it back until I screamed.

"What the fuck are you doing? Let my arm go!" I yelled.

"Lisa do you understand me? I will not stand to lose you, so

144

we will work through this ok?" Victor had a look in his eyes that I had never seen before and that's when I knew I was in too deep.

He let me go and I jerked from him. I stared at him and pulled the covers up over my head. He laid back down and we slept the entire trip with our backs turned to each other.

I made it home and I was so happy to see my kids. I kissed and hugged them while they told me everything they did while I was gone. I thanked Megan and paid her.

"I didn't see your car outside Megan. Did something happen to it?" I asked her.

"No, it's fine. It's technically not my car, it's my aunt's car. She lets me drive it all the time, but she needed it today." Megan explained.

"Ok gotcha. Well I can always help you get a car. And, if you want to take on the full position of nanny, the job is yours." I hadn't gotten any news on Rosa and I had to have someone else soon.

"Yes! I would love to have the job! I love those kids!" Megan said excitedly. She hugged me then her and the kids started dancing.

"Great! I will get everything together so I can put you on payroll." I told her.

"Thank you so much! I can't wait to tell my aunt when she picks me up." Megan hugged me again.

"I would like to meet her if that's ok? I just want to tell her how awesome you are." I asked Megan.

"Yes, she should be pulling up in a few minutes."

I went upstairs to put my stuff in the room before Megan's aunt made it. I wanted to freshen up too. I tried calling Fred again because I was getting worried about him not calling at his normal time. When I called him, the phone went straight to voicemail. That was strange. The entire time that Fred's been locked up I've never went more than 2 days without talking to him.

I tried not to think about it, but I was always afraid of something happening to him in prison and not finding out until weeks after. I heard Megan and the kids calling my name from downstairs.

"Coming!" I yelled out.

I changed my shirt, threw my hair in a ponytail, and went downstairs.

"Ms. Lisa, I want you to meet my aunt Jennifer."

I looked at Jennifer and she looked at me. It was Victor's flight attendant.

"Nice meeting you." I played it off.

"Same to you." She looked like she wanted to pass out.

I mean, this lady just had my pussy in her mouth. It was kind of hard not to think of that when she spoke. Only in my life would the lady I just had a spontaneous threesome with be my nanny's aunt.

"Come in Jennifer and have a seat. Are you thirsty?" I asked. I knew who she was so there was no need to not make her feel welcomed. "I have water, soda, wine, and hard liquor." I said laughing.

I knew that with me being pregnant I couldn't have the hard liquor, but I always had a glass of red wine with my other pregnancies. I pulled out two wine glasses and grabbed a bottle of red wine.

"Megan you are the designated driver." I laughed and opened up the bottle of wine.

"No thanks. I really don't want anything to drink." Jennifer said.

I poured both of our glasses. "Red wine is good for you. Plus, I wanted to celebrate Megan's new job as full time nanny." I told her.

"Wait, Megan you're going to be the full time nanny? What happened with you going back to school?" Jennifer asked Megan.

"I'm going to take online classes." Megan said.

"I'm not going to have her as a slave. She gets days off and I am more than willing to work with her schedule." I looked at Megan to let her know I had her back.

"We have to talk about this Megan. You said that if you were going to stay with me you would go back to school." Jennifer seemed like a totally different person than she was on Victor's jet.

"I'm sorry. I didn't mean to get in family business. Megan is exceptional and I will definitely compensate her for her time with us." I saw how serious Jennifer was so I didn't want to overstep my boundaries. I drank my wine and let them talk.

"I'm not a child Aunt Jen and I respect you enough not to argue in front of anyone but I'm taking online classes," Megan told her. "You said be in school and that is school."

I could see the look on Jennifer's face. She was pissed but she didn't say anything else. There was an awkward silence in the room, so I offered Jennifer a drink again.

"I poured the glass anyway to see if I could tempt you." I said sliding the glass her way.

She grabbed the glass and smelled it. "No, I can't even smell it." She turned her face and slid it back. "I can't drink, I just found out I'm pregnant."

When she said pregnant, I dropped my wine glass. It shattered into a thousand pieces all over the kitchen floor.

Chapter 17

"Shit, I must be tipsy already." I went to get the broom out of the closet.

"I'll get that, don't worry." Megan grabbed the broom and swept the glass up.

I didn't know what to say to Jennifer. I was pregnant and she was pregnant. That may not be a coincidence.

"Congratulations Jennifer!" I tried to sound excited.

"Thank you! I'm so excited. We've been trying for a while but our schedules never let us." Jennifer said.

"Wait so you wanted a baby?" I was confused.

"Yes! Me and my boyfriend have been trying the last year. He drives trucks so it's hard to be ovulating at the right time when he's home." Jennifer explained.

"The last time he was home I was ovulating. The five pregnancy tests I took said positive, so here we are." She laughed.

"That is exciting. I know you will be a great mom. I'm actually supposed to be planning my friends baby shower, so I guess babies are in the air." We both laughed and then Fred Jr walked in.

"Mom have you talked to dad?" he asked.

"No baby what's wrong?" I asked him.

"I've been calling him, but his phone is going to voicemail."
Fred Jr seemed concerned.

"That's what it's been doing for me too." I didn't want to show
him that I was worried, so I let him know that his dad was fine
and that I would call another number to check on him.

"Ok mom." Fred Jr. walked back upstairs.

"I guess I will drink your glass of wine." I grabbed Jennifer's
glass of wine and started guzzling it down.

I thought about Monica and then Big Will all over again. I
couldn't get the image of his head rolling across Chanel's floor
out of my head. Then I thought about Chanel. I knew BJ was
still on a rampage about finding out who killed her.

"Well Jennifer, I don't mean to be rude, but I just flew in and I
have a lot to do today. It was nice meeting you again."

Megan and Jennifer looked at me. "I'm sorry I meant it was
nice meeting you. Blame the wine." I laughed and then they
laughed.

Jennifer gave me a weird look and I smiled as we walked towards the door. "You ladies be careful, and Megan I will call you." I watched them leave and then I went upstairs.

I decided to take the kids skating after my nap. I didn't want them to think I was abandoning them, but my life had turned into a soap opera over the last few months. We had so much fun skating. We all kept skating and falling. Even though Frank was only 5, he was skating better than me. I thought about how excited me and Fred were when we found out I was pregnant with Frank. After I had Freda, I got pregnant again but I had a miscarriage. It really made me depressed and I went through some emotional things that were not easy. I didn't even want to have sex with my husband anymore. Fred kept telling me that he wanted to try again but I was so afraid of going through that pain again. I just didn't even want sex.

I went to a group counseling meeting that my doctor told me about for women who had miscarriages. It was the best thing I could have gone to because they actually knew exactly what I was feeling. They helped me get over my fears and a few weeks after that I was pregnant with Frank. The only thing I hate is that Fred was not there when he was born. He got sentenced when I was 8 months pregnant and I had Frank two weeks later.

"Mom watch out." Freda was coming full speed into me and we

both fell on the ground. We started laughing hysterically. I stood up and helped her up.

"Girl you must be trying to kill me?" I asked her laughing. I knew I shouldn't be skating pregnant but I honestly didn't care what happened.

"I couldn't stop mom I'm sorry." She was laughing so hard she snorted. I saw Fred JR skating over to us and he was laughing too. I was just glad to be with them and couldn't imagine not being here to protect them.

We all decided to leave and go to the best wing place in town, Dean's Wings and Things. The wings were so big and juicy that you literally couldn't eat more than five if you tried. My kids loved the place because it also had an arcade, laser tag, and karaoke. I let them play a little and I called BJ.

"Lisa where have you been?" he picked up the phone.

"Hi to you too BJ," I said sarcastically.

"Hey Lisa, I didn't mean it like that." BJ said.

"It's fine. Me and the kids are at Dean's Wings and Things eating then we'll be heading home." I told him.

"Ok because we really need to talk Lisa. They found Chanel's body earlier." he said.

I immediately got nauseous. I didn't know if it was because I was pregnant or that they found Chanel's body, but I had to vomit.

"Ok BJ, well I will be home in a little bit."

I stood up to go to the bathroom before I puked on myself. I made it and ran to the first stall and threw up. I got light headed so I stood up and went to the sink to put some water on my face. I tried to pull some paper towels out and there weren't any. I walked to the stall to get some tissue and of course there wasn't any in there either. I checked every stall until I got to the last one and I almost threw up again when I saw a dead body.

I held my mouth and stomach because the smell was horrible. I looked closer and it was Ashley. What was going on? This was not happening. I threw up in the next stall and then I heard a vibrating noise. It had to be her phone so I walked back to the stall but I didn't see it anywhere. I pulled my sweater off and picked up her purse with it. The phone had stopped vibrating, but I grabbed it because whoever was calling probably was looking for her.

"Are you fucking kidding me?" I looked at the missed call and what pissed me off was the fact that it was Fred's number.

I tried to slide the screen open but it had a code on it. "Fuck."

I put the phone back in her purse quickly before someone came in the bathroom. Her body couldn't have been there long. All of a sudden I got a weird feeling in my gut. I thought back to Fred and why he was he calling this thot. He wasn't even answering my calls but calling her. I went back down to the other stall and closed the door. I pulled my phone out and called Fred. It rang and went to voicemail. He was purposely not answering my calls. My heart started beating so fast; I had to calm myself down. I flushed the toilet and then walked out and washed my hands. I walked back out and found the kids so that we could leave.

"Mommy is feeling very bad you guys. I just had to puke in the bathroom." I told them.

"Are you going to the hospital?" Freda asked.

"No. I just need to go home, shower and lay down." The kids said ok and we left.

I had a thousand things going through my head. Out of all things I couldn't believe Fred was doing me like this. He was ignoring my calls and Fred Jr's calls, but was calling Ashley. It made me mad every time I thought about it. I had a headache that was getting worse by the minute. I was trying to get home as fast as I could.

"Mom are you ok?" Fred Jr. asked.

"Yes baby, I'm fine." My phone started ringing as I was talking to Fred Jr. and it was Victor.

I sent him to voicemail and he called right back. I sent him back to voicemail because I really didn't want to talk to him and I definitely didn't want to talk to him around my kids. He sent a text telling me to call him ASAP. I didn't know what he wanted but something told me to call him back.

"Hey you guys, I have to take this call about the restaurant. Can you guys be quiet for me?" I said.

Nobody said a word. I looked in the rear view mirror and saw that Frank and Freda were knocked out already.

"Those two never stay woke riding in a car." Fred Jr. and I laughed. I called Victor back and he answered on the first ring.

"Lisa tell me you are ok?" Victor asked.

"Yes I am. Is there a reason you asked?" I was totally confused on why he was asking especially after telling me he couldn't have kids because he was married. It was none of his business or concern what I had going on anymore at this point.

"Where are you?" He had this tone in his voice that let me know that something serious was going on.

"Well I'm headed home now. I was enjoying some family time

with my kids." I looked at Fred Jr. and smiled.

"Ok I understand that you can't talk but Lisa there has been a lady following you everywhere." Victor said.

"I know you didn't want security on you, but I had them watch you anyway." he said.

"Ok, wow! Do you have her name?" I knew in my heart he was talking about Ashley and he confirmed that right away.

"She's dead so I didn't get a chance to ask her name." Victor said sarcastically.

As soon as he said that, I heard someone hitting on brakes but it was too late. A red Cadillac Escalade slammed into my truck spinning us around about five times. My cellphone flew out my hand. Once we stopped spinning I called my babies names.

"Fred! Freda! Frank!" I yelled.

"I'm ok, are you ok?" Fred Jr. asked. Frank start crying and screaming.

"It's ok Frank, don't cry baby. Freda, honey are you ok? Can you grab Frank?"

I didn't want to move too fast myself. Being pregnant, I didn't know what could happen.

"Freda baby, are you ok? Say something!" I got up because Freda wasn't moving. "Oh my gosh!" I screamed.

A guy jumped out his car and walked over to us asking were we ok. Our doors were smashed in and it was a miracle that it didn't smash us.

"Call an ambulance! My baby is not responding!" I screamed.

The guy tried to calm me down and told me that they were on the way.

"Ma'am, I'm a nurse." A lady ran over from a Honda Accord. "Who's not responding?" she asked.

"My baby!" I screamed.

"You should wait until the ambulance comes ma'am," the guy said.

"No, my baby could be dying and I'm not waiting on anybody to show up!" I emphasized to him.

"Come to the other side." I told her.

Fred Jr. jumped out and opened up the back door to grab Frank. The lady got in the truck and slowly slid Freda over then placed Freda's head on her lap. She checked for a pulse.

"She has a pulse but she's definitely unconscious." She said.

I could hear sirens coming closer so I knew that the ambulance was close.

"Oh my gosh!" I screamed.

I climbed over and got out on the passenger side and walked to the Escalade. Before I made it over, I saw the lady open her door up.

"I'm so sorry, are you guys ok?" She asked.

I hit the bitch in her mouth as soon as the words came out of her mouth. I must have shocked her because she didn't even try to hit me back.

"Bitch my daughter is unconscious because you weren't paying attention while you were driving this piece of shit."

I heard a little boy in the background start crying. I looked back and noticed the little boy and he was about 4 years old.

"Shut the fuck up please!" I screamed to the little boy and walked off.

I jogged back to my truck as the paramedics pulled up and they were putting Freda on a stretcher. "What's going on?" I asked the guy.

"Your daughter hit her head pretty hard. We're guessing her

head hit the door during the accident. She could possibly be in a coma," the paramedic explained then he rushed Freda to the ambulance.

"This can't be happening! Noooooo!" I screamed.

"Ma'am, your phone is ringing." The nurse that was helping us said. I ran and found my phone and saw that it was Victor calling back.

"We just had a bad accident and my daughter is not responding. It's not a good time to talk right now." I told Victor.

"I'm so sorry Lisa, please keep me informed." He said.

"Bye." I hung up with him and ran to the ambulance.

"Wait we're riding to the hospital because I can't drive my car." I told the paramedics.

"Ma'am we have to get her there quickly and unfortunately your kids can't ride," he said.

"Well I'm not leaving them, so they are coming too." I told him and then I called Fred Jr.'s name. "Come on you guys!" I yelled out to them.

I saw the police officer waking off from the lady in the Escalade and walking toward me. I swear if he said anything about me punching that bitch in the face I was going to scream.

"Frank, y'all get over here." The boys started walking over and the police made it to the ambulance at the same time.

"Hi ma'am I was doing a report on the accident, but I see that you have an emergency." The officer said.

"I'm trying to get to the hospital and they are not letting me and my kids ride with my daughter. I need to go now!" I sat in the ambulance and watched them finish connecting Freda to everything.

"Well, it is against the law for minors to ride. If you can call someone I can stay with them until they are picked up," he said.

"This is fucking ridiculous." I pulled out my phone and decided to call Megan. I didn't have seconds to spare because my baby's life was on the line.

"Hello." Megan answered.

"Megan we were just in a bad car accident and Freda is unconscious. I need someone to come get the kids because they can't ride in the ambulance." I explained to her.

"Omg, where are you guys? I will definitely come get them!

Poor Freda!" Megan sounded concerned.

"I will have Fred Jr. send you the location from his phone. They will be with the police officer. They don't have a scratch on them thank God. I'm just hoping my baby girl isn't in a coma." I had to fight back tears because I couldn't believe I had to say those words.

"She's going to be fine Ms. Davenport. I am getting in the car as we speak." We hung up the phone and I let Fred and the officer know that Megan was on her way. I waved at them as the officer shut the door and the ambulance sped down the highway.

We made it to the hospital and they rushed Freda to the back. She had minor bleeding from her head, but she had a lot of scratches and bleeding all over her body. The glass shattered on her and apparently her head went through the window and hit the top of the ceiling. The doctors confirmed that she was in a coma. They were going to have to run several tests to see what exactly caused it and what could they possibly do. My heart was beating a mile a minute. I just couldn't imagine anything happening to my kids and there wasn't anything I could do about Freda's condition.

No matter how much money I have, my kids are priceless. I pulled out my phone to call Fred, but I decided to text him instead. I simply texted that Freda was in a coma and I didn't say anything else. I had been calling my husband and he's been calling the next bitch, so really I didn't care how he felt. I was dealing with everything in the free world by myself at this point.

"Lisa is that you?" I turned around and it was Monica.

"Hey Monica." I said.

"Are you ok? What's wrong?" she asked.

"We were just in a car accident and Freda got hurt bad. She's in a coma." I started crying.

"I'm so sorry to hear that. Oh my goodness." Monica hugged me. "I was having some pains earlier, so I came just to make sure everything was ok with the baby. I hate to hear that about Freda." She shook her head.

"Thank you." I didn't even have words to say.

BJ called my phone. I had forgot to call him when I made it to the hospital.

"Hey BJ, we were in a bad accident and now Freda is in a coma." I told him.

"Are you serious? Where are you guys?" he asked.

I told him that Megan is taking care of Fred Jr and Frank and that I was at the hospital.

"I'm on the way to the hospital but Lisa I was calling because somebody told Fred that you have been cheating on him. According to some niggas locked up with him, he had somebody following you." BJ explained.

"Fuck Fred and fuck whoever else! I'm more concerned with my daughter and Fred deserved to get cheated on! Fuck him!" I hung up the phone and suddenly I felt a hundred sharp pains in my stomach. I bent down hoping that would stop the pain, but it got worse.

"I need a doctor." I whispered to Monica.

"Nurse we need a doctor!" The nurses ran over to me.

"Why are her eyes rolling back!" Monica screamed.

The last thing I remember is seeing my kids running and playing around in a garden of flowers. They seemed so happy. They were laughing and waving bye to me. Then everything went black.

Chapter 18

"She's still in a coma, but her vitals look good. All we can do is keep monitoring her for now." I heard a mans voice. I knew I was in the hospital but I had no clue what was going on.

"Hi there." He said. I opened my eyes and started looking around.

"Lisa! I'm so glad you are ok!" Monica said on the verge of tears.

"What's going on?" I asked. The last thing I remember is coming to the hospital with Freda. "Where is Freda? I want to see her now." I screamed out.

"Please calm down because your blood pressure is still pretty high Ms. Davenport." The doctor said.

"I need to see my baby." I said calmly.

"Freda is still in a coma. We are waiting on all her tests to come back so that we can see what's going on with her," he said.

"Lisa did you know you were pregnant?" Monica asked me. I didn't know whether to lie or tell the truth.

"Pregnant?" I tried to sound surprised. Either way it went,

Monica knew that Fred was in prison and I had no explanation on how I could get pregnant.

"The doctor said the reason you passed out was because you had a miscarriage. You lost a lot of blood."

Monica walked over and grabbed my hand. I instantly started crying. I was embarrassed and I was scared for Freda more than anything.

"I had just found out I was pregnant. I have been under so much stress lately, I don't know what to do." I cried harder. Monica just hugged me and she didn't say a word.

I went over everything with the doctor about my healing process and then someone knocked on the door.

"Hi." It was BJ. I wasn't really ready to see BJ, but I knew eventually we were going to have to talk.

"BJ how are you? It's been a while." Monica asked while hugging him.

"Good to see you and the new addition." BJ said laughing and rubbing her belly.

"Yes, you see I have gotten as big as a house." Monica laughed.

BJ walked over to me and I could tell he was surprised to see me in the hospital bed.

"Are you ok Lisa? Did you get hurt in the accident also?" He asked.

"I ended up getting sick when I made it here. I'm sure it's just stressing about Freda." I told him. I looked at Monica so she knew not to say anything.

Someone's phone started ringing and it was Monica's. "Hey baby, I'm about to walk out." She answered the phone. "Oh, well we are in room 340." Monica hung the phone. "My fiancé is walking up, so you guys will get to meet him." Monica sounded excited.

"Well Lisa, I will keep you updated on everything and I will have the nurse come back to check on you. Expect to be here overnight." The doctor said.

"Thank you." I told him as he walked out. I knew Monica's fiancé was Big Will's brother but what I didn't know was if he knew who me and BJ were, especially in the street game.

I heard a knock on the door and Monica walked over to let him in.

"Hey bae with your fine ass." Monica started laughing and let him in.

"Meet my fiancé Tim. Tim this is Lisa and BJ." She introduced us. I had never seen him before and he looked nothing like Big Will.

"Nice meeting you guys." he said.

"Nice meeting you too," we both said.

"I'm glad you are doing a little better Lisa. I will be checking on you but I know BJ will take good care of you." She hugged me and BJ before they left.

"When you get better don't forget we have some planning to do," Monica said jokingly.

"I can't wait to get it all together. Me and Freda will be out of here soon." I told her.

"We had so much going on with the funeral and the police have been investigating everything. It's been so much on Tim mainly, but he wants me to not worry about that." She kissed him on the cheek.

"Sounds like my life right now." BJ said.

"Why you say that BJ?" Monica asked.

"You probably didn't know my baby sister Chanel, but someone murdered her." My stomach dropped.

"Chanel was your sister?" Tim asked BJ.

"You knew my sister?" BJ looked confused.

"Yea, Big Will was my brother. They were dating when he died and she was the last person he called on his phone."

Tim walked over by BJ. My heart rate was going up and the machine started beeping faster.

"Lisa are you ok?" Monica asked.

"I just got upset thinking about someone killing Chanel." I closed my eyes to pretend like I was fighting tears.

"Wait so Big Will was your brother?" BJ sounded surprised.

"This is weird. They were dating and they both ended up getting killed?" Monica said.

"Were they into it with anyone because that's not a coincidence." BJ looked at me and my heart monitor.

"I'm leaving it to the police to find her killer. I'm just working on finding some peace behind it all." BJ said calmly.

169

"I agree BJ because my brother was the opposite of me. He was involved heavily in the streets. I honestly don't know what he had going on because I just moved back here." Tim said.

"The stories I've been hearing is that some girl named Ashley had been trying to set him up. She was involved with somebody in prison and they were using Will as a pawn to get to the bigger drug guys." Tim explained.

"Will knew a lot of correctional officers and he had a business set up through a few of the prisons. However, he was stealing money from some of the guys that were locked up."

I wanted to say something so bad but I kept my mouth shut. It made sense that Ashley wanted Big Will on her side, especially if she was trying to get close to Fred. Will was her connection to the prison. She probably was learning about the businesses so she could take over. That's why she set up Big Will to try to kill BJ because she knew we would retaliate.

"This is too much for me right now." I said.

"I apologize Lisa, I didn't mean any harm." Tim said.

"We are going to get out of here, but Lisa I will be calling you ok." Monica walked back over and kissed my cheek.

"Thanks Monica, for everything." They left out and closed the door.

"Lisa, you are going to kill yourself stressing about Freda." BJ walked over and kissed my cheek.

"You have to take care of yourself or let somebody help you." BJ held my hand.

"I just really wanna be alone." I pulled my hand back from him and turned the other way.

"I just want to help in any way I can that's all, but I understand. It must be rough going through everything you been through the last few weeks." BJ said.

"Very." I said nonchalantly. There was a knock at the door. It was the nurse coming in.

"I didn't mean to interrupt, I just wanted to check your vitals again." She walked over and wrote everything down. "Can I get you anything?" She asked.

"No." I said shaking my head.

She left out the room. I heard something vibrating and I had completely forgot about my phone.

"Can you see if my phone is on that chair? I hear something

vibrating." I told BJ.

He looked on the couch and it had fell out my purse into the couch cushion.

"It was Megan. She's called like ten times." BJ said.

"What? Pass me the phone. She is probably checking on Freda." I called back and she picked up on the first ring.

"Ms. Lisa! Omg! I don't know what happened!!" Megan was screaming and crying.

"Megan what is going on?!" I sat straight up.

"I was downstairs in the kitchen making dinner for the boys and I don't know how it happened!" Megan was crying uncontrollably.

"Tell me what happened Megan please." I said again.

"It's Fred Jr! He shot himself in the head!!" Megan screamed so loud. I knew this wasn't a dream. I could hear Frank crying for me saying he wanted his mommy. I tore the wires off me because I had to get home ASAP.

Chapter 19

The worst feeling in the world is not being able to save your children from any type of pain. Hearing the way Megan screamed over the phone about my son made me vomit on myself.

"Get me home now!" I screamed.

BJ helped me out the bed. "Lisa put on your shoes." he said.

"If you don't get me out this fucking hospital I will literally kill you myself. Let's go!"

I didn't have time for a damn shoe. Fuck shoes. I had one baby in a coma and another one that I had no idea what was going on with. I could hear Megan screaming all over again and I could hear Frank screaming mommy.

"Why my kids? I rather take their spot before they suffer." I couldn't stop crying.

"It's going to be ok Lisa. Let's get to the house and see what's going on." BJ said. We jumped in his car and flew down the highway.

We pulled up to the house and there were about twenty police officers in my driveway. I jumped out the car before BJ stopped it.

"Where is my baby?! Where is my son?!" I was screaming and crying. I knew the worst had happened when I saw Megan holding Frank in the corner.

"Megan where is Fred Jr?" I asked. She just started shaking her head and the tears started rolling down her face.

"Where is my son! How did you let this happen!" I jumped toward Megan and one of the police officers grabbed me.

"Give me my baby!" I grabbed Frank from her and she ran off screaming out the door.

"Lisa, give me Frank so you can talk to the officers." I heard BJ say.

"Where is Fred? I need to see my son!" I held Frank tighter and I walked towards the stairs. They had caution tape blocking the stairs, so I had to go underneath.

"Lisa, Frank shouldn't see that. Please give him to me." BJ grabbed my arm. I couldn't stop crying.

I gave him Frank and walked upstairs. I made it to Fred Jr.'s room but it was empty. I looked down and saw the tape on my door, so I walked towards my room. I instantly thought about when Fred Jr. walked in on me and BJ having sex. I started screaming all over again.

"My baby! Please tell me where my baby is?!" I had so many tears in my eyes I couldn't even see anymore. I wiped my face and an officer stopped me.

"Ma'am nobody is supposed to be up here," he said.

"This is my fucking bedroom and you are not supposed to be up here. Where is my damn son?"

The officers all looked at each other and then I saw another officer, I guess a detective, come out my bathroom. "I apologize for everything ma'am but your son's body is in here."

He moved out of the way so that I could walk in. I saw blood all over the walls and what looked like pieces of his brain. I tried to scream but nothing else would come out. I saw Fred Jr. on the floor with half of his face blown off and my gun beside him.

"Fred why? WHY?! I love you baby! Why didn't you talk to me Fred?" I tried to grab him, but the officer stopped me.

"Ma'am we are waiting on the coroner. Nothing can be touched," he said.

I crawled out the bathroom and I began throwing up everywhere. "Whyyyyyyyyy?!" I screamed again. "Please God take me instead! I can't take this!"

I kept throwing up until one of the paramedics came and got

me. I was kicking and screaming and when BJ saw me he started crying.

"Lisa, is he really dead?" he asked.

"Fuck you!" I spit on BJ. "Fuck everybody!" The paramedic got me and strapped me down to the stretcher.

"We found a note," I heard the detective tell the other officer.

"A note from my baby? Give me the note! I need to read the note!" I couldn't stop screaming and crying! "Untie me please! My baby needs me! What does the note say?!"

I needed to know what happened. Why would my baby want to kill himself?

"Please somebody help me understand." I screamed.

The detective looked around at the officers then he cleared them out. "Ms. Davenport, my name is detective Raymond. You have my deepest condolences. I know this is a very difficult time for you and your family," he said. "Did Fred Jr. ever open up to you about some things that were bothering him?" he asked.

"Look Detective, get to the damn point and tell me what did my son say on the fucking letter!" I screamed at him. "My son is on the floor in my bathroom with his brains blown out, so at this point it doesn't matter." I tried to pull the straps off my arms. The detective grabbed the straps and unbuckled them for me.

"Ok. Did you know that there was a video of your son and another boy from school having sex all over the internet?" He pulled out Fred JR's phone and handed it to me. I thought I was going to shit on myself as I watched my son kissing his best friend.

For the first time in my life I was numb. I was literally heartbroken. I didn't know what to do or what to say. I was trying to wake up from this nightmare, but I couldn't wake up. My first child is gone. My son is dead. I looked down at the phone again and threw it across the room.

"I know this isn't anything you want to hear. I am so sorry about this devastating news, but I wanted to let you know that he had been getting bullied because of this," the officer said.

"Who is responsible for releasing the video?" I asked calmly. "Didn't you say he wrote a note? Where is it?" I asked.

"Yes ma'am, let me get that for you." He nodded his head at one of the other officers and then he walked over towards us.

"The note is considered evidence right now, but it does confirm that this was a suicide."

The note had been put in a plastic cover, but I could tell right away that it was Fred Jr.'s handwriting. I immediately started crying again.

"Are you sure you want to read this?" Detective Raymond asked. I just shook my head up and down and I read the note.

To whoever is reading this,

I have made it to the end. I know right now nobody understands why this has to happen or why it even happened, but I know why. From the time I was a little boy I knew I was gay. I hid this from everybody even myself. I always had to be tough around my dad and he always forced me to play football and basketball even when I didn't want to play sports. When Freda was born I was so jealous that I couldn't dress up like her. I loved my baby sister, but I always wished I was a girl. I would lock myself in the basement at night to play with her dolls and pretend I was a girl. As I write this I can't stop crying because I wish I could have told somebody this before I had to leave here. Unfortunately I can't. I'm sure the video of me kissing Brandon has gone viral by now. I guess all my bullies will just talk to me from the grave. I'm happy my truth will not be hidden anymore and I hope that Brandon can be stronger than me. I ask that my family forgives me for not protecting Freda. She's unconscious now and I rather kill myself than to see her dead because of me. I knew this day would come I just didn't think it would be so soon, but my time is done. I left a book of poetry for you guys to remember me by and to tell my story. I can't take it anymore and I hope everybody that shared the video visits me in hell soon. I just know that hell has to be better than here.

-Fred Davenport Jr

"God!! How did I miss the signs?" I screamed. "My baby is dead! Who are these kids that shared the video?" I asked.

I was ready for war. Kids and parents had to die. I lost one of my heartbeats, so I was feeling heartless.

"I don't know but we will definitely investigate the situation," the detective said.

"We are about to get to the bottom of this now." I said. I walked outside and I saw BJ walking in the driveway crying.

"BJ!" I screamed to him. He wiped his face and walked back

up towards me.

"Lisa, I'm so sorry. I'm so sorry." BJ came and hugged me. I hugged him back. I still couldn't wake up from this nightmare. I started crying harder than I ever had in BJ's chest. I had lost my son and my daughter was in a coma. I had officially lost my mind. Not to mention that Fred has been avoiding me and I had no idea how I would break the news to him.

BJ rubbed my back and we started walking back towards the door. My phone rang. It was Victor. I declined the call. Megan was holding Frank when we walked back in the house and I grabbed him from her.

"Megan you can leave." I told her. "Yes ma'am." Megan started crying again and I hugged her.

"I apologize, but this is the most difficult time of my life. Please understand I don't know what's real and what's fake right now because this feels like a dream." I explained to her. She continued to cry as she grabbed her stuff and walked out the door.

"Do you want me to grab you and Frank some clothes and get you guys a hotel?" BJ asked.

I nodded my head up and down to say yes. I couldn't stay at the hospital with Freda because of the strict visitation hours. I definitely wasn't staying in the house tonight, so I needed a nice hotel room to unwind in.

BJ walked out to the truck and sat us down. Then he went inside to pack us a bag. Two minutes had passed and Victor called my phone again. I answered it.

"Hello." I said.

"Are you ok Lisa? What's going on?" he asked.

"It's not a good time right now Victor. I'm having a family emergency." I told him.

"I'm so sorry Lisa, I hate you are pushing me away but I guess the rumors I've been hearing are true huh?" Victor kept talking. "I know what we had was temporary for you, but please don't cut me completely off because of him."

I was really at my breaking point. "I just told you I was having a fucking family emergency and you still talking about bullshit! Victor, BJ is like a brother and I know you aren't watching me are you?" I looked around the driveway to see if I saw anything unfamiliar.

"BJ? What are you talking about Lisa?" he asked.

"You said the rumors are true and whatever else you said, but honestly I don't care Victor. I have more important things to worry about right now."

Before I could hang up he started back talking. "I've been hearing Fred is coming home early, so I guess it is true?" Victor said.

"What are you talking about?" I asked.

"Yeah, Mo at the barbershop said his brother Maurice is locked up with him and he said that Fred is getting out early." You didn't know?" Victor sounded confused.

What the fuck is going on? I wonder was Fred trying to surprise me and just show up or is he just talking shit to his cell mates. BJ was walking out the front door with two bags.

"Look, I have to go Victor. I will call you later tonight." I hung up the phone.

I just hope that if Fred was getting out early he didn't see the wrong thing.

Chapter 20

We stopped by the hospital so that I could check on Freda before we checked in the hotel. The nurses told me that she was still stable but not much had changed. I was looking raggedy and I know they could tell that something wasn't right.

"My son just killed himself." Tears started rolling down my face.

"I'm so sorry to hear that." One of the nurses said.

"Now I'm here on the verge of losing another one." I was pissed. I was hurt. I was so full of emotions that I couldn't do anything but cry.

"Lisa let's go in and see Freda," BJ said as he grabbed my hand.

"Well, the baby can't go in there but you are more than welcome to leave him with us at the nurses station." The older nurse said.

"He can't what?" I asked with an attitude. BJ interrupted me.

"No problem. Lisa, you go in and we will wait out here. It's for Frank's safety so we will be fine. Just give her a hug for me." He held the door open for me to walk through.

"Ok fine."

I walked back to Freda's room and she seemed to just be sleeping. I couldn't understand how this was happening. When Freda wakes up how will I be able to tell her about Fred Jr. I couldn't help but to cry.

"Uncle BJ told me to give you a hug." I hugged her and I could feel her heartbeat. I held on to her as tight as I could. As long as she had a heartbeat I wasn't giving up until she opened her eyes.

We left the hospital and I asked BJ to stop by a gas station. Fred hadn't answered my phone calls, so I was going to buy a prepaid phone to see would he answer that. I walked in the store and there were two guys standing by the atm. I couldn't tell if they were Jamaican or Haitian, but I got a bad vibe when I saw them. I played it off and went to the back of the store where the phones were. They only had two phones left and they were flip phones.

"They could've at least had a touchscreen." I said to myself.

I grabbed one of the phones and walked to the front counter. "Are these the only phones you have?" I asked the clerk.

"Yeah, we sold out of everything else," he said.

"Well this will work since its only forty dollars." I said laughing.

By this time the two dudes were walking toward the counter. They didn't have anything in their hands, so I guessed that they were buying something from behind the counter. I gave the clerk a fifty-dollar bill and told him to keep the change. I turn around and one of the guys stepped in front of me. If I didn't back up when I did, we would have kissed.

"First of all, you need to back the hell up." I held my hand out. They both started laughing hysterically.

"Wah gwaan?" They started laughing even harder. "Beautiful, I couldn't let you walk away without speaking to you." He said in a very strong Jamaican accent.

"Tonight is not a good night for me ok, now please move." I stepped to the side so that I could go out the door.

"No, let me put your number in my phone first." He tried to grab the phone out my hand.

"Leave the lady alone," the clerk said. I looked back at him. He was a skinny Indian dude, but he didn't seem to be scared.

"Oh, you wanna have problems now?" The dude moved his jacket showing where he had his pistol on his hip.

"You are asking for trouble now." The clerk reached down and pulled out a shot gun. Both Jamaicans raised their hands up. "Get out! I already hit the panic button.The police are already on the way!" He screamed. They ran out the door.

"Who the fuck were they?" I walked back up to the counter.

"They come in here all the time, but I don't know them. The tall one, they call him Ziggy and the other one they only call him Tee," he said.

"So they come here often?" I asked.

"Yes, but they will not be allowed here anymore. I am so sorry. You can explain to the police what happened." Raj told me.

"No, I'm in a rush but thank you." I walked out the door and jumped back in BJ's truck.

"Did you see them motherfuckers that came out the store?" I asked him.

"The two black dudes?" he replied.

"They would not let me leave the store! They blocked me in to get my fucking phone number." I was pissed the fuck off.

"Why you didn't fucking call me or something Lisa?" He sounded pissed off.

"It happened so fast, but I would've blown their heads off if I had my gun."

I looked back at Frank and he was sleeping so peacefully. "You got my son. If something happens to me just take care of my children until Fred comes home." BJ didn't say anything. He just stared me in the eyes and shook his head up and down.

We made it to the hotel and checked in. BJ must have gotten the biggest hotel suite that they had. It was the size of a 2 bedroom condo.

"Is this a hotel or an apartment?" I asked him as I walked around, taking in my surroundings.

"I didn't know how long you wanted to stay so I got something comfortable for you and lil man." He started walking to one of the bedrooms and I followed behind him.

It was a full bedroom with a Lion King theme. "Wait a minute so they have a kid's room? BJ you never cease to amaze me." I started laughing and shaking my head.

He put Frank in the bed and he didn't budge. I walked to the bathroom and it was so cute. It was themed like the jungle and had a beautiful tub and shower. BJ had already tucked Frank in.

"My poor baby is tired." I kissed his cheek and we walked back in the living area.

"Now let's see how your room looks." BJ walked towards the other bedroom and I just noticed how beautiful the living room and kitchen were.

"It looks better than my house in here, hell." We chuckled.

"You have a mansion. Trust me it doesn't." BJ opened the double doors and my mouth dropped. "Wow!" It was absolutely stunning.

The bed was the size of two king sized beds put together. There was all white linens and diamonds everywhere. "BJ, you got a room with a chandelier in it? You are definitely not hood anymore." I said laughing.

"Don't blame me because I like the finer things in life. I just wanted to make sure you and Frank was comfortable." I was so thankful for that. I walked over and hugged him.

"It really means a lot to me, fa real BJ." I kissed him on the cheek. "I really wanna just take a bath or shower right now though." I grabbed the bag and put it in the bed to throw on some clothes.

"Ok, I will take the pull out couch but just let me know if you need anything," he said and walked out the room.

When BJ left out of the room, I locked the door behind him. I decided I needed a long hot bath. I ran my bath water as hot as I could stand it and then set up the flip phone I got. I called Fred. He didn't answer from the new number either. I was worried about him, but at the same time I knew he was good if he was talking to motherfuckers in jail about getting out early. I kept thinking about everything that Victor has been telling me. He is well connected and very well respected, so he can get any information he wants. I really believe he has someone watching Fred closer now because of me. My loyalty will always be to my husband, so I hope Victor doesn't go barking up the wrong tree for nothing.

I had been in the tub for almost an hour when I heard a beeping noise ring from the flip phone. "It must be a text message." I said to myself. I got out the tub and grabbed a towel. I picked the phone up and it was a text from Fred's number asking who it was.

"Your wife." I simply replied.

He was ignoring me but texted this number back right away. I was fucking pissed. All the shit I have been through with him and he can't even pick up the phone when I call. I don't give a fuck if somebody recorded me sucking dick and sent it to him.

I didn't deserve to be ignored. I decided to tell him about his kids. I texted him that Freda was in a coma and that Fred Jr. was dead. After that, I turned the phone off.

I dried myself off and sat on the bed. I started putting my lotion on and then BJ knocked on the door. "Yea!" I screamed out.

"I don't mean to bother you, but Fred just called my phone like four times." I jumped off the bed and opened the door.

"He did?" I asked.

BJ looked me up and down before I realized I didn't have the towel on me anymore. "Don't act like you ain't never seen me naked before now."

I walked back over to the bed. I finished rubbing lotion on my legs and watched BJ try to ignore it.

"I just texted him that Fred Jr. was dead and that Freda was in a coma, so that's probably why." I explained to him.

"Why would he call me though?" he asked.

"Oh, and then I turned my phone off. So just ignore him and tell him you were sleep. Can you put some lotion on my back please?" I picked up the lotion bottle.

"I don't like ignoring his calls but I will think of something." BJ walked over and grabbed the lotion. He looked me in my eyes so deep I had to turn away.

"I need some good rest so I can just understand it all." I still couldn't believe my son was gone. I needed to escape somehow and I needed BJ to help me do it.

BJ rubbed the lotion on my back quickly and handed me the bottle back. "Ok here. I'm going back to sleep." He turned and started walking out the door.

"BJ, I wanted lotion on my entire back." I stood up and then crawled back in bed so my ass could be sticking up in the air.

"Please, I just can't reach those tough spots."

He hesitated for a second, like he really didn't want to do it, but then he walked over. BJ grabbed the lotion, put some in his hands and rubbed them together. He rubbed it all over my ass and back. His hands were so big. They cupped my ass perfectly. He squeezed some of the lotion on my ass cheek and it made me jump.

"That was cold." I said giggling.

"Let me warm you up." BJ said it so sexy my pussy instantly got wet.

He rubbed the lotion in on my back and butt. Then he lifted me up from the back and started eating my ass out. He was eating it like a lunch and dinner buffet. He licked my ass crack while I played with my pussy. I started moaning because I was about to cum already. At the same time that I was cumming, he started licking on my clit. At first he started licking slow, and then he started going in circles. My pussy was jumping like Jordan.

BJ gently sucked on my clit, lifting me up and down. He put his tongue back on the clit moving it up and down until I felt I was about to scream. I started moaning so loud. My pussy was soaking wet! He started sucking my clit again like a baby sucking a bottle and I squirted all over his face. I let out a scream because it felt like my soul had left my body. I couldn't move and I couldn't talk.

"BJ! Bruh, can you hear me?" It was Fred's voice.

Chapter 21

I mouthed the words 'Do not say anything' so that BJ can just ignore Fred for now. If Fred was on speakerphone listening, then he heard that BJ was busy. Busy sucking the soul out his wife. Finally, he hung up the phone.

"Bruh what in the entire fuck? How did you answer the phone?" I was fucking spooked.

I was still mad that Fred had been avoiding me but I damn sure wasn't going to tell on myself like that.

"I must have stepped on it I guess but that shit was close Lisa. What if I was screaming your name or something?" He started rubbing on my clit with his hand. We both chuckled.

"I know how to make you scream my name if that's what you want?"

I grabbed his dick through his boxers. It was already rock hard and ready to go. He moved my hand and stepped back.

"Lisa, I just wanted to release some pressure off of you but you need to get some rest. I will handle Fred." BJ put the lotion on the nightstand and kissed me. He walked out and closed the doors behind him.

I cried all night thinking about the fact I will never see Fred Jr.

anymore. I kept seeing Freda in the hospital bed when I closed my eyes. It killed me knowing that there was nothing I could do to help her either. If she died I would literally go crazy. I know Frank is still depending on me so that's what I'm being strong for. I just had to think positive and do whatever it takes to keep her alive.

I couldn't help but think about the truck that hit us. I was going to fucking blow their brains out. Evil thoughts were crossing my mind as I thought about that bitch who put my only daughter in a coma and made my son feel so guilty he killed himself. I couldn't let that shit slide. I got out the bed to see if there were any snacks or tea in the kitchen area.

BJ was sleep. I walked in to check on Frank and he was sleep too. I looked in the pantry and there were no snacks. There was a Keurig on the counter with different flavors of coffee. I grabbed a French vanilla and made a cup. I knew I wasn't going to be able to sleep tonight so I thought I would do my research on a few things.

My first mission was finding out all about the lady that we had the accident with. I wanted to know all the way down to who her babysitter was when she was a little girl. Once the coffee was done I went back into my room and googled as much as I could find on her. I saw her name on the police report that BJ had, plus I found a background website that would tell me all I needed to know.

I pulled up the site and entered the bitch's name, Gabriela Rodríguez. She was 29 years old and had one son. The website gave me her parents' names and addresses, her current address and even her baby daddy's name and address. It even tells me her criminal history. She had been arrested for possession of marijuana when she was 20, but everything else were minor traffic violations. I also noticed that it said she had a son who was deceased as well. There was an article link connected so I clicked on it.

The heading said, "Woman comes home to fire, toddler and fiancé dead inside." I read the article and found that Gabriela had a son who died in a house fire with his dad. Her fiancé never woke up. He couldn't save his or his son's life. According to the article the little boy was alive at the time of the fire and the dad had dozed off while cooking dinner. They both died on the scene.

"This bitch is surrounded by death," I said to myself. I read everything else that I could find on her to come up with a plan. No matter what, I knew that she had to suffer and everybody around her.

I was able to get about two hours of sleep before I heard Frank crying. I jumped up to go get him but BJ had beat me to it.

"It's ok little man," he said to Frank. "I think he was scared because he didn't know where he was." Frank reached out for me, still whimpering a little.

"It's ok Frank." I got him and hugged him tight. "Mommy not going to let anything happen to you."

I walked in the living room and sat in the big recliner. "Are you hungry baby?" I asked Frank. He nodded his head.

"Ok let's order room service." We all ordered some breakfast and washed up.

"Go brush your teeth for mommy ok Frank." Frank ran in the bathroom.

"Hey, I talked to Fred and he was devastated about the kids. He even got mad at me saying I should have been there to protect them and some other bullshit." BJ explained to me.

"Lisa, I feel so bad about everything and if I could take Freda or Fred Jr's spot, I swear to God I would." BJ sounded like he wanted to cry.

"Fuck him and his opinion, he's not here to protect us either." I was pissed over everything at this point with Fred.

He can't control what's going on himself so how can he blame anyone else.

"He brought up how he knew you had been cheating on him too." BJ shook his head.

"Really? And you should have told him about time she cheated back!" I yelled out.

"Lisa, this shit is serious because whoever you cheating with sent Fred pictures of the two of you kissing." He said seriously.

This could only be about Victor. I knew that getting involved with Victor wasn't a good idea because of his status. He was so well known that it would be impossible to figure out who knew him and Fred.

"Fuck! It makes sense now!" I said to BJ.

"The thing that amazes me is that obviously it's not me that he's talking about which means you have been giving that pussy to somebody else," he whispered as Frank walked back in.

"All done mommy." Frank sounded so excited.

"Good boy!" I gave him a hi five.

I looked at BJ to let him know I don't owe him any explanation about my pussy, especially when I'm married to his best friend. By that time room service was knocking on the door. We got our food and ate. I didn't say anything to BJ and he said

198

nothing else to me.

Once we got done eating, we got dressed to go see Freda. I thought about everything I found on Gabriela and I was ready to act quick. I didn't give a fuck if the evidence pointed back to me or not, I was about to make sure she hurt like I hurt. I wanted to do it on my own, but I knew I couldn't so I called Paco.

"Hey Lisa, how are you?" Paco said answering the phone.

"I've been better Paco, how are you?" I asked him.

"I'm good, I'm out here still handling business. Let me know if there is anything I can do for you," Paco said.

"Well there is, now that you mention it." I tried to ease in the conversation without sounding psycho.

"You know Freda is in a coma and Fred Jr. blamed himself and blew his brains out because of it." I explained holding back tears. "I have to bury my son and if Freda doesn't make it out I'll have to bury my daughter too."

I couldn't stop the tears from coming out. "I have to choose a casket to put my baby in Paco. I am only allowed a certain time of day to see my only little girl because she is in ICU. I need the bitch that caused this and her family dead for fucking up my family." I was crying hysterically by then.

"Lisa, I am so sorry. Give me their names and it's done." Paco sounded like he was holding back tears.

"The lady that hit us is Gabriela Rodríguez," I told him. Frank was on the iPad and I walked in the bathroom to wash my face.

"Gabriela Rodríguez? Do you have an address?" Paco asked.

"Yes. She lives off of Cheyanne Street. I can give you as much info as needed. I can meet you after hospital visiting hours are over," I explained to him.

"Lisa, does she drive an Escalade?" Paco asked. "Yeah, how you know that Paco?" I was confused.

"Because that's my sister Lisa!"

"Your sister?" I asked confused.

"Well my sister- in- law," Paco said.

"Wait, I'm confused Paco. Help me understand this," I asked him.

"She had a fiancé that died in a fire, that was my baby brother." Paco got real quiet.

200

"What in the fuck are you saying Paco?" I really didn't give a fuck anymore.

"I'm saying that's my sister. I can't kill her. She may not be my flesh and blood, but I still consider her family." Paco sounded like he was talking through his teeth.

"She fucked my family up, so I can't feel sympathy at this time for her or anyone." I explained to Paco.

"Lisa, you don't have to kill her to get your point across. What has happened to you?" Paco asked me.

"Life happened to me Paco. Fucking life!" I yelled. "My son took his life and my daughter doesn't know if she's dead or alive." I told him. "So you want to know what happened to me motherfucker?!" I yelled again. "Ask my kids!"

I hung up the phone. I was fucking livid! I don't give a fuck if it was his mother. The bitch is going to fucking die. My phone started ringing. It was Paco calling back.

"Yeah." I answered.

"I know that you gave me an order, but I am telling you that I will not do it," he said.

"Paco you will be handled, but until then you can go home." I told him and hung up the phone. I was in charge and shit was going to go how I wanted it to go. If Paco had to get hit in the crossfire so be it.

I hated seeing my baby lifeless, but I made sure she had the best doctors the hospital had. I let the doctors know that no matter the cost, whatever they saw that she needed I wanted her to have it. The nurses said that she made improvement and they are positive she will make it through. I was so relieved to hear that, but it was bittersweet because I knew I had to start making funeral arrangements for Fred Jr.

We left the hospital and headed downtown to go to the funeral home to start getting things done.

"Good evening. I am so sorry for your loss," a big chubby guy said as we walked into our appointment.

"Thank you. My name is Lisa and this is BJ." I told him.

"My name is Gary. Nice meeting you two. Let me get Mr. James for you." Gary walked to the back. He had more hips and ass than me.

"Gary thick as fuck huh?" I asked BJ laughing. He chuckled and just shook his head.

Gary walked back up to the front. "Mr. James will be right out. He just finished speaking with another family," Gary told us.

"Ok, thank you." I sat down. Frank was sleep so BJ laid him across two chairs.

"We have a daybed if you want to lay the baby in there." Gary said.

"No! I don't want anyone to think he's dead and he's only sleeping. I don't want to bury two sons." I laughed. Gary and BJ looked at me like I was crazy.

"No problem, he's fine where he is." Gary turned around and walked back into another room.

"Are you okay Lisa?" BJ asked.

"I'm good, why do you ask?" I was dying on the inside and honestly scared of life without my son.

"I just want to make sure you are ok, that's all." BJ sat down.

I could hear the door open and voices coming up the hallway. Then I heard a voice say, "It was my pleasure and again thank you." A guy, I'm assuming was Mr. James, shook everyone's hand and a big family walked out the door.

"Good evening. How are you two?" He shook our hands.

"I'm Mr. James, come on back."

BJ grabbed Frank and we went into Mr. James' office. I tried not to notice, but Mr. James was fine as fuck. He was about six feet tall with milk chocolate skin. He was Morris Chestnut brown and had muscles like he played football or something. Mr. James wore a navy blue tailored suit that fit every part of his body. The way his suit fitted, I could see that his dick was the size of a baby leg. It was bulging out his pants. His teeth were as white as milk and his smile would snatch your soul. Damn, I wasn't expecting him to be this fine and I quickly remembered the reason I was there. My baby was gone.

"My condolences to you guys for losing your son," Mr. James said.

"He's my son, this is his uncle." I corrected him.

"I apologize. So sorry," he stated.

"It's ok, BJ was definitely a father figure for him." I started to cry. Mr. James gave me the box of tissues.

"Well I'm not sure if you are familiar with the process but I have a few packages you can choose from. You can tell me your budget and I can show you what's in that range or we can go from lowest to highest," he explained to us.

"There is no budget. I want the very best for my baby," I told him.

"Well that would be the platinum package."

Mr. James showed us everything that came with the platinum package. The casket was gold and had red fabric inside. It was very beautiful. Also included was an obituary booklet. I could put as many pictures or whatever I wanted inside it.

As Mr. James kept talking, Fred Jr.'s death hit me all over again. The tears were flowing down my face uncontrollably. I saw Fred Jr. smiling the biggest smile while dancing in the living room. Some nights, we would all play the Just Dance game and just have so much fun. Freda loved the Michael Jackson dancing game. She always won that round. Before I knew it I was screaming.

"I can't do this! No! Please bring my baby back!" I lost it.

If I had to describe the pain I was feeling, it would be getting hit by an eighteen-wheeler a hundred times.

"I can't do this BJ, not my baby! I can't put him in the ground! I'd rather go!" I was crying hysterically. BJ grabbed me and just put me in his chest.

"I'm right here with you Lisa. I promise I'm not going anywhere." BJ started rocking me in his arms like I was a newborn baby.

I kept hoping it was all a dream, but I knew it wasn't. I just closed my eyes and let BJ keep rocking me until I could calm down. I finally sat up and let Mr. James know that I needed to leave.

"I want to go with whatever package that will send my baby away perfectly. Money is not an issue." I told him.

"No worries. I know this will be a closed casket but please bring clothing, pictures, and whatever you want to be featured. We will do the rest." He stood up to walk us out.

Frank was awake and looking around, but he didn't cry. Normally anything will make him cry but he was so calm that I got nervous.

"You ok Boo Boo?" I asked him. He nodded his head and just put his head back down on BJ's shoulders.

"Here's my card. Please call with any questions," Mr. James gave us his card and we left.

I went back to the hospital to see Freda, but we were too early for visiting hours. BJ needed to run some errands and he took Frank with him so that I could wait and go in the ICU area. I had about a hundred missed calls on my cellphone and tons of text messages from so many people. I'm sure by now Fred Jr. had made the news so I decided to go to the news station website and see. His story was on the front page: *'Teenage boy shoots himself in the head after video of him and best friend making out is released'* They had the video linked to the page and I was pissed.

"Are you fucking kidding me?!" I said aloud.

The other people in the waiting room all looked up at me. I immediately googled the news station's number.

"WKPT this is Mark," a guy answered.

"Mark, I need to speak to whoever would be responsible when I sue the fuck out of your asses." By that time everybody in the waiting room gasped. I got up and walked outside to the garages because I was about to ruin somebody's day.

"Hold one moment." Mark put me on hold and some country ass song was playing. Hell, that pissed me off even more. I don't know why but I was just mad at everything at this point.

"Hello, this is Jerome," he said.

"Are you the one in charge of the news station?" I asked him.

"Yes, I'm the news director. Who are you and what can I help you with?" he asked sarcastically.

"You can start first by getting child pornography off your website." I told him.

"Come again?" he said. You could tell he was one of those men who had money and a fucked-up attitude, but he just met his match.

"I will come again and again and again. I will come in your nightmares. I will come in your dreams. I'm bad enough that I could cum in your mouth and you would love it. I'm calling because you have a story on my son and a video attached on your website of two children involved in sexual activity. I will be calling my lawyer."

I was fucking pissed off to the point that I was shaking. I turned around and as soon as I hung up the phone, somebody grabbed me and put a bag over my head. He covered my mouth with his hand and it sounded like a truck or car pulled up. He threw me in and then he jumped in and closed the door. I couldn't even scream or cry. I sat there and just accepted that whatever happens, happens. I didn't want to give up, but damn could life get any worse. I heard them say something in Spanish. It sounded like a la mansión. I heard mansion, but I didn't know the other shit they said.

"Whoever you are, am I the only one on the kidnap list this month or something?" I asked. They didn't say a word and just sped off.

Chapter 22

They finally took the bag off my head. The guy sitting beside me pulled out his phone. He dialed a number and then he handed me the phone.

"Why are you doing this to me?" I asked. "You will see." I got the phone and who else but fucking Victor answers.

"Victor! Are you fucking kidding me?!" He had me all the way fucked up. "Stop this fucking truck right now or I am calling the police!" I yelled out.

"Lisa, I am so sorry. I meant this to be romantic, but I wasn't thinking. I am so sorry." Victor explained.

"Romantic? Yeah you are crazier than I thought. What's more romantic than being kidnapped?" I said sarcastically.

"Forgive me. I thought after you had visited your daughter you would need something to relax your mind," he said.

"I haven't even seen my daughter and if you make me miss her visiting hours you will need something to relax your mind." I told him.

"Lisa I am so sorry." Victor said something in Spanish and the guy driving immediately turned on the emergency blinkers and did a U-turn in the middle of the street.

"Victor what is fucking wrong with you? I just lost my son and my daughter is in a hospital bed. I don't have time for this." I hung up the phone.

I started thinking about it and Victor was obviously watching me. That's considered stalking because how did he know where I was and when I walked out.

"So, Victor had you two to follow me?" I asked. They didn't say anything.

"I know you can speak English, but that's ok. I'm going to call the police." I pulled my phone out and then the driver said something.

"We were following orders," he said.

"Well now you are about to get a restraining order." My phone started ringing and it was Monica.

"Hello?" I answered.

"Hi girl, I was just calling to check on you," Monica said.

"Thank you. I'm as well as I can be. It's tough." I thought about my kids and I had to hold back the tears.

"Where are you now? I was going to come by the hospital and see Freda." she asked.

"I am about to pull up to the hospital now, it's almost visiting hours." I told her.

"Perfect! See you shortly." I hung up my phone and by then we were pulling back up to the hospital.

"Thanks for nothing you dumb motherfuckers." I got out the truck and slammed the door as hard as I could. I walked back in the hospital and went back up to the waiting room.

Monica showed up a few minutes after me. "Hi girl." We hugged.

"How are you holding up Lisa?" she asked.

"It's so hard Monica. This is the hardest thing I have ever done in my life," I told her. She hugged me again.

"I can't imagine Lisa. I am here for you no matter what you need." Monica said while rubbing my back.

They announced over the intercom that visiting hours were open. We both walked to the back to see Freda. I stopped by the nurses station to get an update. "I was checking on Freda, any updates or anything?" I asked.

"I'm Nurse Travis and I've been Freda's Nurse today. She has been having some activity happening which is a wonderful sign of a full recovery. The nerves are starting to react in the brain and that's a good way to indicate the motor skills are trying to work." Nurse Travis explained.

"Thank goodness. That is awesome news!" I started crying. "Let me go see her."

When I walked in her room, she still seemed to just be sleeping. I kissed on her and fluffed her pillows. I massaged her body the best I could without moving her.

"She is so beautiful." Monica said. Monica walked over and kissed her on the cheek also.

"How's the baby?" I asked her.

"Everything is good Lisa. I'm so excited." she said enthusiastically. "I know with everything going on you won't be able to do the shower, but I still want to include you somehow," she said.

"I still want to help. They kick me out of the ICU and there isn't anything I can do about that, so I still have free time," I told her.

"Whatever you want to do, I would love to have your presence." Monica said.

We talked about the ideas she and I had until visiting hours were up. "Time really flies when I'm in here. I will be so glad when this is over and she's home." I said. I bent down to kiss her and I saw her finger move.

"Did you just see that?" I asked Monica.

"See what?" she asked.

"Her finger moved! I know I'm not crazy," I said. I went to the nurses station.

"My daughter's finger just moved when I kissed her!" I told Nurse Travis.

"That's very common to see fingers, hands, toes, and things like that move when the brain activity starts back working," she explained.

"How long can it take for her to be back fully herself?" I asked.

"Honestly it could be a day or it could be a year, you never know." I finished talking with the nurse and Monica and then I left out.

"I better call BJ and see where he is. He's my ride." I pulled out my phone and saw I had a missed call from him.

"I didn't hear my phone ring, he may already be here." I dialed him back and he didn't answer. "He didn't answer. Let me check to see if he's outside in the front."

We walked out to the front of the hospital but I didn't see him.

"That's weird for BJ not to show up or answer his phone." I was getting nervous. He had Frank and I wouldn't know what to do if something happened to my baby.

"What if something happened?" I asked Monica.

"Calm down, nothing happened," she said. "Come on I will take you wherever you need to go.

We walked in the garage and got in the car. "I guess go to BJ's house." I put his address in the GPS and we headed his way.

We made it to BJ's house and there wasn't anyone there. "This is getting scary girl."

I tried calling him again.

"Think of somewhere else he could be." Monica said.

"Let's go by Paco's."

Even though I really didn't want to talk to Paco, I called him to see had he talked to BJ.

"What the fuck do you want?" Paco answered.

"Excuse me?" I asked him. He must didn't realize who just called him.

"I knew you were going to be calling me you crazy, psychotic bitch." Paco sounded like he had snapped.

"I got your bitch you delusional motherfucker. I will have your ass killed." I screamed at him. Monica looked like she was about to have a heart attack.

"Well, I guess I might as well kill your boyfriend and your other son," he said laughing hysterically.

"What the fuck are you talking about Paco?" When he said other son, my heart dropped to my stomach.

"I want ten million dollars and you can have them back." Paco said.

"What the fuck are you talking about Paco?" I was confused.

"Do you know the definition of hostage? Well I have your son and your boyfriend here tied up. If you don't bring me ten million dollars, they will be cut into ten million pieces." He hung up the phone.

"Oh. My. Fucking. God." I said calmly.

"What's wrong Lisa? What's going on?" Monica sounded frantic.

"Paco has BJ and Frank. He's holding them hostage. He wants ten million dollars or he says he will kill them." I explained to her.

"We need to call the police Lisa." Monica said.

"By the time I'm done with Paco, the police won't recognize him."

I was beyond pissed. I didn't want to involve Monica in what was about to go down, so I had her take me back to the hotel.

"Lisa, you can't handle this alone. Call the police." Monica sounded so scared.

"It's ok Monica. Paco is probably just playing a joke on me so I can come over there." I knew Paco was serious and I was ready to get to his ass.

"Don't worry and take care of you and that baby."

Monica dropped me off at the hotel in front of the door. "Lisa, call me as soon as you get with Frank and BJ or I will call the police myself." she said and blew a kiss to me.

I hopped on the elevator and the only person I could think to call was Victor.

"My beautiful queen. I hope this means you forgive me." Victor answered the phone.

"Victor, this crazy motherfucker has my baby held hostage," I said as calmly as possible.

"What?!" Victor yelled. "Tell me who and I will handle it."

He started saying something in Spanish and then I started hearing all kinds of noises in the background.

"Paco, he has BJ and Frank but he's saying he wants ten million dollars or he's going to kill my baby." I was so pissed I couldn't shed anymore tears. I saw blood and Paco was going to either kill me or be killed.

"The son of a bitch has lost his mind. Ten million dollars? Do you have it or do I need to grab it?" Victor said.

"Well I don't just have ten million dollars laying around Victor."

I heard him snap his finger and say something else in Spanish "en la caja fuerte." Then, I heard a guy say si senor.

"I will bring the money but it's kind of hard to pack ten million dollars in a briefcase. Where are you right now?" he asked. "I'm at the hotel. I can text you the address."

I was looking to see did I have the key to get in and of course I didn't.

"Fuck!" I yelled.

"What's the matter Lisa? Are you ok?" Victor screamed in the phone.

"I can't even get in the room." I told him.

"Go get a key from the desk. Lisa, please know that whatever you need, I will get for you and what I can't get I will pay someone to get. Text me the address so I can show this motherfucker who lady not to fuck with." I knew Victor had really lost his mind.

"Ok, I'm about to text you." I hung up the phone and sent the address.

Victor sounded like he was ready for whatever. I almost wished I would have handled this by myself before getting Victor involved. Victor was ready to go to war and I just wanted to make sure my baby made it out alive. I started walking back to the elevator and my phone rings. It's Megan. I hadn't talked to her since everything happened and I still could not make myself answer.

I knew I would probably have cursed her out even though it was probably more my fault than hers. I couldn't believe I left my gun out so freely around my kids. I always thought that I knew my kids and that they knew better. I missed Rosa. She was the one that really kept us together. I had to make sure I got Rosa back to me someway somehow.

Chapter 23

I waited in the lobby so when Victor pulled up I could just hop in. I was so nervous for some reason I was shaking.

"Are you ok?" The guy sitting in the other chair asked me.

"Yeah, why do you ask that?" I tried to play it off.

"Well your're literally shaking right now." He sounded concerned.

I stood up. "Yes, I'm fine, thanks for asking."

I walked to the bathroom to try and pull myself together. I didn't want to look like a crackhead needing another hit. I got some paper towels and wet them. I placed them on my forehead and neck to try and cool off. Once I calmed myself down, I realized I was about to have an anxiety attack. I walked back and forth until I felt relaxed. I washed my hands and went back out in the lobby. Victor's SUV was pulling up as I walked out. The guy opened the door for me and I got in.

"Lovely as always." Victor kissed my cheek.

"Thank you and you look like you're ready for a homicide." He laughed hysterically.

"Well baby any outfit of mine is ready for a homicide." He

laughed again. "Where are we going?" he asked.

"To Paco's house. Here is the address."

We headed that way and got our plan together. Whatever Paco was thinking when he decided to kidnap my son, he won't ever think it again. I'm pretty sure you have no thoughts when you're dead anyway.

We pulled up to Paco's and I called his phone. "You move fast."

Paco sounded like he was on drugs or drunk. I could hear Frank crying in the background.

"Let me talk to my baby you low down bitch!" I screamed at Paco.

"Now calling me names is not going to make me nicer you know. You are there, and he is with me so be careful Lisa." He had me so fucked up I couldn't help but be anxious to see him die.

"I'm headed in." I hung up the phone.

I didn't know if he had cameras or people watching me as I pulled up, but I tried to play it cool. I didn't want anyone to see Victor because if they did they would know it was something serious going on. Everybody in this area knows that Victor is

222

the plug and he don't come to this side of town unless he wants your head. Literally.

"Lisa be careful," Victor said.

We had discussed how we were going to do everything on the ride there, so it was time to put our plan in action. Paco was in the duplexes where he served on one side and lived on the other. He has a condo downtown that nobody really knows where it is, but I knew almost everything I needed to know about him. I grabbed one of the bags out the car with the money in it. Victor told me it ended up taking more than five bags to fit ten million dollars in and that was mostly all hundred-dollar bills. I went to the door and before I could knock, Paco opened the door and threw me in.

"What the fuck Paco?" I said jerking away from him.

"Frank!" I yelled. My baby started crying so loud, I could tell he was scared.

I walked over to BJ. He just shook his head but he didn't say anything.

"Paco why you have to do this man?" I asked him as I walked closer to him.

"Stay the fuck back! It might be a bomb in that bag." He

sounded like he had lost it.

"Are you ok Paco? You seem like you are on edge." I backed away so he didn't think I was trying to rush him.

"And why would I bring a fucking bomb in here with my son. Be real Paco."

I took the bag off my shoulder and slid it to him. "That's two million and I have the rest, but I need to know I can trust you." I explained to Paco.

"Lisa he's a fucking mess because he's been in the supply and stealing from us," BJ said.

"Who asked you to say a motherfucking thing?" Paco shot in the wall.

"What the fuck you mean he been stealing?" I looked at BJ.

"Tell her why you are really mad Paco? He's stolen about 3 million dollars from us. That's including drugs and weapons." BJ stared Paco in the eyes like he was ready to attack him.

Boom! Paco hit BJ so hard in the mouth with the end of his gun it knocked one of his teeth out.

"So, you going to steal from me and then kidnap my son for the ransom money? You dirty son of a bitch." I said shaking my head.

"I have been dealing with some demons Lisa and you had me killing people. That didn't help me any. So, I feel you should have to fucking pay!" Paco sounded like a lunatic.

I didn't want him to start telling everything to BJ especially about me killing Chanel.

"Just forget it Paco. I can forgive you." I tried to sound as calm as possible because in the back of my mind was murder.

"Look at Chanel. She didn't deserve to die Lisa. You took her life because you were having a fucking bad day!" Paco yelled.

"Now you must be delusional Paco." I just hoped BJ didn't say anything.

"Wait where does Chanel come in at in this Paco?" BJ said.

"What kind of drugs is he on BJ? This is more than coke." I tried changing the subject, but BJ ignored me.

"Paco you telling me that Lisa killed Chanel? How do you know man?" BJ didn't look at me one time.

"Yes, and I hid the body." Paco said.

"Ok if you hid the body where was the body found?" BJ asked Paco.

225

"By the railroad tracks. I buried her by the train station," he admitted.

It got real quiet. It was so quiet I had this little nervous feeling in the pit of my belly.

"Paco you need to get fucking help. Her body was not found there." BJ shook his head.

"BJ why are you entertaining him? He's obviously sick." I could barely breathe. Paco had probably hid so many bodies that he forgot where he put Chanel.

"You need to get fucking help you lunatic. I want my son and BJ out of here now."

I didn't yell or get loud because I wanted him to know I meant business.

"I want all my money at the same time!" BJ screamed.

"You think stealing three million dollar's worth of my shit and money under my nose means I can trust you?" I asked him with a look of disgust. "Nigga untie my fucking son!"

I walked up to Paco and looked him eye to eye. "If I wanted to kill you Paco you would already be dead, but I don't like touching the help." He pushed me backwards.

"Get the fuck back!" He pointed the gun in my face.

I was not doing what me and Victor talked about anymore. I was ready to kill Paco myself.

"Lisa please just back up and go get the money." BJ said pleading with me. "Think about Frank."

I looked over at my baby and he was still crying. I wouldn't want him to witness me getting killed or seeing me kill Paco.

"Ok Paco I will do it your way." I held my hands up and I walked backwards out the door.

I got outside and Paco left the door open. I walked to the truck and grabbed two bags.

"I'm ready Lisa, what are you waiting on?" Victor asked.

"Rush him but don't kill him in front of my son."

I got all the bags and dropped them on the ground. I looked back but Paco wasn't standing in the door, so I just dragged the bags to the door. Money can be heavy as fuck. I walked back in the house and I noticed Paco wasn't in the living room anymore.

"Where did he go and where is Frank?" I asked BJ.

"Lisa go find that sick motherfucker I think he trying to molest

227

him in the back!" BJ yelled.

I ran to the back and I could hear Frank screaming.

"Frank! Where are you baby? Keep screaming!" I screamed back to him.

I got to the bedroom and it was locked. I kicked the door to try and open it. It didn't budge.

"Move!" Victor was in the house and had his gun pointed at the door.

"Back up Lisa!"

He shot the knob off the door and kicked the door off the hinges. Paco's sick ass was walking around with his pants around his ankles and Frank was running all around the room.

"Lisa, he deserves to die right now!" Victor looked and me.

"Kill that sick bastard!" I told him.

Victor shot him in the head. I grabbed the gun out of Victor's hand and I shot Paco in his dick three times until I knew he was dead.

Chapter 24

"You nasty sick bitch! This for my fucking son!" I screamed out.

Frank was in the corner shaking. I couldn't believe Paco was trying to rape my damn son.

"Frank!" I ran over to my baby. He jumped when I got by him like he was scared of me.

"Baby I had to make sure nobody hurt you." I started crying.

Victor came over and hugged us. "I'm so glad you guys are ok."

The two other guys that were in the truck came down the hallway.

"You want us to untie the other guy?" one of the guys asked.

"Yes! Untie me!" BJ yelled.

"Frank are you ok?" I asked.

My baby looked like he had seen a ghost. I did not want to kill Paco in front of him, but he deserved that death. He earned that death. He was stealing from me and he kidnapped my son. Then he had the audacity to try and molest my baby. I wish I could bring him back to life and kill him again. The guys untied BJ and we walked back in the living room.

"I'm so sorry. I was not expecting Paco to turn on me. I fucked up bad." BJ said hugging me and Frank.

"I know BJ, I can't believe it." I shook my head.

"Well it happened and you couldn't even protect yourself, so how could you protect the child." Victor said.

BJ gave Victor a cold look. "I don't know why you had to be called for help but thank you. I admitted I fucked up and I didn't want to take any chances of him killing Frank, so I did what he said." BJ explained.

"So what happened BJ?" I wanted to hear the story and know how did Paco manage to tie them up.

BJ was doing his runs and collecting so he could make deposits. When he made it to Paco, he said he was acting really weird. Paco told him that he had to recount the money because it was short. To make a long story short, BJ said that Paco's friend Kash told it all. Paco was stealing from Kash too. Once they made it in to recount the money, Paco pulled a rifle out on him and threatened to kill Frank. That's when he tied them up. I was just glad my baby was safe I didn't care who got hurt in the process.

When I made it back to the hotel, I remembered that I needed another key.

"Take me around the front because I have to go to the desk." I told the driver.

"I'm so glad you two are ok Lisa." Victor kissed my forehead. "I'm glad you know you can depend on me too."

I got Frank out the truck. BJ went home he said he just wanted to pull himself together. I know he probably feels like he let me down, but I know he was doing what was best for Frank.

"Lisa here don't forget your bags." Victor got out and grabbed the duffle bags out the trunk. "If I was going to give ten million dollars to a pervert, I can definitely give it to a queen."

He grabbed one of the rolling carts and put the bags on there. "I will bring it up for you."

I stopped and got them to reactivate my key then we went up to the room.

"Victor you know I don't need your money right?" I told him. He chuckled.

"Lisa I know this, but if I could I would give you the world." He put the bags down on the floor and I guess he saw something of BJ's.

"So what nigga you had in here? You couldn't call him when you needed help?" Victor said with an attitude.

"The only person that was here was us and BJ. BJ didn't want me to be alone while I was grieving the death of my son." I rolled my eyes and I went and put Frank in the bed because he didn't wake up.

"Having somebody that weak protecting you is not right. I'm going to get you your own personal security from my staff. I won't take no for an answer either."

Victor walked around being nosey, but I wasn't mad at him. He did come through for us today and I really appreciated that.

"So what are you about to do Victor?" I asked him.

"Are you rushing me out the door Lisa? I will leave it's no problem. I'm glad you two are good." He started walking back towards the door.

"I actually wanted you to bathe me." I looked at him and shrugged my shoulders.

"Really?" he asked bucking his eyes.

"Yes, but if you have somewhere to be I do understand." I started walking towards the other room. He didn't say anything but he turned around and followed me in the room.

232

Victor walked in the bathroom and turned on the water. I took my clothes off. I had dried up blood all on me.

"Did someone get rid of Paco's body?" I asked Victor.

"Everything is taken care of when you are with me baby. I just need you to relax."

He walked me in the bathroom and helped me take my bra and panties off.

"I'm going to help you shower to get that blood off of you while I have the water in the jacuzzi tub running."

He washed me off and then grabbed a towel to cover me up.

"I don't need a towel to walk right here Victor." I told him giggling.

"I don't want such a precious thing like yourself to catch a cold." He smiled at me and sat me in the tub.

"It feels perfect." I rubbed the bubbles on me.

"Let me tell the guys to leave. You relax and I will be right in with you." He kissed my forehead and walked out the bathroom.

I sat back and closed my eyes and I saw Fred Jr.

"Mama I'm sorry." He was looking so strange.

His eyes were black. There were no white parts in his eyes at all. His body looked like it was possessed by a zombie. "

Mama I'm sorry," he repeated.

"Don't be sorry." I tried to say it, but the words didn't come out.

"Lisa!" Victor screamed my name. "You were asleep."

He had strawberries and champagne on a cart.

"I must have been sleep a while.

"Yes. I ordered room service and I wanted to join you."

Victor poured some champagne and got a plate of strawberries to sit beside me. He got in the tub and sat in front of me.

"Why you didn't sit behind me?" I asked.

"I want to feed you and look you in your eyes first to admire your beauty."

Victor handed me the champagne glass and then fed me a strawberry. I sipped from my glass and then I kissed him.

"Slow down," he said laughing.

He drank his champagne and fed me another strawberry.

"I just had a weird dream about Fred Jr." I told him.

"What was it?" he asked.

I didn't even want to tell him because I just wanted the image out my head. "It was nothing really. I guess I'm just thinking about everything I have to do for the funeral."

I lost a piece of my heart. I will never get over it and nobody would ever understand how I felt.

"I know and that's why I just want you to relax. Turn around, let me give you a massage."

I turned around and Victor started rubbing my back. I drank all my champagne and let him massage my back so I could loosen up. He kept rubbing and I felt so much better. He kissed my neck and it felt so good.

"Just relax."

Victor turned me around and sat me on the edge of the tub. He lifted my leg up and started licking my pussy so slowly. I could feel every tongue stroke. He sucked my clit then licked it slow. I grabbed his head and pushed him back.

"Stop." I whispered.

"Just relax baby."

His tongue went back to work doing the same rhythm and I just dropped my head back. I had never felt so good. I was so relaxed and whatever Victor was doing was taking my soul from my body. I moaned so loud and nutted all in his mouth. He licked my clit again and that made me jump back so hard I almost fell off the tub.

We both laughed and then Victor picked me up and laid me across the bed. He started right back up and licked my clit slowly at first, then he sped up his rhythm. I lost it. I was moaning and nutting everywhere. He flipped me over and started eating my ass.

"Play with your pussy," he commanded me.

He ate and licked my ass as I played with my pussy. "I'm about to cum again." I moaned out.

He lifted my ass up and then started eating my pussy from the back. I saw my soul leave, but I couldn't even wave bye. I was shaking. Victor got up and grabbed something off the rolling cart. It looked like some massage gel or something. He poured it in the crack of my ass and rubbed it in.

"Just relax." I was so relaxed that I felt high.

I knew I was relaxed because Victor put his dick in my ass and I didn't scream. I jumped but he held me down.

"You have to tell me when you are going to do that Victor." I told him.

"Baby just relax."

Victor got it in and started fucking me from the back. It felt so good that I couldn't do anything but moan.

"Hmmmmm....ohhh shiiiittttt!" I screamed out.

I was about to cum again and so was Victor. I could hear him moaning and then he nutted.

"Shit."

He got up and went in the bathroom. I heard him turn the shower on, so I got up and jumped in with him. I washed him up and admired how sexy Victor was. He kissed me and I turned the water off.

"Come here, I wasn't finished," I told him.

I walked back to the bed and Victor sat down. I got on my knees and I went to work. I started off licking his dick slowly and then I made magic. I made his dick disappear in my throat and he moaned out.

"Fuckkkk!" I stopped.

"Are you ok?" I asked him.

"Yes, don't stop." He grabbed my head and I let him fuck my face until he nutted in my mouth. I swallowed it all and he grabbed my face.

"If you ever leave me I will kill you." I started smiling.

"So I guess I don't have to ask how it was."

I got up, climbed on top of him, and started riding his dick. I bounced and rode his dick until he nutted. We both passed out.

"That was amazing." I said.

I felt so connected and so relaxed with Victor. I have never had that feeling before.

"I'm glad you enjoyed it." He rolled over and kissed me.

My pussy was so wet that I wanted to go another round. "I feel like I took a pill or I'm high. I feel so relaxed." I told Victor.

"Well I did put some Xanax in the champagne so you could really relax," he admitted.

"What the fuck, you drugged me?" I sat up.

"I didn't drug you. I just wanted to ease your mind," he tried to explain.

"You gave me drugs without telling me. That's fucked up Victor. I feel like you could have just offered them to me instead of sneaking them in the champagne."

I knew I was feeling a little too relaxed on my own. I got up and put on a robe from the bathroom. I went in and checked on Frank and he was still sleep. I walked back in the room and Victor had already fallen sleep. I took a shower and ate the rest of the strawberries. Finally, I got back in the bed and I was able to fall sleep too.

I woke up to my phone ringing loud as hell. I looked at the alarm clock on the nightstand and it was seven in the morning. I answered the phone thinking maybe it was the hospital calling about Freda.

"Hello." I answered.

"Lisa this is Gary from the funeral home. Can you come down right away?" he asked.

"Is everything ok? I can be there in the next hour." I told him.

I was worried that something was wrong with the funeral arrangements or they were probably going to have to change

239

the date. I jumped up and Victor didn't hear a thing. I put some clothes on and called an uber. I checked on Frank before I left. He was still sleeping. He ended up on the opposite end of the bed, but he was fine. I figured whatever needed to be done I could handle before either of them woke up. I walked out the door and I saw two guys standing outside.

"Who the fuck are you and why are you outside my door?"

I was about to run back in the room to get Victor.

"We are security for you and Victor. We have been keeping an eye out on everything," the big guy said.

"Well keep an eye on my son. I have to go to the funeral home." I started walking to the elevator.

"Ok. I will have a driver pull around for you and then you will have a security escort." He pulled out his phone to call somebody.

"I already have an uber coming, but you know what I will cancel it." I was going to use the security and drivers because I was so paranoid. I was glad Victor was trying to keep me safe.

"You can wait for him downstairs. Ricky will walk you down."

We got in the elevator. When I made it to the front, the driver was already pulling up. "Y'all move fast. Thanks."

He pulled up in a Rolls Royce. "Wait this is too fancy for the funeral home." Ricky laughed and opened the door.

"Do you know who you are dating ma'am? Mr. Victor is almost a billionaire." He closed my door and I didn't say anything else.

I made it to the funeral home and saw caution tape everywhere. Then I saw Gary and Mr. James standing outside. It looked like the police had just pulled off. I hopped out the car before the driver could open the door.

"What's going on?" I was confused.

I could see that the funeral home had been broken into.

"Good morning. I don't know how to tell you this, but somebody broke in and stole Fred Jr's body," Mr. James told me. I couldn't believe what I just heard.

Chapter 25

"What the fuck do you mean somebody stole his body?" I asked. "How do you steal a fucking body in the first place?"

"When Gary made it in this morning, he noticed someone had broken in. When he checked, the only thing missing was Fred Jr.'s body," Mr. James explained.

"Yeah, and when I checked the cameras all they went for was him." Gary said.

"I want to see the video."

We walked in the funeral home and went to the office where the security videos were set up.

"I still don't understand what anyone would want with a child's body," Mr. James said shaking his head.

Gary pulled the video up and I watched three men come in the back.

"It only shows from this point, when they were searching for his body."

I noticed how they took their time trying to read each name in the dark. Finally, one of the guys found him and then the other two ran over. They pulled him out the sliding refrigerator door.

They unzipped the body bag and I saw a piece of my baby's face.

"What the fuck!" I screamed out. "You have to be one sick son of a bitch to steal a fucking body!" I yelled out.

They grabbed the body bag and walked him out on their shoulders.

"Do you have any idea why someone would want to steal your son's body.

"No I don't! I couldn't even in my wildest dreams think that some shit like this would happen." I was dumbfounded.

"Well Detective Norwood gave me a card for you and said that you should go to the station and file a report." Mr. James gave me the card.

"Detective Norwood should have waited until I got here." I grabbed the card and stood up.

"I apologize. I have never had this situation happen in all my years as a funeral director."

He stood up and followed me back out the door. "If there is anything we can do to help, we will. I hope they get him back quickly so that we can have a beautiful home going celebration."

They shook my hand and I saw them watching me get back in the Rolls Royce. "More money, more problems," I thought to myself. Then the driver closed the door.

I made it back to the hotel and Victor and Frank were exactly how I left them. I decided to wake Frank up so that he could take a bath and eat. When he woke up he hugged me so tight.

"You have been sleeping a long time. You must have had a bad dream." He looked at me and shook his head up and down.

"It's ok, let's get you clean and you can order whatever you want from room service. How does that sound?" I asked him.

"Even ice cream?" Frank asked.

"You know what sure, even ice cream." We laughed.

While he was in the tub I went to wake Victor up.

"Victor it's time to get up."

He moved around a little bit and then he finally sat up.

"Good morning queen," he yawned.

"You need a toothbrush let me order one with room service."

He laughed. "So you got jokes huh?" he said.

"Victor somebody stole my son's body from the funeral home."

He jumped up. "Lisa stop fucking playing." His eyes were bucked open.

"Why would I play about that Victor?" I walked in my bathroom to grab a big towel for Frank.

"What in the fuck is going on? Who would want to steal a dead body? I'm not even that crazy." Victor put his clothes on. "I'm going to head out and see what information I can get so we can get him back, ok baby." He kissed my forehead.

"Ricky is staying with you and Frank from now on." Victor walked to the door and shook the guys hands. "You also will have a Rolls Royce as your car now so that's how you will get around with security." He was telling me all this and I didn't get a word in.

"Wait Victor. How do you know I want this because honestly I rather not have any extra attention on us?"

I wanted to feel that somebody had me and Frank's back, but I also wanted to feel normal too.

"Someone is out to get you and your family Lisa. I just want to protect you." Victor seemed so sincere, so I just decided to go with it.

"I will call you with any information I get. I love you." He grabbed me and hugged me.

"I love you too Victor." I kissed him. He looked so shocked then he turned around to walk off and BJ walked up.

"I didn't mean to interrupt this family moment," he said sarcastically.

"Do we have a fucking problem brother?" Victor walked up to BJ.

"No problem, just came to check on my nephew and sis." BJ put his hands in the air. "I come in peace."

He looked me in my face and I just stared at the ground.

"Ricky take care of them." Victor walked to the elevator and left.

I got Frank out of the tub and BJ followed me in the bathroom.

"So it's ok for me to do what I did the other night but you telling this ese you love him?" he asked calmly.

I knew he was pissed off but BJ knew we couldn't be together because of Fred.

"He is a tremendous help for me right now. Do you know somebody stole Fred Jr.'s body from the funeral home?!" I told him.

"Wait say that again!" BJ looked stunned.

"You heard me. Victor is about to put his ears in the street to find out who did this."

I dried Frank off and got him dressed.

"What's up little guy?" BJ held out his hand for him to shake it. Frank didn't shake it and he didn't speak to him.

"You don't want to speak to your uncle?" I asked him. He shook his head no.

"What did I do little man?" BJ questioned him.

"He's probably still tired but we are about to get room service. Guess who gets ice cream!" I said excitedly.

Frank held his hand up. "That's right so let's order it."

I ordered room service for everybody, even Ricky.

"Frank you can go play until the food gets here."

I started back talking to BJ because he was upset about me and Victor.

"What are you going to tell Fred? According to him, he already knows," BJ told me.

"I knew it was not me because he would have been cut me off or told me he knew. That's how we rock." BJ said.

"Don't act like you didn't fuck and let me suck that dick either. You have a part to play if I get caught too."

I stood up and checked on Frank through the door. He was still playing the game. "Yea you right I did, and I will do it again." BJ tried to touch between my legs.

"It's so wet and warm Lisa. I just want to taste it before room service comes."

I stood up. "BJ what we did was wrong, and I'm done. I will take my chances with Victor but promise me what happened between us stays between us."

BJ didn't say anything.

"Can you promise that BJ?" I repeated myself.

"Lisa if you don't fuck me when I want I will tell Victor and Fred I'm fucking you."

I couldn't believe BJ. "Are you fucking serious right now?"

I walked in the room where Frank was and BJ followed me. "I want to play Frank."

Before I could make it in the door BJ grabbed my arm. "Wait we have that meeting remember." He grabbed my arm hard as fuck.

"You are grabbing me a little rough." I said trying to stay cool.

"Frank give mommy and Uncle BJ a few minutes for our meeting and do not come out the room."

BJ snatched me in the bathroom and closed the door.

"What are you doing?" I yelled at him.

"If you scream Frank will hear you and you don't want to upset him anymore than he already is."

BJ started pulling my pants down. "Stop BJ, what are you doing?"

I pushed his head as hard as I could. When I did that, he slapped me with the back of his hand. "Be fucking still."

He pushed me on the vanity with my pants on my ankles and he pulled his down. He held my head down and he forced his dick in me.

"Stop BJ I said no!" I yelled out.

He kept forcing himself on me until he got his stroke going. BJ was raping me. I was fighting him off as much as I could, but he was just stronger. I could not even drop one tear. I was emotionless. I didn't want to scream and scare Frank, but I could not believe I was getting raped. He kept going until he moaned out and he busted a nut. He was still holding on to me.

"Whenever I want it, or our secret is out." He kissed me on the cheek and then pulled his pants up.

Chapter 26

I felt so weak, the weakest I have ever felt in my life. I was just raped and there was nobody I could tell about it. BJ just took a apart of me that I will never get back. I was not going to let him get away with it that was for damn sure.

"Where are we going today?" BJ casually asked me like he didn't just rape me.

I sat on the vanity chair, speechless. BJ walked out the bathroom and I heard him tell Frank to put his shoes on. I was paralyzed. I could not move.

"Where is my mommy?" I heard Frank asking him. "She is using the little girl's room, but she is coming so put your shoes back on."

I pulled myself together so I could go because I still had to find Fred Jr.'s body. I walked out the bathroom and they were sitting on the couch.

"There is your beautiful mother." BJ pretended like nothing happened. He was acting like he didn't just rape me less than twenty minutes ago.

"Mommy I want something to eat." Frank ran up to me.

"Let's go the car is waiting for us downstairs."

Ricky was still at the door and I knew if I had screamed I could have gotten help. I was just shocked that he would stoop that low. We made it to the Rolls Royce and Ricky opened the door.

"So we riding in the Rolls Royce today?" BJ said and walked around the car. "Ok Lisa I wanna be like you when I grow up." He started laughing hysterically.

Everyone was looking at him like he was crazy. He was acting insane and seemed like something snapped in his brain.

"BJ act like you have been around nice things please."

I got in the car and sat Frank beside me. BJ did not say anything to me, he just got in and put on his sunglasses. Ricky grabbed the front seat and we went to brunch.

I could hear my phone vibrating as soon as we got back in the car. I got it out my bag and it was Victor.

"Hey baby." I said it loud enough so BJ could flinch.

"Hey beautiful. I got some good news and some bad news. Which one you want first?" he asked me.

"The good news." I said.

"Well, the good news is I know who supposedly has your son's body. The bad news is that I heard the plan was to cut his organs out," he told me.

"What the fuck? Why?" Everybody looked at me on the phone.

"You know, that has become a business and people pay big bucks for organs," Victor explained to me.

I was still confused on why they targeted Fred Jr.

"Who has my baby?"

I just wanted to get him back and have a proper burial for him.

"Word on the street is that it's some Zoes, some Haitian guys." Victor said.

"Haitians? Why target my baby's body is the question?" I was still confused by this and I just wanted answers.

"I know Hennrick very well and he is over the Haitian gang here. I am working on getting more answers. You just try your best to focus on you today."

I know he was helping, but it's hard not to stress about some asshole taking your child's body.

"We are headed to the hospital to see Freda so I will talk to you after I leave there."

I hung up the phone with Victor and had a million thoughts going through my head. I didn't understand if this was something against me or Fred. It might even be Fred that had them to get the body so that he could bury Fred Jr. somewhere I could not find him.

"What did Victor say?" BJ asked. I gave him a look so evil he just turned and looked out the window the rest of the ride to the hospital.

Visiting hours had just started when we made it. I went right in and went to Freda's room. "Hi baby, it's mommy." I said as I kissed her cheek.

Freda opened her eyes.

"Ahhhhh!" I screamed.

Ricky was the first person in the room. "What's wrong?!" he asked.

I was shocked and scared. "Get the nurse!"

He ran and got the nurse and they ran back in.

"What's wrong?" It was a male nurse.

I had never seen him before, but he walked right up to check her vitals.

"Her eyes are open look." I pointed to Freda.

"They are open. That is a great sign. We have been seeing rapid change and it all looks good for her," he told me.

"That is so good to hear. What does this mean? Is she going to be back to normal soon?" I needed to know because I needed my baby to be fine.

"Yes. The doctor will actually be here shortly so he can update you with more details."

Freda still had her eyes open. She would look around and then close them. When I spoke to her she would open them back up and she even squeezed my hand. I started crying because I was feeling relieved that she was waking up. The doctor came and let me know that she was fine and that now we just have to wait it out as she comes back to herself.

"I have to go Freda, but mommy misses you so much." I kissed her forehead and she opened her eyes and bucked them really big, then she closed them back. I hated to leave her there but the intensive care unit visiting hours were over.

We were leaving out the door and I saw Monica and her husband Tim walking in the hospital. Monica looked like she was in so much pain.

"Monica are you alright?" I asked as I helped sit her in the wheelchair.

"She said she feels like she is having contractions and is in extreme pain."

I knew Monica had miscarriages before and I was just hoping that this was not the case. Tim checked them in and I just rubbed Monica's back. She was crying and I could tell she was in so much pain.

"It's going to be fine Monica." I kept repeating that to her until Tim came back over.

"They are about to take her to a room." Tim said.

The nurses came and got the wheelchair. They started pushing her to the back and I told Tim that I would call Monica's phone later to check on her and the baby.

"That guy looks real familiar." BJ said.

"Well you know his brother was fucking Chanel." I said smirking.

"What the fuck you say?" BJ said with an attitude.

"Is there a problem Ms. Lisa?" Ricky asked.

"No problem at all, is there a problem BJ?" The car pulled up and I got in.

"Gotcha. So that's the brother of the guy you killed right?" BJ replied and stared at me with this disgusting look on his face as he got in the car. I was at the point that I wanted to kill BJ too.

Chapter 27

We made it back to the hotel and BJ left in his truck. Frank, Ricky, and I went upstairs to the room. Frank wanted to play the game again, so he went in his room and I sat on the couch. I was physically and mentally exhausted. Victor called my phone.

"Hey queen, are you back at the hotel?" he asked. I could barely hear him over the loud noise in the background.

"Yes we are but what is all that noise in the background?" It sounded like chainsaws.

"I'm working on getting information about Fred Jr. Terry is cutting this guy's arm off!" Victor yelled over the noise. "Lisa, I will call you back in a few minutes." He started saying something in Spanish and then hung up. He was a fucking savage and I didn't care as long as I got my son back.

I had dosed off on the couch and my phone rang again. It was my cousin Pam.

"Hello." I answered the phone sounding half sleep.

"Lisa I just saw on the news about Fred Jr. here in New Jersey. Why didn't you call and tell us?" she asked.

Before I knew it I snapped. "I do not have to call and tell you or anybody else a motherfucking thing. I'm grieving my child and I am the only one I am concerned with besides my kids."

I never hear from them unless it's about money. Even at my uncle Charles funeral they were trying to borrow money from me.

"Lisa I'm sorry. I was just concerned because we didn't know what was going on since you didn't come back to Jersey after Aunt Katherine died," Pam said. "You know they still didn't have her a funeral."

I couldn't believe my ears. "Pam it's been weeks since Aunt Katherine died. You mean to tell me she had no funeral service at all?" I had to make sure I heard that right.

"Nobody has any money or any of the information for her life insurance but you."

If I was in front of her I would have slapped the taste out her mouth.

"You people are the most pathetic group I ever seen." I hung up the phone.

I called the funeral home that I thought would have Aunt Katherine to see how much it was to have a small burial service that I could pay for.

"Henry's Funeral Home," a lady answered.

"Hi my name is Lisa and I was calling about a funeral service," I replied to her.

"You want to have the body brought here?" she asked.

"Well, the body is already there." I know it probably sounded crazy to her.

"Okay, what's the name?"

I told her my aunt's name and she put me on hold. I could not believe that my aunt had been there all that time. It's been over a month now since I had been in Jersey.

"Ma'am here is the owner. He wants to talk to you."

A white guy got on the phone. "Good evening, this is Raymond. How are you?" he asked.

"I'm fine, just trying to handle getting my aunt buried. I was not aware she had been at the funeral home this long," I explained to the owner.

"Well, what happens is after six weeks we have to make room for new bodies. When nobody claims a family member we cremate them." He sounded like he did not want to tell me that.

"You what?" I asked because I could not believe what I just

heard.

"We had to cremate the body. I do have the remains here for you to pick up."

I was hurt and pissed at the same time. My aunt and uncle always said when they died to make sure their graves are side by side so that they can Rest In Peace together.

"Will someone be able to pick them up?" Raymond asked.

"I will be in Jersey in a few days. I will pick them up." I hung up the phone and just started crying. I was letting everyone around me down. I was even letting everybody down in the afterlife. It was time to shake back.

Knock! Knock! I looked out the peephole and saw Victor.

"Baby, you look better and better every time I see you." He kissed my forehead.

"Ricky go ahead and handle your business. You know what time to be back."

Victor's security guard took the post after Ricky left.

"Have you two had dinner yet?" he asked.

I went in the other room and saw that Frank was on the floor sleeping.

"No, we both dozed off." I shook my head and laughed.

"No problem I know you must be exhausted. I can order something for us to be delivered." Victor pulled out his phone.

"Just get me a steak and potato from room service. Frank is asleep so whenever he wakes up I can order him something."

I really did not have much of an appetite, but I needed to eat. We ordered room service and I told Victor about my aunt being cremated.

"I am so pissed that I could not depend on one person to take care of my aunt while I deal with my own fucked up life." I told Victor.

With so much going on I forgot about my aunt. She was one of the few people that never forgot about me. I have been through some crazy shit these last couple months. I just needed my children to be safe and healthy.

"When Freda is completely better I think it's time to relocate."

I looked to see what Victor's reaction be.

"You should baby. Where do you want to go?" he asked.

"Somewhere nobody would come looking for me. I will go to Iceland."

He chuckled. "Just promise me I can go with you Lisa."

He grabbed my hand and kissed it. Then he started kissing up my arm and then he kissed my lips. I knew what he was about to do so I stopped him.

"I'm not in the mood right now bae." I stood up and walked to the kitchen area.

"Are you alright? Is it that time of the month?" he asked me looking confused.

"Why does it have to be that time of the month for me to not be in the mood?" I was a little offended.

I really could not believe I was still involved with Victor. I had put myself in one of the most dangerous situations to be in. Fucking with my husband's plug was personal. This man is the way we eat. Two powerful men in love with the same woman, it was not going to end well. I had betrayed my husband by fucking Victor in the first place but to actually have him fall in love with me was cold blooded. It is going to seem to the world that we planned this shit and in reality, it just happened.

"I did not mean anything by that Lisa. We can cuddle. I just want to be near you." He walked over and grabbed my hand.

"I just have so much on my mind and I need to know where

Fred Jr. is" I couldn't rest knowing my baby could be getting slit open for organs.

"Do not worry about that at all. I am always working no matter where I am. I will get your son back to you, I promise." Victor's phone started ringing. "See."

He answered the phone and put it on speaker. "If you don't have his body hang up the fucking phone."

It got quiet.

"I have it boss, but I was too late," he said.

"What do you mean?" I yelled out. "He was too late? What does he mean Victor!"

I knew what it meant but I did not want to believe it. Victor took his phone off speaker and went in the hallway. I followed behind him because I did not want to believe what I just heard.

"Why are you coming in the hallway? Where is Fred Jr.? Let's go get him now Victor!" I was screaming and crying.

I walked back in and woke Frank up. I heard the door open and room service had made it up as well. It was being delivered by a very petite white girl. When she saw my face, you could tell she was scared.

"I'm so sorry. I almost forgot I ordered room service." I grabbed the tray from her and moved it by the sofa.

"No problem. Is there anything else I can get for you?" she asked.

"No but wait let me give you a tip."

I went to my purse and I didn't find any cash. I remembered the ten million dollars Victor gave me and I got nervous.

"One second."

I went in the bedroom and grabbed one of the bags. I had them all just sitting out so I decided to hide them all over the room and bathroom. I kept one bag out that I would probably spend on a few things. Since Victor was generous to me I decided to be generous to her. I pulled out a thousand dollars to tip her with. I tried to zip the bag up but it was stuck. I just kicked it out the way and it all fell over.

"Fuck!"

Frank ran over and grabbed one of the stacks.

"Frank!" I yelled to him. He took off running around the room. "I don't have time to chase you Frank."

Knock! Knock! The girl from room service stuck her head in

the door. The door wasn't closed so I guess she thought it was ok to stick her head in. She was holding my phone in her hands and it was lighting up. I saw how big her eyes got when she saw all the money on the floor.

"Is my phone ringing?" I walked to her and grabbed it out her hand.

"Yes, I am sorry. It rang about seven or eight times and the door wasn't closed. I am so sorry," she apologized.

"You are fine and here you go." I handed her the tip money.

I grabbed the money from Frank and put the money back in the duffle bag. I put the bag on my shoulder and walked out the room. I was not going to even let her think I was leaving it behind.

"I wish I knew we were leaving so I could have had this to go." I told her. "I know I look a mess, but my daughter is in a coma and we are doing whatever it takes to get her home. It's stressful with all the money we have to spend out."

I could see it on her face that she was nervous. I don't know if it was because she saw the money or seeing me crying.

"What is your name?" I asked her.

"Stephanie." She looked like a typical rich white girl.

"How long have you been working here Stephanie?" I asked.

"I been here about three years now."

She had brown hair with blonde and light brown highlights. She was about five feet four inches and petite. It looked like she had a boob job because her boobs were the same size as Dolly Parton's.

"You in college?" I was getting a good look at her because I could sense that something was not right about her. She looked innocent, but I was normally a good judge of character.

"No, I had my son and I started working here."

I saw she had a tattoo on her wrist and I could make out the name.

"Is that your son's name on your wrist?" She tried to hide her arm.

"No, a name I wish I could get removed." She turned red in the face, so I knew it had to be an ex.

"My son's name is Spencer."

I do not like judging people, but she gave me a vibe that I could not shake. "Nice meeting you Stephanie."

I walked her out so that I could let Victor know I was ready. He was the one blowing my phone up. He was gone. "Where is Victor?" I asked.

Stephanie walked on out and went to the elevator.

"He left ahead but the Rolls Royce is waiting on us downstairs."

I grabbed my purse off the table and we all waited on the elevator to come. I noticed Stephanie had on Gucci loafers. She also had a necklace on from Tiffany's. I recognized it because I had the exact same one that Fred bought me years ago. They stopped making those necklaces because I wanted one for Freda for her birthday one year. She had to have had that handed down to her.

"I have that exact necklace, where did you get it?" I asked.

"It was a gift," Stephanie replied awkwardly.

She grabbed the necklace and tucked it in her shirt. I thought that was weird for her to do. The elevator opened up and she went one way and we went out the door.

Chapter 28

Victor played games with me the rest of the night. He never would let me know what was going on but promised me that he was taking care of everything. He would never tell me where he was or where Fred Jr's body was. I did get to see Freda again and she was doing so much better. Eventually I decided to go back to the hotel. Ricky met us at the hotel when he was back on duty. It was after midnight and Frank was knocked out. Ricky carried Frank like a rag doll and we got in the elevator, headed to the top floor.

"What the fuck." The door was wide open.

"Get back on the elevator."

Ricky handed me Frank. He pulled his gun out and went in the suite. I texted Victor and he called me right away. I pressed ignore because what if somebody was still in there. I could hear Ricky opening and closing doors.

"It's clear." I walked off the elevator into a tornado.

"The money!" I yelled out.

I put Frank on the couch and went in my bedroom. I looked in all the places I put the bags and they all were gone. "Are you fucking kidding me right now!" I hit myself in the head. "That bitch did this! I'm going to fucking kill her!"

The only person that saw that money was Stephanie.

"I knew I got a bad vibe from that bitch!" I looked again to make sure I did not overlook any of the bags. I knew they were gone.

"Who are you talking about Lisa? What did they take?" Ricky asked.

"Just a few million dollars." I was pissed to the fucking max.

"Are you serious? Who else knew about that money?" Ricky asked.

"Nobody knew about it but that white bitch that walked in on me when it fell out."

All my karma was hitting me at once. I was at the point of no return. "Ricky I am about to spazz the fuck out."

I walked in the living room and picked up one of the vases and threw it across the room. I saw Frank jump but he stayed asleep.

"Fuck!"

I walked out the suite. I was ready to burn this fucking hotel down to the ground.

270

"Lisa calm down, I am about to call the boss." Ricky ran out behind me.

Everything that could possibly go wrong in my life was going wrong. "What the fuck have I done so bad that I have to deal with this bullshit!" I screamed out.

"Yeah boss, somebody fucking trashed the place and she said they took a few million dollars." I heard Ricky on the phone telling Victor.

It was more than just the money. It was the fact that some son of a bitch targeted me. Everything that I am going through right now is pulling me deeper and deeper in hell. Everybody thinks because you have all this money that life is perfect. Whoever fucking said more money more problems did not lie.

Victor finally made it and I was still sitting up on the couch. I was not about to lay my head there anymore. I felt violated and I did not want to take any chances staying somewhere that was just burglarized.

"I need the fucking cameras now." Victor was so mad you could see his vein sticking out. I didn't say a word.

"Is everybody fine?" he asked. I could tell he was in a serious mood. He barely looked at me as he walked in all the rooms.

"I am moving you to one of my condos. Leave everything here and you can go shopping." He walked over kissed my cheek and patted Frank on the head.

"I am just glad you two were not here. I know Ricky would risk his life to save yours and Frank's." Victor patted Ricky on the shoulder.

"You know I would boss," Ricky replied.

Ricky seemed nervous around Victor. I guess if he was my boss, I would be a little nervous too. He had the power of life and death in his hands. He had so many people working for him and so many willing to die for him.

"Vamonos." Victor stood in the door waiting on me to get up.

Ricky walked over and picked up Frank off the couch. "I can get him." I walked over to grab Frank from Ricky.

"Lisa he will get him. We are all walking together anyway." Victor said with an attitude.

He had something he was dealing with and I could see it all over his face. I let Ricky hold him. I grabbed my purse and duffle bag and we left.

We pulled up to some beautiful high rises on the other side of town. "These are stunning. How long have you had a condo here?" I asked as we pulled into the parking garage.

"I have had these about five years now."

Ricky pulled right up to the elevators and parked.

"They must not tow cars around here?" I asked sarcastically.
"You must have more than one condo here baby?"

Ricky got out and opened the door for us.

"I own the building Lisa. I own the ones across the street too."

He got out the car. I knew Victor was known for having millions
of dollars, but I might have underestimated him.

"So you have one empty that I can stay in?" Victor nodded his
head and hit the button for the elevator.

He was not saying anything and it made me think he was
hiding something about Fred Jr. I know he had plenty of
money, but he might have been upset about the eight million
dollars being stolen. Whatever it was, it had Victor in a mood I
had never seen. He was serious as ever and it scared me, but
secretly it turned me on. We all got on the elevator and went
up to the condo.

The condo was drop dead gorgeous inside. There were

windows all over and marble everywhere.

"Wow this is beautiful." I walked all around looking. It was fully furnished. You could tell it was some expensive shit. "You have an apartment this nice just sitting around?"

The thing about men with money is that they feel as if they can do whatever and whoever they want.

"I rent it out mostly."

Victor walked into the magnificent kitchen and looked in the refrigerator. The entire kitchen was stainless steel. The refrigerator even had Bluetooth on it. There was a huge island with a built in sink in the center. The countertops were black and gray marble top that was right out of a magazine.

"This kitchen looks better than mine." I walked through the entire condo and every room was exquisite.

"I could totally live here Victor." I was not expecting this condo to be as nice as it is. It was easily over half a million dollars in gold and marble throughout the house.

"Well you are welcome to stay as long as you want. Whatever you need we can get this afternoon or whenever you wake up."

Victor pulled out a stack of money. "Here is something for

breakfast and to get some clothes. I will be back around noon or after I handle this situation."

He still had a look on his face that I could not figure out. "Is everything ok? You never told me what was going on with Fred Jr.?" I asked him.

Victor walked to me and grabbed my hands then kissed my forehead. "Lisa do you trust me?" He looked me in my eyes so deep that I looked away.

"What do you mean?" I replied to him.

"Exactly what I said, do you trust me?" he asked again.

I wanted to trust Victor, but he had a closet full of skeletons. I still replayed everything about his wife and his other life in Mexico. That whole situation was still holding me back.

"I trust you Victor. I would not have put my life and my kids' lives in your hands." I did trust him. He was a man of his word and he was a protector.

"You make me feel so safe, but I worry about you when you won't talk to me."

He kissed my forehead again and turned to walk out the door.

"I will see you at noon." Victor left, and Ricky closed the door behind him.

I woke up a few hours later and Frank was already up watching tv.

"Mommy you still sleepy?" he asked and hit my back with the remote.

"Frank that hurt!" I yelled out.

I sat up and I noticed Frank had a bowl in front of him. "Where did you get that bowl Frank?" I asked.

"Rick gave it to me." He hit the bowl with the spoon. "I want some more cereal mommy."

Frank was watching cartoons and on his second bowl of cereal, so it was safe to say he was doing good.

"Sure thing."

I got up and grabbed the bowl. I walked in the kitchen and I saw Ricky at the table drinking a cup of coffee.

"That's exactly what I need a cup of coffee." I fixed Frank's cereal and took it back to him.

"Thanks mommy," Frank said to me with a big smile.

I got my cellphone and turned back around. He was into the television show so hard that he didn't care when left back out. I sat and had a cup of coffee with Ricky and then I called the hospital to check on Freda. The nurse told me she was still moving fast in the right direction. I let her know I would be there at the next visitation and that I wanted to see the doctor. I was glad to finally hear good news, but I wanted more details from the doctor.

"Have you talked to Victor?" I asked Ricky.

"No, I thought he said he would be here at noon," Ricky replied

I know he said noon, but I decided to call him anyway.

Voicemail.

I tried again and still got his voicemail. "It's not ringing."

I sent him a text because I'm sure his phone was probably dead.

"Do you know the other security guy's phone number?" I was worried about him but I did not want to overreact.

"Yeah, let me call him." Ricky pulled out his cellphone. "His phone is going to voicemail too."

I really got worried when I saw an incoming call from a number

I didn't recognize. I answered and it was Victor.

"Lisa, this is Victor. I'm in jail."

Chapter 29

Jail!?"

Victor in jail this was not good at all.

"Calm down Lisa. I had a small altercation and they just booked both of us. I need somebody to come bond us out." He sounded really calm so I trusted that he was ok.

"I'm on my way." I jumped up and went to grab Frank.

"Lisa you can just send Ricky, it's no big deal. I know you are tired," he said.

"No, we are on the way. Where are you?"

I got the information from him and hung up the phone.

"What's going on with boss?" Ricky asked.

"He said they were in an altercation and got arrested. He wants us to come bond them out." We jumped in the car and headed to bond Victor out.

Once we made it to the jail, I hesitated about going in and bonding him out. I told Ricky to do it and I just waited in the car. Almost an hour had passed and nobody had came out. I decided to go in and make sure everything was alright. Me and Frank walked in and I saw Ricky sitting down.

"What's going on? Why haven't they released him?" I asked him looking around.

There were no officers at the front at all. "Something happened in one of the zones and that's all I know. Everybody took off to the back and we have just been sitting here." he explained.

I heard some talking coming up the hallway and it was four officers walking back in. "Sorry about that good people. Who was next?"

It was a female officer and she looked like Tyra Banks. She had these brownish green eyes. she stood about five feet ten and was gorgeous. I could not help but notice how her uniform fit her. It was hugging her hips and ass. She was built perfectly. She could easily be a model and she was the fucking police. The other three officers were white guys that looked like they beat black men for a sport. I hated being in the police station or around police officers unless I grew up with them. I have seen on so many occasions where they abuse black men just for being black. They smiled and spoke to me as they walked by. I smiled and nodded my head.

"I am here to get Victor Sánchez." Ricky sounded nervous.

"Ok on what charges, do you know?" she asked him as she typed on the computer.

"I'm really not sure." He looked at me with his shoulders shrugged.

"I am not sure the exact charge, he only told me about an altercation." I walked over closer to the counter.

"I found him, Victor Sanchez. Charge is, oh wow." She stopped talking.

"Oh wow? What does that mean?" I asked.

"His charge is solicitation of prostitution." She looked at me like she was sorry.

"What do you mean?" I was totally confused. I know I did not hear her correctly.

"Solicitation of prostitution charge basically means that he was caught trying to pay for sex." I was fucking shocked.

I know it had to be an explanation for this. Victor is rich as fuck, so he didn't have to pay for sex. Women throw themselves at him.

"It has to be a mistake on those charges. I'm sure he will be in contact with his lawyer."

I was not about to believe that. I knew Victor would be able to explain this. Ricky paid the money and about twenty minutes later Victor was walking out.

"Are you good?" I walked over and hugged him.

"Yes, I will explain later."

We walked outside and got in the car. Frank was acting cranky, so I knew he was tired. Before we got on the highway he was asleep.

"Pretend it's later and start explaining now. Telling me why your charges say that you were buying pussy is a good place to start."

I was not about to let this slide. I know I have been dealing with everything with my kids and not been myself lately. I just thought he would go find some young girl out the strip club or something and let her suck his dick.

"Somebody? Anybody?" Nobody said anything.

"That's why you asked me did I trust you? So that you could go buy some pussy? Sad." I shook my head and looked out the window.

"Let it go Lisa, I will explain later," Victor said very calmly.

I have been letting him get away with whatever. This man had somebody kidnap me and thought it was romantic. I was done being nice.

"No, I'm not letting shit go. You owe me a fucking answer. Why were you buying pussy? You look desperate as fuck right now."

I rolled my eyes and looked back out the window. Before I knew it, Victor had grabbed me and put me in a chokehold.

"When I say leave something alone bitch I fucking mean it, do you hear me?" He had my neck so tight I could barely say a word. I tried to nod my head but his grip was too strong.

"Do you hear me bitch? I will give you the world, but you stay out my business unless I put you in it. Comprende?"

He let me go and I saw Ricky's face in the rear view mirror. He looked back down and just kept driving. I looked at Frank and he didn't move or make a sound.

"Fuck you Victor."

I had tears falling from my face. I was pissed. I knew I needed Victor and I knew how powerful he was, so I didn't make any crazy moves. He had so many sides to him I never knew what I was getting. He grabbed my face and reached in to kiss me.

"Don't worry you will."

We made it back to the condo. Victor was having some clothes delivered for us.

"Go ahead and take your bath. I will have some things for you to choose from by the time you get out."

Ricky put Frank on the bed. He was still asleep. I just looked at Victor and went in the bathroom and closed the door. There was a built in radio with an intercom on the wall. I turned on the radio and ran some bath water. The tub was huge. It could easily seat two or three people in it. The bathroom was so glamorous. It was all black and white with gold fixtures. It was mostly white, but it had this black and white marble from the floor to the shower. There was also a bench in the shower that was big enough to fit about five or six people easily. I got in the tub and soaked my body until I drifted away to sleep.

Knock! Knock! "Lisa!" I heard Victor yelling.

I jumped up. I don't know how long I had been sleep. I got out the tub and grabbed a towel. I wrapped it around me and walked out.

"I dozed off."

Frank was still sleeping and I could hear women voices in the living room.

"You have been in there over an hour but I will have Natalie come in and show you what she has." I saw her rolling in a rack full of clothes.

"Victor you could have just went to the Target and got me some clothes."

Natalie wheeled right in and the rack was jam packed. "I am so sorry, I just grabbed everything we had in your size when Vic called."

She grabbed another bag that was filled with shoes and placed them on the floor.

"I will leave you two ladies alone." Victor walked out and closed the door.

"I love me some Vic. That is one charming man. Well obviously you know. Look what he's got me doing for you." Natalie laughed out loud.

She was not someone that I would see myself hanging with ever. She was dressed like a punk rocker and she had dreadlocks. Natalie had colorful tattoos all over her arms and a nose ring. I really couldn't tell you what her ethnicity was, but she was beautiful. She had this larger than life personality. I was curious to see what she had for me to wear.

285

"Yes, he is something. So, what do you have for me to wear?"

I changed the subject because Natalie was talking like she wanted to fuck Victor right there on the floor. He was very charming, but I was doubting myself when I said I trusted him.

"I have some of everything. I have something from day to night you can choose from." Natalie started laying out clothes on the bed.

"I didn't even see little man right there. He is soooooo handsome." She pulled out everything from track suits to evening gowns.

"I will try on a couple track suits and then go from there."

I grabbed the Gucci and Fendi one and went in the bathroom. I liked the way they both fit, but I decided to keep the Gucci one on.

"I love them both, but I will rock this one today."

I looked at everything she had, and I found some Gucci sneakers that matched my outfit perfectly.

"Whatever you want to keep it's yours. Victor already paid for it."

I decided to just keep it all and I could try it on later. "Just leave everything then Natalie. Thank you so much."

I walked to the door to let her know she can leave.

"I'm doing your hair and makeup too. Come on and have a seat."

We walked in the kitchen and a salon chair was set up. "Sit here and I will get you glammed up then I will be out of you guys way." Natalie winked at me and Victor.

There was a guy that was hemming Victor's pants and I saw the kids clothes.

"Are those for Frank?" I asked.

"Yes, I will put all of his clothes in his room." Ricky grabbed the clothes and the shoes to put up.

I must admit Natalie was very talented in makeup. I let her know that I wanted something natural and she delivered. It was not over the top, it was really perfect.

"Wow Natalie! Girl you got talent. Thank you." She added some wand curls in my hair and I was ready.

"You would make anything look good girl, thank you."

I looked over at Victor and he still had this strange look on his face. "Baby, how do I look?" I asked Victor. He looked up at me.

"You look beautiful as always." He blew me a kiss.

"Ok, well that's my cue to leave. Thanks Vic." Natalie chuckled.

She got all her stuff and started putting it in her truck.

"Natalie give me a card so that I can call you to do my makeup again for my son's funeral." I walked behind her.

"Yeah, no problem. Sorry to hear that. My condolences."

She handed me a card and I walked back inside.

"What was that about?" Victor asked. "You following behind Natalie?"

"I was trying to see did she have business cards?" I replied back to him.

"She works for me so she doesn't need business cards. I will get her anytime you need her."

I thought that was strange for Victor to not want me to get in contact with her. If he was hiding something about him and her and I was definitely going to find out.

Chapter 30

I got Frank dressed and we headed to the hospital to see Freda. I was still pissed that I didn't know what was going on with Fred Jr's body and it was making me think the craziest thoughts. I just needed to put him to rest and make sure his name lives on forever. I wanted to go to the news stations and radio stations to tell them what was going on. I knew that would never go by with Victor, so I played it cool. I had to try to focus on Freda and Frank and make sure they were well taken care of. I was hoping to walk into Freda's room and she would be sitting up and talking.

Ricky dropped me off at the front entrance. Frank was not allowed in ICU, so they were going to park and come up later. I made it to her room and her eyes were open.

"Freda." I just spoke her name.

She did not move. Her eyes moved back and forth so fast I almost got dizzy.

"Baby say something to mommy." I walked up and hugged her. Her fingers started moving. She began to wiggle her toes and feet.

"Nurse!" I yelled out. I hit the nurse button on the hospital bed and I started rubbing Freda's feet.

"Blink twice if you can feel this baby." I rubbed every toe on both of her feet. Freda's eyes stopped jumping around and she blinked twice.

"Yes baby! I knew you would survive this!" I was screaming and crying.

I started shouting for joy. The nurses all ran in and all look scared for their lives.

"What is going on?" one of the nurses asked.

I could barely talk because I was so happy. Tears of joy ran down my face.

"She can move her feet and fingers!" I caught my breath so I could tell them what was going on. "She understood what I said because I told her to blink twice if she could feel me rubbing her toes and she did!"

I started back rubbing her toes and feet.

"Freda blink three times if you can feel this." Everybody looked at her and she did it. She blinked three times.

"Get the doctor here now!"

I kissed Freda's cheek and hugged her. I knew she still was not back to normal, but my baby was awake. I knew that things were about to get better.

"This is so awesome. It's like seeing a miracle happen right before your eyes." One of the nurses said.

She was young and I had never seen her before. They had new nurses almost every time I came.

"It's definitely a miracle and I needed this miracle." I told her.

"I could not imagine what you are going through," she replied.

I looked at her and she looked like she had the good life. She was about twenty-two years old with blonde hair and blue eyes. She had the whitest teeth and prettiest smile. You could tell she used to be one of those southern pageant girls. She had a ring on her finger, so she was married.

"Do you and your husband have kids?" I asked her.

"No, we have only been married three months." She giggled.

"When you have kids please talk to them and love them. Ask them about their day. Listen to them when they are not saying anything. Their actions tell a lot. If you are not ready, do not have them until you are."

I never thought I would be going through this with my kids but it has been an eye opener for me.

"We agreed to wait about five years so no worries, but you are right."

I kissed Freda's cheek again.

"I will let you know when the doctor is coming and give you some time with your daughter."

Everybody left and she closed the door. I sat there with Freda and I did not say one word. I just kissed and hugged her until the doctor came.

"Good afternoon. I am so pleased with the progress Freda has made. She is doing a full recovery and I hope to have her in a regular room soon."

He told me about some more things they have been monitoring and how fast her brain is moving in the right direction. I was just so thankful to hear good news. Visiting hours were over and it was so hard for me to leave. I stayed and kissed and hugged on her until the nurses came and got me.

"We let you stay thirty minutes over, but you have to leave now," the nurse told me.

I kissed Freda again and I told her goodnight. "You will be out of here soon princess."

I left out and met Ricky and Frank in the waiting room.

"My baby can move her feet and fingers. She even understood me when I told her to blink." I told him what happened as we were leaving the hospital. In the midst of everything going on, it felt good to have something positive happen.

We stopped for dinner at one of newest restaurants downtown called Lava. It had three levels and there was a big aquarium throughout the entire place. The lighting was mostly lava lamps which gave off a really cool illusion. Victor met us at the restaurant.

"What's up you guys? How is Freda?" he asked.

"She is great! She is moving her hands and feet and she understood what I was saying to her." I was ecstatic.

"That is awesome. So what happens from here?" He stopped the waitress and ordered a bottle of Ace of Spades.

"Well the doctor said her brain activity is moving fast so hopefully she will be back to herself and can leave soon."

I really had no idea but I just wanted my baby out that hospital.

"If there is anything I can do baby, do not hesitate to ask."

The waitress came back with the bottle on ice and glasses.

"What would you like to eat sir?" She pulled out her notepad.

Victor ordered lobster and steak for everybody.

"Frank is not going to eat lobster Victor. You could have ordered him a cheeseburger." I said.

"He is a growing boy, he needs some meat. Right Frank?" Frank shook his head up and down.

I laughed at them and pulled out my phone. I went on my news app to see if they had removed the video off the website. The first thing I see is Fred Jr's face. The top story was about his body being stolen from the funeral parlor.

"How can they fucking do this?" Everybody turned and looked at me.

"Lisa is everything alright?" Victor asked.

"They have my baby's face plastered all over the news. That's not right. He is a fucking minor." I explained to Victor.

"Anything for a damn story. The media is pathetic." He shook his head. "Lisa I have been trying to get Fred's body sewn back up for you. They destroyed him." Victor put his head down.

I had a feeling that was why he had been acting strange. To

hear those words it just broke a piece of my heart. I let my son down. I never protected him.

"I am a horrible mother. I let my son down." I said aloud.

"You are a great mother. You are a great woman period Lisa." He stood up and kissed my forehead. "Some people are evil baby. I mean, I am evil but even I would not steal a child's body. I have killed families yes, but when they are at the funeral home I do not care anymore." Victor started speaking something in Spanish and shook his head.

"Where is he?" I asked.

"Not far from here."

I was going to have a closed casket anyway, but I just wanted to give my son a burial to honor him.

I could barely eat once the food came. Everybody else ate though. I even cut up Frank's steak and he ate almost all of it.

"Is there anything else I can get for you?" The waitress cane back.

"Yes, the check please and a carry out."

I was not waiting on Victor. I needed to see Fred Jr.

"I need to get my son back to the funeral home."

I pulled out my wallet to pay for dinner.

"What are you doing?" Victor had this look on his face like I just spit in his face.

"I'm paying for our food. Is that a problem?"

The waitress brought the check and I handed her a thousand dollars. "Keep the change."

She bagged our leftovers and I stood up to leave. Victor did not move and he poured him a glass.

"Did I say I was ready to leave Lisa?" he asked calmly as he sipped from his glass.

"I need to get to my son. You know what, you can stay but I need the address."

I pulled my phone out to get the address. "Better yet give it to Ricky, he's the driver."

I turned and started walking towards the door. I walked out the door and it was a long hallway that connected to the parking garage. As I started walking, somebody yanked my head so hard I almost fell.

"What the fuck!?" I screamed.

I turned around and it was Victor. "You think you are more

than me?"

He had my hair wrapped around his hands. Ricky kept walking with Frank and Victor pushed me against the wall.

"I am the man in this relationship so I make the decisions."

Victor slapped me so hard I lost my balance. I slipped down and he grabbed me by my collar.

"You do not pay for shit when I am around. You want people to think I'm broke or something. You are showing me you are a dumb bitch."

He grabbed my neck and then he started rubbing on it like he was massaging it.

"I should make you suck my dick right here to show you who the man is in this relationship."

I couldn't form any words. I was in shock.

He grabbed my hand and made me rub his dick through his pants.

"Hmmmmm damn you turn me on baby." He wiped my face and kissed me in the lips.

"Don't do that anymore baby. Come on before Ricky and Frank get worried." We walked to the car like nothing happened. He got in with us and we headed to Fred Jr.

We pulled up to this butcher shop.

"Park over on the side Ricky." Victor pulled out his phone and called someone.

"Open up the side door."

He hung up the phone and opened the door.

"Ricky stay here with the kid."

He reached for my hand to help me out. I acted like I didn't see him. I got out the car and he grabbed my hair. "I thought I just told you about that disrespectful shit."

I tried to play it off. "What are you talking about, I just got out the car."

He let my hair go and pushed my head. "You saw me hold my hand out for you. Do not play dumb with me."

Victor was turning into a monster. I was not about to be abused by a man. That was not something I tolerated.

"You are not going to keep putting your damn hands on me." I walked forward and opened up the door. It was pitch black and I had no idea where to go.

"See, if you don't follow my lead, you will end up in the dark alone if you go against me."

He turned on a flashlight and grabbed my hand. We went through a door at the end of the hallway that led to the kitchen. There was an older Hispanic guy standing by a big freezer. He looked at Victor and then he open the door. He rolled out what appeared to be a body bag.

"My baby." I knew it was Fred Jr.

I started crying as I watched my child get rolled out on a table. I was mad at myself for not seeing the signs.

"You sure you can handle this sweetheart?" he asked me.

I really had no idea what to expect. I just had to make sure that was his body. When he unzipped the bag, I lost it.

"Who did this to my baby?! I want them all dead! Do you hear me?! Fred I am so sorry!"

I couldn't help but cry and scream seeing my son mutilated for no reason. I walked over to my baby's body and it had been gutted like a pig. I vomited on the floor.

"Who the fuck is responsible for this?" I looked at Victor.

The old guy handed me some paper towels to wipe my mouth

with.

"I told you I am on it Lisa. I am so sorry." Victor slammed his hand on the table. "Sorry is not good enough when your child is dead. I am about to put fire on everyone until we kill every last son of a bitch involved with this."

Victor zipped the bag back up and gave the man some money.

"Lisa, this man owns a funeral home and has all his licensing. He will take care of the arrangements."

I looked at Victor and I stopped him. "I want his funeral to be how I want it." I told him.

"It will be baby. I understand that. I am not trying to take that away from you." He kissed me on the forehead.

"We want the supreme package. Cost does not matter." Victor grabbed my hand. "Come on baby lets get home and get you some rest."

We made it back to the condo and I was just drained. All I could picture was how Fred Jr.'s body was cut all open.

"Lisa, what can I do to make you feel better?" Victor asked.

"Bring my son back." I replied.

I put Frank in the other bedroom. He was knocked out. I tucked him in and walked to my bedroom.

"Something a little more realistic Lisa."

Victor followed me into the room. I stripped naked and ran my bath water.

"Let me run your water for you. You have to let a king lead when you are the queen."

Victor poured bubble bath in the tub and grabbed some towels for me.

"Lead then Victor." I put my hair up in a messy bun.

"Come on get in."

I walked back over to the tub and Victor grabbed my hand to help me in. I put one foot in and then he stopped me. He kissed my thigh. I stood still and let him. He opened my legs up and started kissing my pearl tongue. When he began licking my clit, I could not help but to moan.

"Hmmmmmm!"

I grabbed Victor's shoulders. He bent down lower so that he could get in the perfect position and then he went to work. He licked and sucked my clit until it was throbbing. I nutted all in his mouth. I could barely catch my breath. He sat me in the tub and began to wash me.

"One second." Victor got up and left out the bathroom.

Victor putting his hands on me was bullshit. Fred used to do me like that before we got married. He would get drunk and accuse me of cheating on him. He was the one that was actually cheating, but he put the blame on me. Years of fighting the person you love is not a good feeling. The last time we fought I left him. I only left for a week, but he knew I was serious about never coming back. Fred signed up for anger management classes to show me he was serious. He stopped drinking on his own and after that he never hit me again. When he asked me to marry him I knew he was ready. Victor hitting me triggered those old emotions and I would kill him before I let him beat on me.

"Here you go." He had a wine glass and some fruit.

"Well you are full of surprises." I grabbed the glass and he put the fruit down.

"Enjoy your bath and I will be back." He kissed my forehead.

"Where are you going baby?" I asked. "Just handling some business. I won't be gone long." He left out and closed the door behind him.

I got in the bed. I knew if Victor was leaving this time of night he was not coming right back. I knew how the streets worked but in the back of my mind I kept thinking that he was going to be with another woman. Or even worse, a fucking prostitute. I shook those thoughts out my head and I fell asleep.

I felt something on me and it woke me up out my sleep.

"Victor?"

I could feel kisses on my toes and then he started sucking them. I put my head back and closed my eyes. He licked up my thighs and immediately started eating my pussy. He was being so aggressive and I was loving it. I tried to grab his head, but he grabbed my hands and held them down.

"Ohhhhhhh!" He made me cum right away. He was putting the tongue stroke in extra time. He grabbed my ass and started eating it. Then he scooped me up and I had to fight back screams. I grabbed a pillow and covered my face. Victor was definitely apologizing for what he did earlier. He finally put his dick in me and I lost it. He started out with three slow strokes and then he pounded me until I was screaming in the pillow. He was going deeper than ever and I swear his dick felt bigger. I threw the pillow off my face and let out a moan. I tried to grab his face so I could kiss him, but kept moving back.

"Kiss me baby." He kept going and I guess he nutted because

303

he started shaking.

"Did you just cum?" I asked.

He did not say a word. He got up off me and zipped his pants back up.

"Baby are you ok?" I sat up and asked. He opened the door and my heart started beating a mile a minute. It was pitch black in here, but I could see a light in the hallway. What I was not expecting to see was the light to be shining on Ricky's face.

Chapter 31

"Victor!" My eyes were playing tricks on me.

I touched myself to make sure I was not in a horrible dream. I was very much awake. I went in the bathroom and splashed water on my face.

"Get it together Lisa."

I dried my face off and went in the living room. Ricky was on the couch like he was asleep.

"Ricky! Where is Victor?" He didn't budge.

"Ricky! I know you are not fucking sleep! Where is Victor?" I repeated. He pretended like he was waking up and rubbing his eyes.

"Nevermind." I went back in the room and locked the door.

I called Victor on my phone. No answer. "You have to be kidding me." I said to myself. I called three times and he never answered. I sent him a text telling him to call me as soon as possible. Ricky had just come in and took advantage of me. The sun was starting to rise and I heard the door opening up in the living room. I waited a minute before I got up but then I heard Victor's voice. I ran out my room and into the living room. They both looked at me and then Ricky sat down.

"Victor I need to talk to you right now." I was disgusted and I rolled my eyes at Ricky.

"Yes baby, what is it?" Victor walked to the kitchen and looked in the refrigerator.

"We need to talk in private. Please." I grabbed his hand and walked in the bedroom.

"I think Ricky had sex with me and I thought it was you." I told him.

"What are you talking about Lisa? How can you think someone had sex with you?" he asked me looking confused.

"Well I'm pretty sure he had sex with me Victor. I thought it was you and when I saw his face in the light he was leaving out the door." I was fuming.

I wanted to go cut his dick off and feed it to him.

"Is this a sick joke?" Victor didn't seem to believe me.

"Well If you don't say anything to him I guess I will." I walked back in the living room.

"Ricky you came in my room this morning and fucked me. You heard me saying Victor's name." I confronted him as Victor walked in the room.

"Is this true Ricky?" he asked him.

Ricky looked at Victor with a strange look. I turned and looked back at Victor. He had pulled out his gun.

"But Victor you told me..." POW! POW! Victor shot him in his mouth. I looked at Ricky fall down to his knees and I couldn't help but kick him while he was down. I spit on him.

"Nasty motherfucker."

I heard Frank crying. "My baby can't see this mess." I ran to the back with Frank.

"What was that noise?" he asked.

"I dropped something baby and I am so sorry I woke you up." I kissed him and hugged him.

"I want some cereal," he said and got back under the covers.

"One bowl of cereal coming up."

I went back in the kitchen and Victor had sat down.

"Why are you sitting down and there is a dead body in the middle of the floor?" I asked.

"Oh, Jose and Jerry are almost here to clean up." He kept his eyes glued to the phone like it was not a big deal.

I fixed the bowl of cereal and went to give it to Frank. He had went right back to sleep. I put the bowl on the nightstand by his bed and left out of the room. I was not expecting him to kill Ricky. I kept replaying it in my head. I wonder why Ricky said those last words...'but Victor you told me...' I wanted to know what exactly Victor told him. I guess I would never know and of course Victor would lie. What if Victor told him to fuck me? I did not want to believe that, so I got that idea out my head quick.

Knock! Knock! Somebody knocked on the door.

"I'm going back to bed." I left out the living room because I did not want to be a witness to anymore murders unless I was doing the killing.

I could hear them laughing and talking in the living room. You would never think they were cleaning up a dead body. I remember Jerry from hanging with BJ. A long time ago he used to do business with Fred. Then he started doing the supply and got hooked. He lost almost everything. I decided to get in the shower and scrub myself. The thought of knowing Ricky touched me and was inside of me made my flesh crawl. It was so fucking creepy. I was starting to believe I was going crazy. I let him come in and do whatever he wanted and I never saw his face.

I turned the water on as hot as it could get. I wanted to just bleach my entire body. I washed my hair, shaved, and just sat and let the water run on me. I heard a knock on the door.

"Mommy." It was Frank.

"I'm coming baby." It was hard to let that water go but I got out, wrapped a towel around my head and another around my body.

I walked out and Frank had started eating the cereal on the nightstand.

"Ewww! I know that cereal is soggy by now." He ate another big spoonful, then looked up at me and smiled. I shook my head and grabbed his cheeks.

"You are so handsome I can't be mad at you. If you like it I love it." I kissed the top of his head.

"I wanna see Fred and Freda." He ate another spoonful of cereal.

I was so concerned on how I would tell Freda, I never realized that I would have to tell Frank. I really was not ready to have that conversation.

"Well sweetie you are too little to go in the room." I tried to be as vague as possible.

"So does that mean Fred and Freda both in the same room?" He sure asked a lot of questions.

"Freda is in ICU and Fred Jr. is somewhere else." I knew I was going to have to tell him.

"Where is he? I want to see him," he said. I took a few deep breaths to try to be as strong as possible.

"Well, Fred Jr. hurt himself so he will be gone forever." I explained to him the best way possible.

"You mean with the gun?" He held his head down.

"Yes baby. I left the gun where he could get it. I blame myself." I could not hold back the tears.

"Don't cry mommy." Frank wiped my face. "Why did Megan put the gun on the table mommy?" he asked me. I was confused.

"What do you mean Frank? When did she put the gun on the table?" Frank may actually know more about that day than I thought.

"She put the gun on the table and Fred got it off." He ate another spoonful of soggy cereal.

"Frank please don't eat anymore of that soggy yucky cereal." I got up and went in the bathroom. I saw blood.

310

"That bitch knows more than what she is saying. I pulled myself together and walked back out.

"When Megan put the gun on the table, was she mad about something?" Frank stared at the cartoons on tv. He shook his head no.

"Well, was Fred Jr. mad about something? Is that why he got the gun?" I needed answers and Frank was the source.

I knew it was something strange when Megan said she forgot to turn the cameras on. Those cameras should have never been off in the first place. Frank kept watching tv.

"Is that why he got the gun Frank?" He shrugged his shoulders.

I knew I had to wait a few hours to get his attention again. Megan is the reason my son is dead. She basically handed a child a gun and told him to blow his brains out. What other explanation could she have on why she put a gun on the table. Fred Jr. may have been confiding in her. If he told her that he wanted to kill himself and she didn't try to stop him, she deserves to die too. I walked in the bathroom again to pull myself together. I kept seeing my son blow his brains out. I just sat at the vanity and cried.

Knock! Knock!

I guess Victor had cleaned up the mess. I got up and opened the door.

"I was checking on you two. I have a new driver and new security guard coming now." He kissed my forehead.

"What's up little man? I want to hang with you today. Think of something fun for us to do and whatever it is we will do it." He gave Frank a high five.

I had nothing to say. The less I knew the better.

"Go ahead and get ready and we will take the Rolls Royce," Victor told us and closed the door behind him.

I really had got myself involved in something crazier than I could imagine. Victor really was living in his own world. I can't even remember the last time I saw him actually sleep. He had so much money, he could buy what and whoever. I was not falling into that trap with him. I knew he had fallen in love with me, but I had to let him go. I hated I had to bring Frank around him. I did not want him to get comfortable around my kids. I was still a married woman and technically he was still a married man.

We finished getting dressed and I met everyone in the foyer.

You could not tell that there had just been a murder here less than two hours ago. I looked at Victor and he smiled at me.

"There they are. You look fantastic baby. You are just too cool little dude." He gave Frank a fist pump.

"Thank you." I smiled and looked at the new driver and guard.

The driver was a woman. She had a short haircut and a caramel complexion. She was shorter than me and she was very pretty. She looked like Nia Long's long lost sister.

The security guard was a big white guy. He looked like one of those guys that lived and breathed the gym. He probably put steroids in his cereal.

"Lisa this is Yasmin and Rod." He introduced us.

"Nice meeting you both." I flashed a smile, but I was ready to get out the house.

"Ok well let's go." Victor opened the door for us to leave.

Nobody said anything on the elevator and it was very awkward. We all got in the car and Victor asked Frank again what he wanted to do.

"I wish we lived closer to Disney World," he said.

"Would you like to go to Disney World? Have you ever been?"

I looked at Victor because I know he is capable of anything.

"No sir, do not even do it." I said.

"What if I told you I have my own airplane and I can fly anywhere in the world."

Victor pulled out his phone. I saw Frank's eyes light up.

"I need the jet gassed up for a flight to Disney World. If he cannot fly this trip he will not fly any other trip either. I will be ready in one hour." He hung up his phone.

"We are not going to Disney World. Have you lost it." I saw Frank's eyes get big.

"Why not mommy?" he asked.

"Yeah, why not mommy? Everything is on me, I promise." Victor had this sinister grin on his face.

"I need to be here for Freda. If they call me from the hospital, I want to be minutes not hours away."

Frank put his head down.

"You can only see her at certain times anyway Lisa. Let's go check on her now and then I will fly us back tomorrow morning."

I looked at Frank and I knew it would be so much fun for him. I still needed to make sure Freda was progressing before I said yes or no.

"Let's go to the hospital first before I make a decision."

Yasmin put in the address and headed to the hospital.

We made it and there were a few minutes until the next visiting hours. Frank and Victor were playing some game as I waited for the doors to open. My phone rang and it was Monica. With my crazy life I forgot she had some complications.

"Hi girl. How are you?" I was so scared to hear if she lost the baby. I know how bad she wanted a child and I wanted it for her too.

"I have been better Lisa. I wanted to check on you and see how Freda was," she said.

"I am waiting to see Freda now but we are fine. How is the baby?" I needed to know what was going on.

"The baby is fine but I have just been very sick. I am taking it one day at a time."

I was so happy to hear that. "That's great Monica. Not that you are sick but that the baby is good." I heard them announce the doors were opened for visitors.

"I hate to cut you off, but they just opened the doors to the ICU."

We got off the phone and I went to Freda's room. I walked in and her eyes were wide open, and her feet were twisting.

"Is that my princess?" I gave her a kiss on the cheek. She started moving her eyes and feet really fast.

"Slow down baby." I grabbed her feet and started rubbing them. She started moving her hand like she was waving.

"Hey my baby." I wanted to start crying and screaming but I held my composure.

"Blink once for yes and twice for no ok." I told her. "If you understand blink once."

Her eyes were moving everywhere and then she closed them. She held them close for like ten seconds before she finally opened them. Then she blinked once.

"Ok so are you hurting?" She blinked once.

"Is your entire body hurting?" She blinked twice.

"Ok is your head hurting?" She blinked once.

"Do you know who I am?" She blinked once.

"Baby that's great!" I was so excited I could not hold the tears back anymore.

"Do you know who Frank is?" She hesitated and then she blinked once.

I didn't want to flood her brain with questions so I left it at that.

"Frank misses you so much. He just asked about you. We all miss you and are ready for you to feel better." I kept massaging her feet and then the nurse assistant walked in.

"Just checking vitals." She checked Freda's blood pressure and other vital signs. I noticed Freda's eyes were going crazy again. She kept looking at me and then back to the nurse assistant.

"Freda, I heard some great things about you. I hope you continue to get better." The nurse smiled at me and left out. Freda may not be able to talk but I could tell something was not right.

"Has that nurse been doing something to you?" I asked. Freda stopped moving her eyes and blinked once.

"What the fuck has she been doing?" I knew it. I could tell how Freda was looking that she wanted to say something to me.

"Did she touch you somewhere bad?" I asked. She blinked

twice.

"Did she hit you?" She blinked once.

"I will kill this bitch!" I got up and walked to the nurse's station.

"Where is the nurse assistant that just left out of here?"

Before I could get the words out of my mouth good I saw her walk out another patient's room.

"You been putting your hands on my daughter?" I punched her dead in her mouth. "Bitch you got life fucked up."

I tripped her and she fell down. I got on top of her and beat the bitch into a pulp. Security finally got me off her.

"I dare you to look at my baby again!" I yelled out. Security escorted me out and threatened to call the police on me.

"That bitch needs to be fired!" I saw the head nurse walked toward me.

"What in the world is going on?" She looked so concerned and confused.

"Freda told me that your nurse was hitting her. So since she likes to abuse kids, I showed her I like to abuse adults." I wanted to kill that trifling bitch.

"I will get to the bottom of this but for now we have to ask you to leave or I will call the police." She handed me my bag I left in Freda's room.

"Look, I will have this hospital shut the fuck down. I could care less about the damn police. You will be hearing from my lawyer." I put my bag on my shoulder. "When I come back to see my daughter that bitch better not be here." I turned and walked outside.

Victor and Frank were walking back toward the car with slices of pizza. "We got hungry, you want a bite?" Victor tried to put the pizza in my mouth.

"How is Freda?" he asked. I was so pissed off I ignored the question and got in the car.

"What did I say?" he asked Frank. Frank started laughing.

"You good?" They got in the car.

"Freda told me that one of the nurses has been hitting her." I kept seeing me kill that bitch.

"Hitting her? Hitting her how?" His mouth dropped.

"I don't know exactly how but I asked her was she hitting her, and she said yes. I beat the bitch ass until they kicked me out the hospital." She got no licks in at all so I was not worried about any bruises.

"We will get a lawyer for this and you will own this motherfucker," he said.

"I have to get her out of this hospital immediately. They really might try to hurt her now."

I was not leaving until I could discharge her. "If security removed you then you can't come back on the premises for at least twenty-four hours," he explained to me. They had messed with the wrong fucking child and this was not over with.

Chapter 32

I was not about to wait to get Freda out of there. I called the hospital and asked for the head administrator. The receptionist put me on hold.

"I am going to shut this hell hole down." We pulled off.

"Are we going to Disney World now?" Frank asked.

"Hello, this Andrew. How can I help you?" An older black guy answered the phone.

"I need to file a complaint. Are you the right person to tell that you have employees hitting children!" I yelled.

I really had no problem with protecting my daughter by all means.

"Is this Freda's mother?" he asked.

"As a matter of fact it is. I was kicked off the premises when my child was telling me she is getting abused." I wanted to get my baby and burn the whole fucking place down.

"I do apologize. I am just hearing of what transpired and just so you know, that person is no longer employed here."

He sounded like he was sympathetic, but they were going to pay for this shit.

"Well, I would like to file that complaint and discharge my baby." I waved my hand to let Yasmin know to stop the car.

"You have the right to do whatever you want with your child, but I am not going to go without a fight to keep her here," he told me.

"You mean the same damn way that bitch ass nurse was fighting my baby?!" I was not hearing that bullshit.

"I understand your anger, but Freda's brain activity is getting better every minute. If you move her to a new facility you will be really taking a big risk. She could end up with permanent brain damage."

I wanted to do what was best for Freda. I was glad they fired that bitch but what if she was not the only one.

"Tell them we want our own security there and unlimited visiting hours." Victor said. That was a great idea.

"She can stay under one condition. My own security guard will be present at all times and no rules on visitation for family."

Yasmin pulled over and everybody stared at me. I put the phone on speaker. Andrew got very quiet.

"I have to run it by my board, but I know they will say no to the visitation. I may be able to get away with security because they have access any time." he said.

"Obviously you have people working for you that know when to harm innocent people and a children on top of that."

I could hear him typing something on the computer.

"I will get an official letter together. Can you give me twenty four hours? I promise that Freda will be treated like royalty."

He seemed very sincere, but I did not trust a soul.

"I want a security guard there starting now." He kept typing.

"Send him to my office. I will give him a hospital uniform. This is only for twenty-four hours," he explained and he typed some more. "What size does he wear?" Andrew asked.

"His muscles are about the same size as Hercules. When he gets in your office he can find what size works best. Thanks." I said sarcastically and hung up the phone.

"I cannot believe they think I am supposed to be fine with my daughter getting abused. I am going to gladly take them for everything they have. I'm going to make sure my great grandkids nieces and nephews are rich off their dumb asses." We all laughed.

Yasmin drove back to the hospital and Rod got out.

"Watch everything. Please!" Rod gave me a salute like they do in the army and walked in the hospital.

I was so pissed I had ran out of words to say.

"We might as well take the kid to Disney World. I already have the jet waiting on us. We can buy new things when we get there," Victor said.

I wanted to stake out at the hospital and just sneak her out. Having Rod there was not the same as having me there.

"I have to protect my daughter. Disney World will still be there next week." I said.

"Nobody cares about me." Frank said sadly.

"That is not true baby. Why would you say that?"

I was hurt by him saying that. I always made sure my kids had the best everything.

"I want to do something fun, but you won't let me." Frank folded his arms and stuck his lip out.

"Your sister is just very..." I stopped and looked at Frank's face.

I know he was spoiled but for some reason I just gave in. He had been through a lot these last few weeks and months.

324

"Let's go. Vamonos!" I exclaimed. "If I stay here I will probably end up in jail." I laughed.

"Si! Vamonos!" Victor gave Frank a high five and then me.

"You both have been through so much, you need this too Lisa." He gave Yasmin the address and we headed to his jet.

We loaded up on the jet and I still had this feeling in my gut to not leave.

"I still feel like I should stay here. My son just died, and Freda is in the hospital. I have so much I need to take care of. I think we should wait."

I was losing it. I know I have to take care of Frank but how could I enjoy Disney World.

"Let me give you something to help you relax." Victor handed me a pill.

"This is definitely not the right time to do drugs." I whispered.

"It's just some anxiety medicine, a prescription from a doctor." he told me.

I took the pill and Victor called the flight attendant to bring me some water. It was a new girl I had never seen before.

"She's new?" I asked. She was a white girl with blonde hair

and big boobs.

"That's Becky," he said.

"I would have never guessed that." I said.

I felt a vibe that I immediately did not like about her.

"You just wanted one bottle boss?"

Becky was chewing on her gum obnoxiously. She looked like she was right out of the playboy mansion. The closer she came to me, I could tell she was not a natural blonde and her spray tan was horrible. She was the girl that you kept away from your man. Men always fell for her type.

"Thank you." I grabbed the water from her.

I popped the pill and drank some water. I wanted to relax and just not worry about what was going on around me. Becky walked back up to the front. Her dress was so short that I could see her panties.

"You need to hire better help." I sat back in the chair.

"Wait!" I shouted.

"Is everything ok Lisa?" Victor looked concerned.

"Did you know Jennifer was pregnant? She said it's her

boyfriends or whoever but that was strange that we both ended up pregnant."

"Who is Jennifer baby?" he asked.

"Remember that one time on the plane. Me. You. Flight attendant." I whispered.

"Ohhhh, but what does that have to do with me?" He looked confused.

"I was just wondering did you know since she is an employee of yours." I took another sip of water.

"The bitch just stopped showing up to work, I do know that. That's how I got Becky." Victor shook his head.

I looked over at Frank and he was already asleep. I thought he would be so excited that he would not even want to sleep. I could feel the pill kicking in because before I knew it I was sleep too.

Chapter 33

We finally landed in Florida and we had a car service waiting for us. Our destination was about ten minutes away from the landing strip. We made it to a beautiful beach house.

"How did you find such a beautiful place to rent last minute?" I asked. It was breathtaking.

"I own this," he said proudly.

I was amazed that Victor had so many properties and business ventures.

"You own everything don't you." I giggled. "How far are we from the park?" I asked.

"Not far at all." He replied.

We walked in the house and it had everything. It had a huge arcade room with a pool table.

"Mommy look!" Frank hollered and took off running.

"We might not have to go to Disney World." Victor said chuckling.

I walked around and Victor gave me a tour.

"You have amazing taste; or did you hire someone to

decorate?" I paid attention to all the details and everything was matched so well.

"I pay the price and I get results. I am not the best interior decorator, but I did pick out the color scheme," he said.

"It's beautiful here but we better get to the park so we can make it back home tonight."

I waked to the arcade to get Frank.

"Come on baby, let's go." I grabbed his hand to walk out the door.

We headed back outside and got in the car.

"So wait, we won't have security while we are here?" I asked.

"We can if you want me to get some. I just wanted to blend in but let me arrange that now." He pulled out his cellphone and started calling someone.

"No!" I exclaimed. "It's perfectly fine without it."

I was tired of having somebody following me. I had a target on my back but I rather deal with things as they come.

"Let's just enjoy the magic of Disney."

We made it to Disney World and Frank was having the best

time of his life. We went to Magic Kingdom and of course Victor bought everything that Frank said was cool.

"This is so awesome," Frank said.

"I am glad you are enjoying yourself. It is almost midnight I think it's about time to go."

I looked at Victor to let him know. "Ok well let's head out," he said.

We had tons of stuff and it could barely fit in the car.

"I cannot believe you bought all this stuff. You spent way too much money." Victor spent money like it grew on trees.

"I can't spend it when I'm dead." He shrugged his shoulders. His phone rang and it was Rod.

"How is everything going Rod?" I sat up and moved the bears and inflatable sword out my way. "One second." Victor handed me the phone.

"What's wrong Rod?" I asked.

"Freda just had a spike in her blood pressure and they are saying it's very high. The nurse tried calling you."

I grabbed my phone out my bag and I saw that I has no service. "We are on the way." I handed the phone back to

Victor.

"This is what I was afraid of. Please get me to my baby!" I cried.

We made it to the landing strip and nobody was on the jet. "Where is the pilot?" I asked.

"I have to get him because I thought we were leaving in the morning." Victor replied.

"I told you I did not want to stay long. Here I am hundreds of miles away from my daughter in ICU. If something happens to her I will never forgive you for this," I said.

"I'm sorry mommy." Frank said sadly.

"Not you baby. This is not your fault. I had so much fun. I promise I did." I hugged him and kissed his cheek.

"Mommy loves you so much. I love Freda and Fred Jr. too, so I want to make sure you guys are all safe." I hugged him again.

He didn't say a word. I had so much on my mind I could not even focus on anything but getting on this jet.

"Where is the fucking pilot?" I asked again.

Finally, I see a SUV pulling up and two guys jumped out.

"Ok let's go." Victor said.

We got on the jet and you could tell the two guys were pissed. It looked like the one with the pilot uniform had been drinking.

"Are you ok to fly a plane?" I asked.

"Yes ma'am, I am fine. I had dozed off that's all."

I saw the other guy give him a strange look. I got on the jet and I had a very strange feeling.

"Victor I think the pilot has been drinking." I told him. "No not him. I don't even think he drinks Lisa." Victor fastened his seat belt.

"I am being serious right now. The man is fucking drunk." I whispered.

I looked over at Frank and I would not risk his life or mine. "Find another pilot. Come on Frank." I grabbed Frank's hand and we started walking back off.

"Where are you going? Are you serious right now?" Victor asked.

"I am not risking our lives. Are you fucking serious right now!" I replied.

He got out his seatbelt and followed behind us. "Wait Lisa."

He went into the cockpit where the pilot was. They all walked out and looked at me.

"What the fuck y'all looking at me for?" I said.

"I am not drunk. I was just waking up." The pilot said. I knew when a person was drunk, and it was pissing me off that they were trying to play me.

"Look even if you are sleepy I do not want you flying me or my son. I will wait outside."

I walked off the plane and stood outside. Victor and the other two guys walked behind me.

"Lisa let's not forget Freda," he said.

"Exactly! I want to get to her!" I exclaimed.

"If it helps, I also have my pilot license," the other guy said.

"Well why are you just now saying something?" Victor yelled at the guy. "You don't need a damn uniform just get us out of here." Victor walked back on the plane and we all followed him.

"I am not drunk but fine." They switched seats and we buckled our seat belts and waited for takeoff.

A two- hour flight turned into three because of turbulence. We finally landed and rushed off to the hospital. Yasmin was waiting as we landed and got us there in a few minutes. I called Rod back and he made it sound so bad.

"Just get here as fast as you can guys," he said.

Once we pulled up, I jumped out and ran upstairs. I knocked on the doors because they had them locked.

"Rod! It's me Lisa! Somebody let me in!" I yelled.

They unlocked the doors and I saw Rod.

"Where is she?" I asked.

"She's still in her room."

I got to her room and saw the nurses surrounding Freda. "What is going on?" I asked.

They were sitting around like she was dead.

"Hi. Freda's blood pressure went up really high and it did some additional damage to her brain," the nurse explained.

"What kind of damage?" I asked.

"She has gone back into a vegetative state for now, but her brain activity has not slowed down dramatically," she said.

I wanted to scream as loud as I could. "How did this happen!" I hollered.

"She could have been stressed by the situation about the abuse and it spiked her pressure. Anything that could have caused her anxiety or stress could have also triggered something in her brain," the nurse explained to me.

I walked over to hug her and kissed her cheek. "You will make it out of this baby girl. I will not leave your side."

Everyone stared at me but I was not leaving. It was four in the morning and I was exhausted.

"My baby needs me, and I am not leaving. I really want her out of this fucking hospital. You bitches might be trying to kill her."

I got up and pulled out my cellphone. I called Victor because I was fed up.

"I am moving Freda from this sick ass hospital and I am suing their ass." Everybody started leaving out the room.

"What happened baby? Is she ok?" Victor asked.

"Hell no! My baby is worse than before. I think they are trying to kill her and I want her out of this place."

I had no idea what to do or where to take her, but she was leaving now.

"Lisa think about what you are doing. I know you want to protect her at all cost but moving Freda could be risky," he warned.

"Leaving her here is a risk too." I had to do what I felt was right.

I immediately started removing the cords off her. "Find the closest hospital and meet us at the back door." I told him.

Rod came back in the room. "What are you doing? Are you crazy?" He looked at me in utter shock.

"Just grab her!" I ordered him.

I took my socks and shoes off and put them on her feet so that they would be warm. I wrapped her in blankets to hide her, but I knew the nurses would know what was going on.

"I hope you know what you are doing." Rod ran out the door.

I walked out slowly and there were no nurses at the nurse's station. We got to the back door without anyone seeing us.

"You are out of your fucking mind Lisa." Victor opened the door for us.

"I found a hospital six minutes from here." Yasmin said.

"Get us there in two." I said. "Make sure you get us there."

Frank was staring so hard at the blankets, but he never said a word. If he knew it was Freda, he would probably scream his lungs out.

"Good thing I told her to bring the SUV." Victor said.

I blocked out everything they were saying. I had just basically kidnapped my own daughter, but I was willing to do whatever it took to save her life, even if it meant losing mine.

Chapter 34

Yasmin pulled up to the back of the emergency room so me and Rod could jump out. I wanted Frank gone so he never saw Freda's face. Once they pulled off we threw the blankets off and ran in the front entrance.

"Help!" I screamed. Nurse! Doctor!" I yelled out.

"I am Doctor Patel. What is going on?" An Indian doctor walked out.

"My daughter needs help right now! She's in a coma!"

He grabbed a stretcher and we laid her on it.

"What happened? Why does she have hospital bands on?" he asked. They rolled her to the back and hooked her up to some machines.

"I can explain all of that, but right now I need to know if is going to be alright?" I said.

"What did they diagnose her with wherever she was?" the doctor asked.

"She was in a coma but she was getting better. The nurses and doctors there told me her brain activity was improving." I replied back to him.

Nurses and doctors kept coming in and out. They did all kinds of testing and took a lot of blood from her. Her heart rate was perfect but her other vital signs were not stabilizing.

"When you say she was getting better, what was she doing?" Doctor Patel asked.

"She was able to understand me. I told her to blink once for yes and twice for no and she did it." I explained to him. "She started moving her hands and feet also."

I know Freda was getting better and I was going to make sure she kept getting better.

"I don't care what it costs to keep her alive but give her the best treatment you have." I told him.

I was not playing anymore games. "I also want around the clock security on her." He bucked his eyes. "We cannot accommodate those type of requests," he said.

"I can provide everything I need with no problem. I also will definitely consider making a very charitable donation to the hospital if you could make those accommodations happen sir."

Rod stepped up and smiled. "Well I want to be security," he said. The doctor looked up at Rod like he was Hercules.

"That decision is not up to me. I am doctor here yes, but you must talk to the head director of administration about your requests," he advised us. "Her name is Joy Ricci. You can walk back in the front door and go on the right side, her door is the first one on the left," Doctor Patel said.

"I have no idea what you said but I think we will find it." We all laughed and walked out the door.

We made it to Joy's office and luckily, she was in.

"How can I help you?" she asked.

Joy was a heavy set Italian lady. She looked like she was mean and stubborn.

"I was told to talk to you about having security here for my daughter." I told her.

"What are you some celebrity or something?" she asked.

"No, my family has been on the news lately and we want to make sure she is safe." I replied.

"So macho man here is your security guard?" She looked at Rod with a cold eye. He smiled and flexed his muscles.

"I am willing to make a very charitable donation to the hospital if you can promise me the best service to her."

My daughter was depending on me and I was depending on

Joy. She sat up a little better in her seat when I said donation.

"Of course. I am very firm on quality service and customer service. We have the most skilled doctors and nurses here with multiple degrees. We also make sure our parents know everything involved with treatment for children." I listened to her speech and at this point I had to put my trust in their hands and God.

They moved Freda to the intensive care unit and gave us a special room. It had a bathroom and a little area where Rod could be and still have privacy.

"I like this better already." I pulled out the phone to check on Frank and Victor.

"Hello." Frank whispered.

"Are you sleep?" I asked.

"Yes, we were waiting so long that we dozed off."

I know everybody had to be exhausted because I was definitely drained. Freda has stabilized and that was great news.

"Well they have Freda stable, but she is back in that vegetative stage." I looked at her and she just looked sleep.

"Well at least she is stable that is great. So are you coming out or what because we cannot sleep in the car."

I could hear Frank start whining in the background. "It's ok little man. We are headed home soon." I heard Victor whisper to Frank.

Victor was really amazing. He was helping me do whatever I asked and even helping with my kids. I was still trying to understand how he ran a multi-million-dollar drug ring and everything else he did.

"I am headed to you now baby." I hung up the phone and kissed Freda.

I walked outside to the SUV and got in. I kissed Victor like I never had before. Whatever Fred heard about me or whatever he knew about us I did not care anymore. I have been holding him down for years through cheating, prison, and all kinds of abuse. I deserved the world and to be able to enjoy it with someone that was willing to cater to my every need. Fred provided us a great lifestyle but all the time I have lost, I will never get back. I needed this physical connection that I have been yearning for. Frank never had Fred in his life and BJ was the only other father figure the kids had. I was choosing me and my children this time around. I was officially in love with Victor. I have never had these feelings for anyone else besides Fred. I was ready to take it to the next level with him and I was not letting anyone or anything come between us.

Chapter 35

We slept in the next day. I think everybody was exhausted after such a long night. I got up and showered and decided to cook breakfast. I made Frank's favorite, chocolate chip pancakes. I knew he would love those. I thought about Rosa and how she always made those for Frank. I had to find a way to get her back. I missed her and I could trust her.

Once I was done cooking everything, I found a number online for the Department of Immigration. I talked to several people before I finally got to someone who found Rosa in the system.

"I have her information here and it's saying that she filed an appeal for the deportation order," the agent said. "So what does she need to do? Is there something that she can pay to make this go away?" I asked.

"Well she has over ten thousand dollars in fees and fines, but I can not release any personal information to you over the phone."

I needed to know how to get in touch with her. "How can I talk to her and pay her fees then?" He gave me the number for the facility that they were holding her in. I was able to get the address and was told I could pay her fees to stop the deportation order. I cried because I needed someone around me that I could trust right now. Fred Jr.'s funeral was in two days and if I could get Rosa home by then it would make things so much easier.

We ate breakfast and I asked Victor about the funeral arrangements.

"You sure that everything is good with the burial right?" I asked.

"Yes baby, everything is perfect." He winked his eye and smiled at me.

"Oh yea I finally talked to the people to get Rosa home." I told him.

"That is wonderful. So what do you have to do?" he asked.

"Well, I am going to pay all her fees and fines that she has." I said.

"Those ICE assholes always trying to deport somebody. My people come here just to make a fucking living!" Victor exclaimed.

"Do you have all your paperwork up to date?" I asked him.

He started laughing. "I am a businessman baby. I am definitely up to par on my citizenship," he replied.

"Well, I want to get her out today hopefully. That would really help me get through this funeral for Fred Jr."

Tears were rolling down my face. When I thought about losing my son, I wanted to wake up from this nightmare. I need to lay him to rest so I could try to move on with life without him.

"We can get dressed and go. Are we going to see Freda first?" Victor got up and put our dishes in the sink.

"Yes and then we can go there." I said.

"Comprende." Victor replied.

"How were those pancakes Frank? Are those still your favorite?" I asked him.

"Yeah! They were yummy!" He hugged me. I hugged him as tight as I could and kissed his cheek. "I love you." I told him.

"I love you more mommy."

We made it to the hospital and Freda was stable. They said that surprisingly she was doing well.

"For the trauma she has, making her get in a bouncy car to come here was a big risk you took." Doctor Patel said. "Once I let everything scan her consistently I noticed how her brain activity was working." He continued, "It is moving very fast and

I have never seen anything like it before actually." He explained.

"Is that a good thing or bad thing?" I asked.

"Very, very good but the way her brain is working, her body should have caught up." He had a very weird look on his face.

"Does that mean she should be waking up very soon?" I did not want to hear any bad news.

"More than likely she should. Her movements will start coming back in slowly I assume." He wrote something on the chart and washed his hands. "I will keep a close eye on her but other than that she is fine."

I was relieved to hear that. I was going to think positive about today. I needed everything to go right.

We left and went to the facility to hopefully get Rosa. Once we made it there, of course Victor saw all the officers and decided that they would just drop me off at the front door.

"We will probably go get a snack while you are in there and then wait outside for you," he said.

"Yasmin whatever you do please have my man and my son back here." We laughed then I walked inside.

There were people everywhere. Some people standing in line. Some people sitting on the floor. You had people sleeping in the chairs. It was ridiculous.

"Where do I go to pay in full for someone's fines?" I asked one of the security guards.

"One of those lines. They accept cash, credit and debit.," he told me.

"Thanks."

I walked to the other side of the room and the lines were all long. I jumped in the one that looked the shortest and waited. I finally made it to the front and gave them Rosa's name. Her total fines and fees were over thirteen thousand dollars.

"So she will be able to use my address right?" I asked.

"Yep." The lady had such a nasty fucking attitude, but I played it cool. "So when will you release her?" She looked up at me and popped her gum.

"You just paid the money. There is a process that has to take place you know," she said with a stank attitude.

"I am well aware of the process, that is why I asked when you will release her. Will it be today, tomorrow, next week?"

She definitely had the wrong one to be fucking playing with and she had no clue.

"Ma'am, you can have a seat and we will let you know what to do next." She started picking papers up and slamming them.

"Are you upset about something?" I asked her.

"I have no reason to be upset ma'am. You can have a seat," she replied.

"You must hate your fucking job and your fucking life. I have been extra nice to you and you have constantly been giving everybody a damn attitude."

I really wanted to choke her but I remained calm.

"People are dealing with enough with their loved ones and you are not helping." I said calmly.

"Lady, you are not Iyanla so dammit you cannot fix my life now have several seats," she said.

"You know what, you right. It's hard to fix dumb bitch." I said and turned and walked away.

I sat down and an officer came to escort me to the immigration side. I made it over there and they put me in a room. I wanted for almost an hour and then I saw Rosa. I immediately started crying tears of joy.

"Is this real Ms. Lisa? Is this real Ms. Lisa?" Rosa kept repeating. I nodded my head up and down and the tears kept coming out.

"It is real Rosa. I am so happy to see you. I really need you." I hugged her so tight.

"Gracias! Gracias!" Rosa jumped up and down crying with her hands in the air.

"I am so happy right now!!" She started saying something in Spanish and the tears were coming out her eyes. She dropped on her knees like she was kissing my feet.

"Rosa if you do not get off my feet." We started laughing.

"I owe you my life right now, my freedom." She stood back up.

"Let's get you out of here and get you pampered." I hugged her again and we left out.

We made it outside and Frank saw us in the window. He started jumping up and down. Victor opened the door and Frank got out and ran to Rosa.

"Rosa!" He screamed.

"My Frank!"

They hugged each other and tears were streaming down her face.

"Rosa this is Victor. He is a close friend of the family." I said.

"I have heard nothing but great things." Victor shook her hand.

"I am so happy." Rosa said.

It was such a sigh of relief to have her back.

"No I am so happy to have you back. Things have been hectic since you have been gone. A lot has changed in just a short timeframe."

It was so hard for the words to form in my mouth about Fred Jr.'s funeral. I decided I would tell her after we got home.

"Well let's go. Do we need to take you anywhere?" I asked.

"I lost everything Ms. Lisa. They took everything from. I have nothing," she said.

"Material things can be replaced but at least you are okay." I told her.

"You are right. I will work free until I pay you back everything I owe you. I promise," she said.

"Rosa let's just get you out of those clothes and get you a good meal before we worry about you working." She smiled and hugged me and Frank again. We got in the car and headed home.

I had Yasmin stop at the store to buy Rosa some clothes and toiletries before we made it home.

"Where are we going? Did you move?" Rosa asked.

"We had an accident at the house, so we are staying here for a little while." I told her.

"What accident you have?" she asked.

"I will tell you later. Right now I am about to run your bath water."

I went in the bathroom and ran the bath water and even lit some candles.

"Rosa!" I hollered out.

"Here I am Ms. Lisa," she said walking in the bathroom. "This looks so romantic." she said admiring her surroundings.

"Well I guess I am trying to set the mood for you to relax." I told her. "The towels and everything you need are right here." I showed her.

"Thank you so much. I feel like a princess." She hugged me again.

"We will be in the front when you are done."

I walked out and went where Victor and Frank were. Frank had fallen asleep and was laid across the couch.

"She is so happy and I feel like things are coming back together one way of another."

Ring! Ring! My phone started ringing but I did not recognize the number.

"I don't know who this could be."

I watched it ring a couple times but decided to answer it. "Hello," I answered.

"What's up Lisa?"

It was Fred. I had no idea why my heart started racing.

"Who is this?"

I knew my husband's voice better than mine, but I asked anyway.

"Your husband," he said.

I walked outside to talk to him. He has been ignoring me for weeks and now wants to decide to call me. I had a lot of shit I wanted to say to him, but I did not want him to hear Victor's voice. I walked off from the condo together some privacy.

"You have a lot of fucking nerve calling me like everything is peaches and cream!"

I let him have it. I have been the best fucking wife to the son of a bitch and this is how he repays me.

"I did not call to argue. I called because my family would like the funeral arrangements for my son," he said.

"Your family? Hello! What about your family Fred? You know your wife and your other two children that's still living," I told him.

"My wife has been perfectly fine getting dicked down by some peon," he hissed back at me.

"Are you fucking kidding me? I have been holding you down damn near my entire life and you think you can just cut me off because of a rumor?" I said.

"Lisa everybody told me you and Paco were messing around. You thought nobody knew but people took pictures of the two of you together," he told me.

"You have to be kidding me right now." I burst out laughing.

I know he was joking about Paco. I thought about the times that I was around Paco and most of the time was when some shit went down. Who saw us and who the fuck took pictures to give Fred?

"Paco is a fucking worker. I like bosses," I said.

"You are a piece of fucking work. You not loyal. You not holding me down fucking the help" he said.

"Who told you then? Did they tell you BJ was in the hospital and I was handling the street business for you? Did they tell you every damn thing Fred!" I exclaimed.

I had fallen for Victor and Fred really could do his time and leave me alone.

"How is Freda?" he asked.

"Great," I said calmly.

I have been nothing but good to this man and he turned his back on me because of what someone else said. I know that I was being unfaithful, but he had it wrong. Regardless, he still stopped checking on me and his children.

"I know I am in here and you are living your life so I really do not blame you Lisa. I just thought you knew better than to fuck a fucking do boy," he said. "You went from the top to the bottom," he chuckled.

I wanted to scream in the phone and tell him I was fucking his boss but I remained calm.

"I am not about to deal with this," I told him. "Frank is sleeping but he is great. I will text the address of the burial to this phone number for your family. Anything else?" I asked.

"No, I will let you get back to your errand boy," he laughed. "I will be home sooner than you think and the truth will be exposed. Believe that."

I was completely silent while he talked. I started walking back toward the condo. "Hello!" he said.

"Goodbye Fred." I hung up on him.

I had a guilty conscience for cheating, but it just happened. Meeting Victor was unexpected but I knew he was the one I needed. I made it to the door and something told me to call Fred back. He picked up on the first ring.

"I know damn well you did not hang up on me!" he hollered on the phone.

"Yes I did. I forgot to tell you I want a divorce." Then I hung up on him again.

Chapter 36

I wanted to be free. Fred has been locked up and I have been too. Emotionally I was exhausted. I deserved to be held and cuddled whenever I wanted. I was holding him down and he was holding me back. I was tired of feeling alone and with Victor I was not alone anymore. I walked back in the house and Rosa was in the kitchen.

"Is this really you?" I asked and hugged her again.

"It is really me Ms. Lisa. Where is Freda and Fred Jr?" she asked.

I knew I would have to do this and I really was not ready but I would never be ready.

"Rosa come sit down."

We walked in the living room and sat on the sofa.

"Is something wrong? Please do not tell me something is wrong," she said.

"Freda is in a coma..." Before I could finish the sentence, she screamed.

"Noooooo! No! No! What happened?" Rosa started speaking

Spanish and crying.

"Please calm down Rosa." She started crying hysterically and I was more afraid to tell her about Fred Jr.

"Is everything okay?" Victor walked in from the back room.

"I just told her about Freda."

I looked at him and tears were forming in my eyes. I knew this would not be easy for her because she has been with them since they were babies.

"Rosa, I need you to be strong," I said.

Victor sat down beside me and started rubbing my back. When he did that I broke down. I saw my son's body ripped up. I saw his head blown off. I kept replaying that letter over and over in my head and I could not hide my emotions.

"I am so sorry Ms. Lisa." Rosa said crying.

"Victor please tell her," I told him.

He looked at me like he really didn't want to tell her, but he nodded his head.

"Ms. Rosa, we have been faced with tragedy these last couple weeks. La familia is very important and that is why we wanted you here to attend Fred Jr.'s funeral service. He committed suicide," Victor explained.

Rosa lost it. She started saying words in Spanish and Victor hopped up and grabbed her.

"She said she thinks she is about to pass out!" Victor translated.

"Rosa please calm down," I begged her.

She walked to the kitchen screaming and crying. Victor grabbed her a bottle of water out of the refrigerator.

"You have to try your best to calm down. I know this is very difficult." He grabbed her and sat her on a bar stool.

Victor started speaking to Rosa in Spanish. I could only make out a few words but whatever he said it helped. Rosa started wiping her eyes and drank her water.

"Yes and we need you more than ever," he said. He hugged her then I walked over and hugged them both.

"I am here for you Ms. Lisa. I am so sorry you have to deal with this, but I will be strong for you," Rosa said.

"Mommy." I heard Frank whimpering.

"Did we wake you up baby?"

I walked over and picked him up. He nodded his head while he rubbed his eyes.

"I am so sorry," I said.

Rosa walked out and went back to the bathroom.

"What did you say to her?" I asked Victor.

"I just told her you needed her and that she was the missing piece we needed to get your life back together." He kissed my forehead.

"I love your forehead kisses," I told him. "I also like your lips too." I leaned in to kiss him.

Rosa walked in while we were kissing. "Would you like me to get dinner started?" she asked.

Her eyes were red and puffy. I knew she had a million questions seeing me with Victor.

"No, we are treating you out to dinner," Victor said.

"You really have done so much already, I do not mind." she said.

"Rosa you deserve to be waited on hand and foot after what you have been through. Just enjoy it." I told her.

She looked up at me, but she didn't say anything else. She just smiled and nodded.

We went to a fantastic restaurant uptown called Brent's. They served seafood and all types of steaks.

"Rosa order whatever you want. Get you a margarita if you drink too," Victor told her.

"Hi, what can I start you off to drink?" the waitress asked.

We placed our orders and I got a text from BJ saying to call him. "I need to go to the ladies' room."

I got up from the table and went to the bathroom to call him.

"Yo, why I ain't heard from you?" he picked up the phone.

"I have been handling the services for Fred Jr." I told him.

"I want to see you tonight. Where are you staying?" he asked.

"It's none of your business where I am staying." I told him.

"Everything about your whore ass is my business. You got with the fucking Mexican and lost your mind I see," he said.

"BJ you raped me and you think I will tell you where I am. You are fucking sick and I should call the police on you," I told him.

"What if I told you I am outside your stall." I could hear his voice echo.

"Open up the stall Lisa or I will climb underneath." He reached his hand under the stall door.

"Somebody is going to walk in here any minute." I tried to kick his hand.

"Not with the out of order sign on the door." He grabbed my ankle and tried to pull me.

"Just stop. I am unlocking the door," I told him. I opened up the stall door and walked out.

"What is wrong with you BJ?" I asked him.

"The question is, what is wrong with you!" he exclaimed.

"How did you even know I was here?" I was weirded out. BJ had started acting like a fucking psycho. He raped me, and I let him get away with it. I guess he was back to do it again.

"You know iPhones do a lot sweetie," he said.

"Ok well I have to get back to dinner before someone comes looking for me." I tried to walk pass him. He grabbed my arm.

"Not before you do something for me first." He started unbuckling his pants.

"I am not about to do this. I will fucking kill you BJ!" I yelled.

I started walking back toward the door and he grabbed me and slammed me on the wall.

"You think I won't kill you Lisa? I will kill you and be cell mates with Fred. Now you are about to suck the skin off my dick and if you don't I will blow your head off."

He pulled out his gun and he leaned against the sink. "Come on baby, please daddy."

I did not move.

"Bitch you think I'm playing." He took the gun off safety and cocked it back. "Get over here now."

I walked over and he made me get on my knees. He pulled his dick out and forced it in my mouth.

"Suck it before you die bitch," he whispered to me.

He moved my head back and forth until I just started sucking it on my own. I ran my teeth across his dick and then I bit down on it.

"Bitch!"

I kicked him so hard in his dick his eyes looked like they were ready to pop out. I grabbed his balls and started squeezing them.

"You have fucking lost your mind trying to blackmail me and stalking me is about to stop," I told him.

"I told Fred I want a divorce and I am with Victor now, so try this shit again and you will be the next one on the hit list."

I let his balls go and dug my fingernails in his eyes.

"Ahhhhhhhhh!" he yelled.

BJ dropped down to his knees. I grabbed his gun and put it to his head.

"I should fucking kill you right now." I said. I started to pull the trigger, but I had my family waiting on me. "I am about to go back to dinner and pretend this never happened. You need to do the fucking same."

I put the gun on safety and dropped it in my bag. I washed my hands and put some water in my mouth to rinse off BJ's dick.

"You are disgusting." I walked out the door and left him

crouched over in pain.

Once we left dinner we went by the hospital to see Freda. I was still pissed about BJ and I made sure my location was turned off my phone. I have never seen BJ act like this. I was dumb enough to fuck him willingly and now he feels that he can have sex with me whenever he wants. I had never seen this side of him before, but I heard stories back in the day about him being abusive. I tried to shake it off, but I really wanted to tell Victor.

"You ok Lisa?" Victor asked.

"Yes. I am just emotional for Rosa to see Freda that's all," I said.

"I am nervous myself but I want to see her," Rosa said.

We walked back to her room. She just looked sleep.

"My baby." Rosa walked to her and hugged her.

"What are they saying about her recovery Ms. Lisa?" she asked.

"We are just taking it one day at a time but she is getting better," I told her.

Rosa started holding her hands. It looked like she was praying.

I walked out and went to the nurse's station.

"I am checking on Freda." I told one of the nurses.

"Do you know who her nurse is?" she asked.

"No. I forgot but Dr. Patel is her doctor," I replied.

"I know who you are talking about now. Everything is going good with her. Dr. Patel will be back in the morning to see her again," she told me.

"Thank you." I walked back in the room and Rosa was hugging Freda and crying.

"Rosa are you going to be alright?" I asked.

"Yes, I just want Freda to be ok," she said.

She hugged her some more and kissed her cheek. Then Rosa stood up and wiped her eyes.

"A lot of things can change very quickly," she said.

She was absolutely right. My life has changed so fast. I still think I am in a dream. It mostly feels like one big nightmare that I will never escape. I was terrified of my children being hurt. Now, I have lost one and I'm trying to hold on to another one. I was always scared to let Fred go. I have been with him half my life. The pain will not go away easily, but I know I have to move on. Victor is a major part of my life and all of these changes happened in less than a year.

I hugged Rosa. "Thank you for being a part of my family and helping me raise my kids. I love you so much Rosa," I told her.

If Rosa had been here, Fred Jr. would still be alive. I was not done with Megan because I know she knows more about what happened and I was going to find out what.

We made it back home and Rosa went straight to bed. She had a long day and she was tired. I got Frank ready for bed and read him a bedtime story. He finally fell asleep and I kissed him goodnight. I went back into the living room to sit down and watch tv. I have not had a moment to myself in so long. Reruns of Martin were on so I decided to watch that.

Victor walked out dressed in all black. "Where you headed?" I asked.

"I have a lot of business I need to handle. Do you need anything before I go?" he asked.

"Are you going to be gone long?" he had an overnight bag in his hands.

"I might be away for a day or two. Yasmin and Rod are still here to do whatever you need and Oh, I almost forgot," he reached in his wallet and handed me a card. "Use this card for whatever you need," he said.

"So are you going to miss Fred Jr.'s funeral?" I asked him.

"I am going to try my best to make it Lisa, I promise." He put the bag on his shoulder and kissed my forehead. He started walking out the front door.

"Start looking for houses too. This condo is too small for our family. We need something spacious." He winked at me. "I love you. Call you later." Victor walked out the door and I locked it behind him.

It was the day before Fred Jr.'s funeral and I was so nervous I could puke. The first thing we did was visit Freda then we headed to the mall. We went shopping to buy Rosa and I fabulous dresses and I bought Frank a black suit. The casket was not going to be open, so I stopped by the funeral home to put a note that I wrote to him inside his coffin. Everything turned out beautiful. He was going to be celebrated as the prince he was. I stayed up late the night before and I was feeling depressed, so I started writing a letter. The same way he left a note for me, I wanted to give him one back letting him know I was sorry. I was able to put it all on paper and free myself from the guilt trip I was going through. I just needed a way to feel that I connected with him one last time before he turned to ashes.

Me and Rosa went to the nail and hair salon and got pampered. Frank was able to get a haircut. He played in the kids area until we were done.

"I feel like a princess." Rosa said.

"You are," I told her. "No, we are queens!" I exclaimed. I drank my glass of wine that the salon gave me and then we left.

"We have had a long day. How about we order pizza and have it delivered?" I asked.

Everybody agreed and we went home. I tried calling Victor and no answer. I had only talked to him once today and it was very briefly. I knew he had a lot of business to handle so I tried not to bother him, but I wanted him to at least check in with me.

"Men can be so difficult," I told Rosa.

"Yes they can. So who is this Victor to you?" she asked me.

She had a look of concern on her face. I knew she was confused and I really had no idea how to tell her.

"Well I am moving on from Fred now Rosa, for good. Victor is my man now." I explained to her.

"This is none of my business I know, but Ms. Lisa that man is very dangerous," she said.

"How do you know that Rosa?" I was trying to figure out why would she say that and she just met him.

"I remember him from when he was younger. He looked very familiar and I thought all night and I find out who he is," Rosa said.

She was talking so fast her English was really broken up. "Calm down Rosa. I am having a hard time understanding you. What did you find out?" I asked.

"Him and his gang killed a lot of people in Mexico. They are said to have killed my ex-husband too." She had a look of terror on her face.

Knock! Knock! It was the pizza delivery guy with our food.

Frank came running out and almost knocked me over. "Calm down little boy before I drop everything."

I put everything on the counter and I tipped the delivery guy.

"Let's eat you guys."

Rosa still had a strange look on her face, but I ignored that. Victor has some skeletons in his closet and I have a few dead ones in mine.

We all crashed on the couch after eating. I was stuffed and was half asleep.

"Breaking news" I heard the news reporter say on the television.

"Several buildings on fire after hundreds of gunshots heard on a busy street." she said.

I kept listening and then she said something that made my stomach drop.

"Did she say Haitians?" I asked Rosa.

"Si." Rosa said.

Somebody had burned the entire area where the Haitians live and own businesses. The gunman shot and killed over twenty people and injured over fifty.

The reporter finished, "Right now there are no suspects but if you have any information please contact local law enforcement."

This had Victor written all over it. "Fuck!" I exclaimed.

I got up and called Victor again but still no answer. Frank was sleeping and I saw Rosa pick him up to take him to bed.

"Let me get him in the bed," she said and walked off.

I just wanted to make sure Victor was okay. I had no sympathy for anybody that could cut up the body of a dead child. You fuck with my family, you better believe you will get dealt with.

Victor finally called me back. He let me know that he was almost here and to keep all the doors locked. I took my bath and got ready for bed. Rosa had gone to her room and I stayed on the couch until he came. About three hours later, he finally made it.

"Are you alright?" I asked him.

"Yes baby. I've just been handling a lot of business that is all. I missed you."

Victor started kissing me and grabbed my ass. He kissed and licked on my neck and started pulling my gown up. I stopped him.

"Babe did you hear about the Haitians that got killed tonight?" I asked.

"Yes I heard." He walked to the bedroom and put his bag down.

"I have to get somebody to stay here with you guys. Rod can't be back and forth from the hospital. You will have new security hopefully tomorrow." He took his clothes off to get in the shower.

"I don't need security and I don't want security." I told him. "I can handle myself."

He looked at me and shook his head. "Lisa you are in a whole new league now. Trust me, you need security." He walked in the bathroom and got in the shower. I followed behind him.

"Did you have anything to do with what happened tonight?" I asked him. He said nothing.

"I know you hear me." I waited on him to say something, but he ignored me.

"Fine!" I exclaimed and walked out the bathroom.

I went in the kitchen and poured me a shot. I knew it would be hard for me to sleep knowing that the funeral was in a few hours. I took a few shots so that I could relax.

"Can I drink with you?" Victor walked in the kitchen with his towel wrapped around him.

I slid the bottle and the shot glass to him. He took about five shots and then I took one more.

"Let's go to bed." He grabbed my hand and we went in the bedroom.

"Did you look at any houses today?" he asked.

"You were serious about that?" I replied.

"Lisa, I do not play games. We will look at some another day, but we have to get you something more spacious than this." He started kissing me again.

"Wait baby, you never answered me. Do you know who had something to do with those Haitians getting killed or not?" I wanted to know if it was him or not.

"Lisa, I told you everything would be handled with Fred Jr., right? I love you so that means I love your seeds because they are a piece of you," he said.

"Damn that was deep baby." I started kissing him again.

I kissed on his neck. Then I made a trail with my tongue to his chest down to his navel. I snatched the towel off him and grabbed his dick.

"I missed you." I whispered to him.

While looking him dead in his eyes, I started licking the tip of his dick. I licked all over it and then I spit on it. I put his dick in my mouth as far back as I could. Since I have no gag reflexes, I deep throated his dick and juggled his balls with my hands.

Victor moaned out something in Spanish and then he gripped my hair. I moved his hands back and then I started giving him the wettest head I could give.

"Lisa I am about to cum." he moaned.

I sucked faster and then started sucking on his balls. He almost flew to the headboard. "What's wrong?" I asked.

"Are you trying to take my soul woman?" He was shaking.

"I want your mind, body, and soul," I told him.

"Now, you lay down," he said.

I laid back in the bed as he commanded, and he began kissing between my thighs. Victor licked my pearl tongue slow and gentle. He started sucking it and rubbing it with his thumb. My pussy was wetter than a waterfall! Our connection seemed stronger than ever before because I was nutting back to back.

He kept eating me out and then he slowly licked my ass. He lifted my legs and slid his dick in me so gently. I grabbed him and held him tight. He slowly stroked me as I held him. We started kissing passionately. The way he was throwing his dick made me feel like I was floating.

Victor turned me over and started fucking me from the back. He put his hands in the center of my back so that I couldn't move. He pounded his dick in me and I couldn't help but moan out. "Hmmmm baby."

He was fucking me like he had a point to prove. He pulled his dick out and started back eating my pussy. My clit was so sensitive. I was trying to push his face away. He kept licking and sucking until I squirted in his face.

"Shiiiiittttttt!" I moaned.

My toes were curled and my body was frozen in place. I was shaking.

"I had to get you back," he told me. "You had me shaking like a bitch." He laughed and kissed me. We both fell back on the bed and went to sleep.

I woke up sick. My body was in pain and I was vomiting everywhere. I was a nervous wreck. My anxiety had taken over and my body was shutting down.

"I know it is hard to deal with this day but it's time for him to rest," Victor said. He grabbed a medicine bottle out his bag. "Take this." He handed me a pill.

"Just take it and trust me when I say I am not trying to kill you."

I looked at him and walked in the kitchen. I got a bottle of water and took the pill. I honestly did not care what it was. If it could help me calm down and make it through this funeral I was fine with that.

"Mommy!" Frank ran up to me.

"Hi baby. You look so nice in your suit," I told him.

He spun around and I clapped for him. "Nice job." We laughed.

Rosa walked out and she looked so pretty. "You look very nice Rosa." She smiled.

"It is time to go, the limo is outside," Victor told us.

I put my shoes on and grabbed my sunglasses. "I can do this."

I started crying. I was weak. I had no way to pretend this was going to be alright. I had to face the fact that I was burying my son today. Victor and Rosa grabbed my hand and we walked out the door.

We made it to the burial site and I could barely focus. I felt like I was walking in clouds and everybody was beneath me. I could hear everyone's voices from a distance. It seemed like they were far away.

"Lisa!" Victor screamed at me. "I just called you like five times.

Are you ok?"

I just nodded my head and they sat me down in a chair. I saw the casket and it looked wonderful. It was gold and had ivory lining and there were gold and ivory flowers everywhere. There was a picture of Fred Jr. on a stand sitting by it. There were a few people from his school there and that was it. I never texted the information to Fred Jr's family because they were never in my children's lives. I did not feel bad about them not being there to mourn his death.

I started feeling like I was floating. Whatever was in that pill Victor gave me made me feel like I was hallucinating. "I need some water."

My mouth was so dry that I could barely talk.

"I have a bottle in my purse." Rosa whispered. She handed me the bottle of water and I drank it.

I was so doped up that I was moving in slow motion. They were about to lower Fred Jr. in the ground and that is when I lost it.

"Noooo! I am not ready! Pleeeaaaase come back Fred Jr.! Pleeeaaaase take me instead!" I cried.

"I can't do this! I need my son!" I hugged the casket and kissed

379

it. "They bullied my son until he killed himself! This is all your fault!"

I pointed at the people from his school. I was crying so much that my eyes were blurry.

"Lisa come on, please have a seat." Victor grabbed me and sat me down by him.

I cried hysterically as they lowered my son in the ground. They started shoveling the dirt on him and I started kicking and screaming.

"Give me my baby back! Fredddd!!"

I tried to get in the ground on top of the casket and the men all picked me up and took me to the limo. I was screaming and crying. The reality had set in that my son was gone forever.

"I know it's hard baby, but we are going to get through this, Victor assured me.

Rosa and Frank were walking to the limo and I could see the tears in their eyes.

"I want Frank!" I yelled.

They opened the limo door. I grabbed Frank and just started

hugging and kissing him.

"Mommy I am scared." Frank put his face in my shoulder and then hugged me.

"I got you baby." I hugged him tight.

"I am ready to get out of here." I said. "Let's go." The driver pulled off and we went back home.

Chapter 37

I woke up and my mind was in a haze. I grabbed my phone and saw that it was four thirty in the morning. I was in bed but Victor was not here. I got up to use the bathroom. I could barely recognize myself in the mirror. My eyes were so swollen it looked like I had gotten beat up. I cried so much that I just cried myself to sleep. Seeing them put dirt on my son was something a mother should never have to see. I had to make everybody suffer and I was still going to get rid of Gabriela. Paco was not here to save the bitch now. I was so depressed I could not eat yesterday. I would never forgive myself for not being there for my child. I would have to live with that for the rest of my life.

I checked on Frank and he was sleeping peacefully. Rosa's door was closed so I did not bother her. Everything looked normal in the house. I wanted to call Victor but I decided not to. Instead, I went to the refrigerator to find something for my swollen eyes.

I put some ice in a zip lock bag and made an ice pack. I put the bag on my eyes for a while to see if that would help, but it seemed to make it worse. I had no clue what to do so I got back into bed and decided to text Victor. I asked him where he was and was he coming back today.

A few hours passed and he finally texted that he was working. I looked at the text and put my phone back on the nightstand. I sat back and thought things over again. Victor is here in the flesh, but he is still a very busy man. I could text him and he could be in another country if he wanted to be. His lifestyle is very dangerous and even though I am used to the street life, Victor was on another scale. He creates wars. He wins the small battles and he wins the wars. Taking his opponent completely out. Taking the Haitians out was also beneficial for him because that is another area he can set up with his product. The only thing about the Haitians is that they believe in revenge. They will definitely retaliate at some point and I hoped Victor was on alert.

I went back to sleep for a few hours and Frank came and woke me up. "Mommy I want some cereal," he told me.

"Ok let me get up baby." I got up and I guess I looked worse than I thought. Frank started screaming and crying like he had seen a monster.

"What is wrong baby?" I asked. He just pointed to my face.

"Mommy had an allergic reaction, but I am ok." I laughed to myself and then I looked in the mirror.

Damn I was looking crazy as hell. I had to figure out something because I could not go out the house like this.

"Let's get you something to eat."

We walked in the kitchen and Rosa was making coffee. "Good morning you two," she said.

"Good morning Rosa," We both said to her in unison.

"What happened to your eyes?" she asked while bucking her eyes.

"I cried myself to sleep and woke up like this. It was worse earlier," I told her.

"I have a remedy for that. Give me one second." Rosa grabbed some things out the fridge and handed them to me.

"I will whip up this mask and the swelling will be gone in less than an hour," Rosa said. "Can I make anything special for you this morning for breakfast?" Rosa asked us.

"Yeah! Chocolate chip pancakes!" Frank yelled.

"I knew you would want those but there are no chocolate chips. I can do a store run," she said.

"No Rosa, he can eat some cereal. When we go see Freda we can grocery shop afterwards," I told her.

"I not mind Ms. Lisa," she said.

"Frank will be fine." I looked at Frank and he crossed his arms and stuck his lip out. "You better not get an attitude either," I told him.

He walked over to the table and put his head down on the table.

"Frank, go brush your teeth and wash your face while I make this cereal for you." He made some noise and stomped in the bathroom.

"Frank! Do not try me!" I yelled to him.

"He is so handsome," Rosa said chuckling.

"He is so bad." I laughed and shook my head.

Ring! Ring! It was BJ calling.

I was so disgusted with him. I pressed ignore and sent him to voicemail. He called three times back to back and then sent a text saying call him. I did not respond to anything. BJ had raped me and was trying to control me. I was done with him and I wanted no parts of anything dealing with him anymore. Fred and BJ could have each other for all I cared. I just wanted this divorce so I would not be locked down any longer. It was time for me to live my life.

We had a great visit with Freda. She was already starting to move her feet again. I knew she would progress once she stabilized and she was moving much faster than Dr. Patel thought. I was ready to bring her home and that was my biggest concern at this point. Once visitation was over we stopped by the grocery store so Rosa could get everything she needed for the week.

"Is that all you need?" I asked her.

"This should be enough to last for the week," she replied.

We got everything we needed and checked out. We were putting the groceries in the car when I saw the white bitch from the hotel.

"That's Stephanie." I thought to myself.

She was with this older black guy and they had just got out of a BMW. I kept my body turned to the side so she could not see my face. There was a sushi place beside the grocery store and that is where they walked into.

"Hey, I am about to order some take out for lunch, do you guys want anything?" I asked.

"No, I will cook for us Ms. Lisa. You need good home cooked meal," Rosa said.

"I just want a few California rolls so I will be right back." I handed Rosa the keys and closed the door.

I had to find a way to get close enough to the bitch without her noticing me. I walked in and they were sitting in one of the booths in the middle of the restaurant.

"Hello how many?" the hostess asked me.

"I just want to place a to go order," I replied.

"Very well. What would you like?" She pulled out a notepad.

"Is there a menu I can look at?" I glanced over to see if they were looking at me but they were busy talking to each other.

"Here you go, take your time." She handed me a menu and I pretended to look through it. I noticed the guy Stephanie was with was wearing a Rolex and they both had on red bottoms. I instantly got mad all over again because I knew they probably had just been balling out with the money Victor gave me.

"I want the California rolls with some of the spicy mayo," I told the hostess. I paid and told her to keep the change.

"About ten minute," She told me. She had a very strong Asian accent. I could barely understand her.

"Where are your restrooms?" I asked. She pointed to them and I went in to waste time.

I waited ten minutes before I came back out to get my food.

"You do this to me while I am fucking pregnant!" I heard a woman's voice screaming.

"I call police. They on way," a short Asian guy said.

I made it back to the counter and it was Jennifer. She was talking to the guy that was with Stephanie.

"Let me explain baby, I promise this is not what it looks like." he said, begging her to listen to him.

"Fuck you Patrick." Jennifer turned and started walking out the door. Stephanie sat there not saying one word.

"Jennifer you are not leaving!" he yelled and followed her. He grabbed her arm.

"Do not fucking touch me!" she screamed.

"You know what, you think you are hurting me by cheating with another bitch while I am pregnant? This is not even your baby." She snatched away from him. I put my head in the menu and she walked out the door.

I walked back to the car with my food and I could not believe what I just witnessed. I was even more surprised by what Jennifer said.

"What took so long mommy?" Frank asked.

"Sorry baby it was a few people ahead of me," I replied. "You guys ready?" I asked. They both nodded their head and we headed home.

When we made it home, Victor was back and was asleep on the couch. I guess we were loud because he woke up when we came in.

"Sorry did not mean to wake you," Rosa said.

"No you are fine. I had no idea I had dozed off." He got up and stretched. "You guys went grocery shopping?" he asked.

"Yes, Rosa is ready to cook. She is tired of eating out." I chuckled.

"I am so glad to be out of the hell hole prison they had us in. I need some authentic Mexican food." She laughed.

"Lisa, let me talk to you," Victor said.

"Ok is anything wrong?" I asked him.

"No baby, I just want to talk to you." We walked in the back bedroom.

"Why are you going out without security?" Victor asked and closed the door.

"I cannot wait on somebody to come take me to the grocery store Victor." I told him.

"Look Lisa we did some major damage to the Haitians. I do not want to take any chances with you guys. I do not want you going anywhere without protection," he said.

"Victor I am a big girl," I told him.

"Listen to me and trust that I am only doing this for your protection." He grabbed my face and kissed my forehead.

"I understand baby," I said. "Guess who I saw while we were out?" I still was shocked at what Jennifer said.

"Who?" Victor asked as he walked toward the bathroom.

"The white bitch that I think stole the money you gave me," I told him.

He grabbed his toothbrush and a washcloth to wash his face. "Did you say anything to her?"

I walked in the bathroom to tell him what happened. "No, I was sneaking up behind her and she was with this black guy, so I tried to be discreet," I said.

"While I was ordering my sushi I saw Jennifer walk in and she headed straight to their table." I explained to him.

"Jennifer the flight attendant?" Victor asked.

"The one and only. She catches them together and calls him out right there in the restaurant."

Victor turned the water on to brush his teeth.

"Here's the best part. She tells her boyfriend that the baby that she is carrying is not his!" I continued.

Victor looked at me with his eyes bucked and spit out the toothpaste. "Damn really?" he said and started back brushing his teeth.

"Yes and she just walked out the restaurant after that. I was hiding my face so neither of them would see me," I told him.

Victor finished brushing his teeth and washing me face. "You have the craziest things happen to you," he said.

"I swear I have no idea why the most bizarre things happen to me. The world is so small. It's crazy that the girl from the hotel is fucking with her man," I said. "If the baby is not his there is a chance it could be yours Victor."

I hated to tell him that, but it was true. I got pregnant and as dumb as it sounds we did not use protection in the threesome.

"Look she probably said that shit to make him mad. I did not nut in her I promise," he said.

"I am about to take a shower and take a nap. Wake me up in a little bit." He turned the shower on and took off his clothes.

"I want to take a shower with you." I started rubbing on his dick.

"I am so tired baby. I really need some rest." He moved my hand off his dick.

"Well, I will not bother you." I told him.

He grabbed my hand and kissed it. I noticed that my hand was shining with glitter. I looked at his dick and he had glitter in his pubic hair.

"Why the fuck do you have glitter on your fucking dick?" I asked.

He looked down at it and just shook his head. "Do not start any drama Lisa." Victor walked in the shower and let the water run on him.

"Are you fucking kidding me right now? The only way glitter gets on your dick is if you are fucking with some skank!" I exclaimed.

He ignored me and started washing off. "So you going to play it like that? Ok fine Victor." I walked out and went back in the kitchen.

"Mommy we are making homemade enchiladas!" Frank said excited.

"Wow! That is so cool." I hugged him. "It already smells good in here." I told them.

"Rosa I also want to let you know I will be giving you an advance and a raise." I told her.

"Ms. Lisa are you serious?" she asked.

"Very much so."

She started speaking in Spanish and crying. "How can I ever repay you?" She wiped her face.

"You have no idea how lost we were without you." I hugged her and then she kissed my cheek. "You are family and I am forever grateful."

She hugged Frank so tight that he screamed. "Rosa are you trying to kill me?" Frank asked.

We looked at him and started laughing hysterically. "Frank shut up." I told him and rubbed his head. They started back cooking and I sat in the couch and dozed off.

After dinner I got Frank in the tub and ready for bed. I was still not talking to Victor and he could feel the tension when I walked in the bedroom.

"Lisa, I have no idea where the glitter came from. Probably from my shirt or something. I promise you I have been working," He tried to explain.

"Ok." I said dryly.

"I see how this is going to go, I need a cigarette fucking with you." He got up, walked out and slammed the door.

I ignored him and went in the bathroom to take a bath. I closed the door. When I looked in the mirror, I had a breakdown. I just cried. I was feeling like nothing was going right for me. The man who I loved the most had ruined me and now the man I thought I loved was blatantly cheating on me. I wanted that fairy tale ending, but the men that surrounded me were not Prince Charming's. They were all fucking villains.

I locked the door and got in the tub. I just sat there. I needed to be alone. I wanted Victor to take Fred's spot, but the grass is not always greener on the other side. I thought long and hard about what needed to be done. Finally, I came to the conclusion that it was going to only be about me and my children. Luxury things were no longer desirable to me. I rather have peace and happiness. Looking in that mirror, I could barely recognize who I was anymore.

When I was a child around Freda's age, I had dreams of being a nurse or a teacher. I never thought things would end up like this. Money is good to have but it will never buy happiness. I had a plan to take my life back and I was going to follow through with it.

Once I was done taking my bath I got in the bed. My phone was on the nightstand and it vibrated. I picked it up and saw I had a missed call from the hospital. There was a new voicemail and I listened to it. I started screaming.

"Thank you God!" I jumped out of bed.

I started putting my clothes and shoes on.

"Lisa where are you going? I told you not to go anywhere without security," he said.

"The hospital just called and said that Freda just spoke and asked for me!" I exclaimed. Tears started running down my face. "I knew my baby was going to make it." I was filled with so much joy.

I went in Frank's room and woke him up. He started whining and then Rosa opened the door and walked in. "Is everything alright?" she asked.

"Freda is talking! I am headed to the hospital right now!" I was so excited.

"I am coming too, let me throw something on." Rosa walked back out of Frank's room.

"I am getting the SUV sent here so we can all go to see her. Are they going to let us in to see her?" Victor asked.

"I don't know but from the voicemail I received, I do not care what they say."

I grabbed Frank and sat him on the living room couch. It was truly a miracle. I never would have thought she would go through this, but to know she is out of that coma made me reassure myself that it was time to do what was right for my children.

Chapter 38

We all made it to the hospital and I was so excited to see my baby. They only let me come to her room which was perfectly fine with me. When I walked in, Freda was wide awake.

"Freda." I said calmly. She turned her head to me and she started crying.

"Mommy." Her voice sounded raspy, but she could talk.

We both started crying. I hugged her so tight. I would not let go.

"Mommy you are smothering me," she said giggling.

"Baby you can talk! I can't believe this!" I had the biggest smile on my face.

"What happened to me?" Freda seemed confused.

"We were in a really bad accident and you have been in a coma for weeks." I told her.

"I want to go home. Where is Fred and Frank?" she asked.

My heart dropped to my stomach. I was not about to tell her about Fred Jr. right now because it would literally kill her.

"Well, Frank is too young to come in here but he misses you

like crazy." I told her. "Let me go talk to the nurses and I will be right back ok baby." I left out and went to the nurses station.

"Can we help you?" one of the nurses asked. "Yeah, I was trying to get some information on my daughter and see when she can be released." I was feeling very anxious.

"You're Freda's mom, right?" she asked.

"Yeah I am," I replied.

"She has had amazing progress but it is not quite time to release her. We are going to move her to another room and take her out of intensive care first," the nurse explained.

"When will that happen? Is the doctor here?" I asked.

"He will be in at seven. Once he checks everything, she should be moved."

I was fine with that as long as I knew my baby was a step closer to coming home.

"Will I be able to stay with her once she gets a different room?" I asked.

"Yes, definitely. The rules are not as strict as intensive care," she said.

The nurse told me I could spend a little more time with Freda and that I would have to come back when Dr. Patel was available. I went back in the room and I talked with Freda some more. I asked her a lot of questions. She answered everything! I was happy that there was no memory loss.

Knock! Knock! Someone came to the door.

"Hi. I am so sorry, but we have to cut the visit a little short," the Nnrse said.

I nodded my head because I knew they were really only doing this for me.

"Ok Freda, I will be back in a few hours and hopefully I will not have to leave you here. Rod is in and out. He is your security so just know that I have someone in the hospital keeping an eye on your room." I kissed her on the cheek.

"Mommy no, I don't want you to go." She started crying.

"Get some sleep and I will be back before you wake up, I promise." Freda nodded her head and I hugged her again before I left.

"We will take care of her. I promise," the nurse said.

"Please do because I would hate for something to happen to any of you beautiful people here," I said with a smile and left out the hospital room.

We made it home, but I could barely sleep. I was thinking about Freda. I was up all night, excited about the things I wanted to talk about with her. I was also thinking about how I would I tell her about her big brother killing himself.

Fred Jr. was so protective of her and she loved him so much. I remember I told Freda that I was going to get her for talking back to me and she was so scared. Fred Jr. came and had a belt in his hand but told me to use it on him rather than Freda. He loved her just as much as she loved him. They were extremely close. I knew that this would not be easy and that no time would ever be the right time. I hate she missed his burial, but I was overjoyed that my baby girl was doing fine.

"Why are you still up baby?" Victor asked. I looked at him and I stayed silent. I turned my back towards him.

"So that is what we are doing? I see. Whatever Lisa." He turned around and went back to sleep. I could care less how he felt, I was ready to get my daughter home.

I woke up the next morning, got dressed, and went back to the hospital. I left everyone asleep and went alone. When I made it to the intensive care unit, it was about fifteen minutes before I could go in to see Freda. I sat in the waiting area. There was this guy sitting on the opposite side looking out the window. He looked so familiar, but I could not remember where I knew him from. They announced over the intercom that it was ten minutes before visiting hours started. He looked over where I was and waved. I looked around to see who he was waving at then he started laughing.

He got up and started walking towards me. This man was so damn fine I instantly got nervous and my leg started shaking. He was about six feet four and had tattoos all over his body. He was light skinned, had curly hair and the sexiest beard I have ever seen. He could have been Chris Brown's twin brother. As he got closer I saw his beautiful gray eyes and he just smiled at me.

"If it isn't the queen herself. How are you Lisa?" he said. I was shocked that he knew my name.

"I am not trying to be rude, but do I know you?" I asked him.

"Wow. I am so sorry. You probably have no idea who I am. My name is Kash. I work with Paco and BJ sometimes." He held his hand out for me to shake it.

"Yeah I have heard of you. Nice meeting you." I shook his hand.

"I heard about your daughter and I hope she gets well soon," he said.

"Thank you." I smiled.

"My grandma is here. I think they are about to pull the plug on her," he said.

"I am sorry to hear that." I told him.

"Thanks. She is in her nineties. We have had a lifetime with her and I rather her not to suffer you know?" He licked his lips while he was talking and I had to look the other way.

He was obviously a worker and I was not going that route with him, but he was rather handsome.

"Sad about BJ huh?" he asked.

"What do you mean?" I replied.

"You haven't heard? He is addicted to opioids and now he is on cocaine hard," he told me.

This was my first time hearing about this. "Not BJ. He told me that you told him about Paco and how he was stealing money," I said.

"No I confronted BJ, not Paco. Once I found out about BJ, he told me about Paco stealing money from me too. I hire people to pay attention to these things, but everybody was getting over on me," he explained. "I could have had them killed right then but I spared their lives."

I was shocked. BJ was definitely not himself lately and if what Kash was telling me was true, I needed to get BJ away from these million dollar deals.

"I have been knowing BJ for years and he has never been on any drugs. He smokes weed and drinks but nothing heavy like coke," I said.

"Well, he told me that after he got shot he got addicted to the medicine they had him on. It created a downhill spiral from there," Kash said.

That would definitely make sense. I did not want to believe it, but BJ basically raped me. I was not giving him an excuse for what he did but that would explain a lot.

"He called me a few days ago trying to give me my money back," he said. "He told me he had a million dollars for me and that he wanted to introduce me to a new plug and everything."

Kash pulled out his phone and showed me the texts to back up everything he was saying.

"Where would BJ get that kind of money from is the question," I said. Then something hit me. "He stole my fucking money too!" I exclaimed.

I stood up. "Wait one fucking minute!" I yelled out.

The people looked back at us in the waiting room, but I did not give a fuck.

"What you talking about?" Kash asked.

"The last time I saw BJ, I had eight million dollars stolen from me." I whispered.

His eyes bucked. "Whoa!" he said.

"If I find out he is responsible for stealing my money..." Before I could finish they announced that we could come to the back for visitation.

"Lisa look before you jump to conclusions with that let me do some investigating myself. I haven't seen Paco in a few days, but once I do I will get more information from him and see who the culprit really is."

Kash pulled out a card and handed it to me. "Here is my card. Give me a call in a day or two and we can meet for dinner or something to discuss everything."

I looked at the card. It was for a carpet cleaning business. I slipped it in my purse.

"I am married so I do not want to give you the wrong

impression." I told him.

As I was saying that a woman walked up to us. "Sorry bae traffic was backed up."

She kissed Kash and then looked at me and smiled. She was so beautiful that I almost felt that I looked homeless. This girl looked like she had literally just stepped off a runway. She had on a fitted dress with six inch pump and was decked out in diamond jewelry. Her makeup was flawless.

It was not even eight o' clock in the morning but she was glowing. Her hair was done perfectly in a bun and she smelled like fresh flowers. She was damn near perfect.

"That is ok babe, glad you made it safely," he told her. "This is Lisa and Lisa this is my fiancé Dior." He introduced us. We smiled and shook hands.

"Very nice meeting you two but I have to get to my daughter." I said.

"Make sure you call me so we can have dinner," he said. I nodded and left them in the waiting room. I went to the back with Freda.

Chapter 39

Doctor Patel gave the okay for Freda to be moved into another room. I was so glad that she had made progress because that meant she was that much closer to coming home.

"How are you feeling?" I asked her.

"I'm ok, but I wanna go home," she said. I was so excited to hear her voice I could cry.

"You will be out of here shortly." We talked for hours and then I just held her until we both ended up falling asleep.

"Sorry to wake you two." A very slim nurse walked in. "I am Nurse Schwartz and I am here to check on Miss Freda," She explained.

"I guess we were both tired. I am Freda's mom, Lisa." I introduced myself.

"I have never seen a case like this before. Freda is definitely a miracle," she said.

"I agree. We just want to get her home," I told her.

Nurse Schwartz checked Freda's vitals and everything was perfect. "I will be back to check on her before the end of my shift." Nurse Schwartz walked out the room.

"Where is Frank and Fred?" Freda asked. I knew I had to tell her sooner or later so I pulled out Fred Jr's obituary.

"Freda there will never be an easy way to say this. Your brother is no longer with us." Tears ran down my face as soon as I started talking. "He's gone baby."

I wiped my tears off my face. Freda looked at me like I was speaking another language. "He's gone where mommy?" she asked.

"He is in heaven baby girl," I said to her. I never heard my baby scream as loud as she did.

"Noooooooo! Not my brother!! I want my brother!!" Freda cried. "Mommy bring my brother back from heaven! I want him now!!" Freda hollered.

"Please calm down baby. I am so sorry." I could not hold back my tears.

"Nooooo! I need my brother to get me out of the hospital mommy!" she said.

Knock! Knock! "Is everything alright in here?" Nurse Schwartz and another male nurse came in.

"I want Fred! I want my brother! Tell him to come and get me out the hospital!"

Freda was crying so loud that her heart rate machine started to beep. "You have to calm down Freda or you will make yourself sick," Nurse Schwartz advised.

Freda started kicking and screaming. She pulled the wires out the machine and tried to get out the bed.

"Freda stop! You can't do that!" I exclaimed.

The nurse walked over and held her back down. "Nurse Norman, help me hold her down please."

They got Freda and held her down but she was still crying.

"She could really make things worse if we do not calm her down. She is making her blood pressure rise," Nurse Norman said.

"We may need to give her something to get her to sleep with your consent." Nurse Schwartz advised me.

"Freda please calm down. I should have waited to tell her. This is my fault." I tried to hold back my tears, but they kept falling out. "Do what you have to do," I told them.

"No! No! Please don't do it mommy! I want my brotherrrrrrrr!" Freda screamed out.

Nurse Norman left out and came back with a needle. "This will sting just a little."

He stuck Freda while me and Nurse Schwartz held her down. It took about five minutes and Freda was knocked out.

"This is my fault. I knew I should have waited until she was out of here before I told her." I got up and got some tissue to wipe my face.

"What made her so upset?" Nurse Schwartz asked.

"I told her that her brother passed away." I wiped my tears.

"I am so sorry, I had no idea." They looked at me with sympathy.

"There was not going to be a right time or place, but she asked where he was and I told her." I looked at his obituary and I put it back in my purse.

"We would like to extend our condolences to you and your family." Nurse Norman disposed of the needle and they washed their hands. "Is there anything else we can do for you today?" Nurse Schwartz asked.

I shook my head no and they left out the door. My phone started vibrating and it was a New Jersey number calling.

"Hello." I answered.

"May I speak with Lisa please?" It was a female's voice.

"This is Lisa, who is this?" I asked.

"This is Kenise, how are you?" she asked. It was the lady who saved my life.

"Hi, how are you? I thought I had saved your number." I told her.

"I have been dealing with a lot since I talked to you last and I ended up getting a new number," she explained.

"I understand. I have been dealing with a lot as well. I actually have to come back to New Jersey soon. I still want to meet with you," I told her.

"Well I am glad you said that because I did not know if you had been trying to contact me or not," she said.

"No, I haven't yet but is everything ok?" I asked.

"Well, I told you about what happened to my boyfriend and his brother right?" she asked.

"Yes you did," I replied.

I instantly got nervous. I did not have time for any more drama and anymore problems. My life was already going downhill.

"You told me that anything I needed, you would help me. Well I'm not asking for money, but I do need a favor," she said.

"Ok, what do you need then?" I asked her.

"I need a friend." She sounded like she was holding back tears.

"Yes, we are already friends Kenise." I told her.

She started crying on the phone and I just listened as she let it all out.

"Thank you Lisa." We talked a little while longer and agreed on a day to meet up before we hung up.

I had been staying at the hospital everyday nonstop with Freda. She could talk perfectly but they were putting her in physical therapy to help her walk correctly again. She could only walk so far before she would collapse so I made sure I did whatever it took to make her legs strong. I was right there rooting her on.

Victor, Rosa, and Frank would come and stay for hours and sneak us in food too. Things were finally looking up for us. I was starting to feel normal again. Victor flew to Jersey for me and got my aunt's ashes so that I could have some closure. He bought a beautiful gold urn and had it sitting on the fireplace in the new house he bought for me.

Victor was not perfect, and I know money is not everything, but I had fallen in love with him. He made my family feel complete and he protected us at all costs. Fred had basically abandoned me and BJ was nowhere to be found.

I had people in the streets looking for BJ and the rumor was that he went to rehab and bought a house in Mexico. He was in too deep to run away now and the longer he stayed away the worse it would be for him. I had given up on getting revenge from anyone. I knew the only way to make things right is to forgive the people that hurt me. I just wanted my family to be together and I had just that.

I would always have an empty spot in my heart for Fred Jr., but I was finally happy again because my kids were happy. Rosa being back made my life so much easier. Freda coming home was the icing on the cake. I could not ask for anything more. I was counting the days until she was released so I never had to look at this hospital again.

———————————————————————

Three months had passed and the day had finally come for Freda to come home. Freda was back to herself and I could not hold back my tears.

"It has been a long journey and I am so glad to take you home." I kissed Freda on the cheek. "What's the first thing you want to do when you go home?" I asked her.

"I want a peanut butter and jelly sandwich and I want to go to Dave and Busters." she told me. Everybody in the hospital laughed.

"I also want to thank all of the beautiful nurses that worked so hard and made us feel like family. I had issues at another hospital and you all did not turn us away, you made my baby a priority. I am so grateful to this wonderful hospital staff. I want to present a check for one million dollars."

They started screaming and clapping. I handed the check to the director and we took pictures. I had food catered for them as my way of letting them know how thankful I was. I hugged each and every one of them before we left.

"Baby I will get the truck pulled around." Victor said. "

You mean you did not get a driver?" I asked him laughing.

"I gave everyone the weekend off because I just wanted to spend time at home with you and the kids." He kissed my forehead.

"You not want to spend time with me?" Rosa joked.

413

"Rosa you are family you automatically count." We all laughed.

Victor walked out the door and grabbed some of Freda's things. She had so many gifts and balloons that it was going to take a couple nurses to help walk some things out.

"Freda, I have a big boy bed like you." Frank said.

"We are going to jump in it as high as we can when we get home," she told him.

"Yay!" Frank exclaimed.

"Frank you sit here with Rosa so we can get Freda in the wheelchair," I told him.

"Yes ma'am mommy," he said.

"You are such a big boy. I love you." I gave him a high five.

He sat down and started eating his cupcake. We got everything situated by the time Victor walked back in.

"You guys ready to go?" he asked.

"Yep, let's go," I said.

"Let me get the wheelchair and you grab the rest of her stuff," Victor told me.

We loaded everything up and Victor put Freda in the car.

"Go ahead and get in. I will get Frank and Rosa." Victor walked back in the hospital and I sat in the back with Freda.

"How does it feel to finally be out of that hospital?" I asked her.

"It feels weird." She giggled.

"You guys are all I have so I just want to protect you from everything. I wish I could keep you in a bubble." We both laughed.

"I miss Fred so much mommy." She held her head down.

"I miss him too. I think about him every day. I want to have a big celebration for his birthday in a couple months. Will you help me plan it?" I asked Freda. She shook her head up and down.

"There they go. Let me get out so Frank can get in the back.

I hopped out the truck and the next thing I heard were gunshots. I looked up and there was a white SUV coming full force down the street the hospital was on. Everybody started screaming.

"Everybody get down!" Victor screamed.

He grabbed Frank and Rosa and I hopped back in the truck.

"Get down baby." Me and Freda ducked down as far down as

we could.

I heard some shots hit the truck and all I could do is just cover Freda up with my body.

"Get a Doctor! Nowwwww!" I heard Victor yell.

The truck sped off and disappeared. "Are you ok baby girl?" I asked Freda.

"Yes. Mommy I'm scared." She started crying.

I looked out the window and Victor was holding Frank in his arms.

"Frannnkkkkkkkkk!" I yelled.

I jumped out the car and ran to Victor. "Was my baby shot? What's going on?" I screamed. I looked at Victors hands and blood was dripping all over them.

"Helllpppp!" Victor ran back in the hospital.

The nurses came with a stretcher and Victor laid Frank's lifeless body down.

"My baby! Not my baby! Not my baby!! This can't be happening to me!!" I cried out.

"We need to get him to the back immediately. He is losing a lot of blood," the nurse said.

I saw Dr. Patel walking towards us and I was shaking so bad that I could not talk.

"What happened? What is going on?" he asked.

We were all running with the nurses as they pushed Frank to the back. "We are losing his pulse. We need to get him to surgery now!" the nurse said. "He has a gunshot wound to the chest," she said.

"Noooooooo! Please God! Please take me instead!! Please don't take my child!!" I cried out.

I could not take losing another child. I was so dizzy I was about to pass out.

"Hook him up to the machine now!" the doctor yelled. "Do not let this baby die do you hear me!"

They got him to the machine. "Clear!" he yelled. I heard his heartbeat on the monitor and it was very faint.

"God please save my baby!" Victor grabbed me and hugged me.

"Victor, were you shot too?" His arm was bleeding.

"I will be fine. I need Frank to be ok." He had a look on his face that scared me even more.

"He is flatlining! Do not let this baby die!!" I heard the doctor yell out again.

"Flatlining? No! Noooo! Save my baby!!" I ran over to Frank and one of the nurses grabbed me.

"We are going to have to ask you to wait outside," she said.

"Hell no!! I am waiting right here!!" They all grabbed me and walked me out.

"Frannnkkkkkk!!" I dropped to my knees and cried out his name.

I could not stop crying. I saw the floor moving and I laid back on the floor. I could hear Victor telling me to get up. I felt him pick me up and slap my face.

"Her eyes are rolling to the back of her head! I need a nurse!" I heard Victor yell.

I looked up and I saw Fred Jr. grabbing Frank's hand. They ran off and then Frank looked back at me.

"I'm going to play with Fred mommy!" Frank said excitedly. He smiled and then waved at me. I tried to talk but nothing came out. Then everything went black.

TO BE CONTINUED...

Made in the USA
Middletown, DE
20 June 2018